THE SPAIN TOURMALINE

An Ainsley Walker Gemstone Travel Mystery

J.A. JERNAY

ISBN (electronic): 978-0-9836852-7-2

ISBN (print): 978-1-960936-20-2

CHAPTER ONE

As her blood began to drip onto the cutting board, Ainsley cursed under her breath.

It was nearly eleven in the morning on the first day of her beach vacation. She was somewhere along the Costa del Sol, the long concrete strip of tourist resorts on the southern coast of Spain. Joaquim, her boyfriend, had gone swimming an hour ago, and even from here, standing in the kitchen of her rented oceanfront condo, Ainsley could hear the Mediterranean waves crashing against the sand below.

She'd been trying to make lunch.

Though she and Joaquim had been together for three months, she hadn't yet cooked a meal for him. It hadn't been easy to find the time, not with their different schedules, different homes, stressful jobs, work travel, and a multitude of other obstacles.

This morning was Ainsley's first real opportunity to play housewife.

She'd settled on an asparagus-and-cheese frittata, partly because she'd started following a vegetarian diet for the last month. She didn't know exactly why she'd begun it except for the fact that she'd simply lost her taste for meat. No other reason. This wasn't unusual. Most of her girlfriends had gone vegetarian for periods of time in their lives too, and they hadn't been able to enunciate exactly why either.

Ainsley had turned on the television and listened to the news while chopping the vegetables and beating the eggs. Before long she'd found herself immersed in a news report about a bullfighter who'd been gored the previous night in Madrid. There, onscreen, was the raw footage of the injury— the slow-motion image of a bull's horn sliding into the abdomen of an unlucky matador, his feet lifting off the ground.

Then the knife had slipped.

Now she studied the diagonal slit running across her left index finger. It was long and fairly deep and blood was already seeping out of it. Ainsley lifted her hand, elevating it above her heart. The blood began to run down her hand and soak the edge of her shirt sleeve.

Cursing again, Ainsley used her good hand to reach for the paper towel in its vertical stand. She yanked hard, but the base wasn't heavy enough. In the blink of an eye, the entire dispenser toppled to the floor with a crash.

Ainsley swore again.

Crouching, she placed her foot onto one edge of the paper, tore off three squares of the absorbent paper, and quickly wrapped it around her finger, gripping it tight. Then she collapsed onto her bottom, leaned her back against the oven, and looked around.

The cutting board, the counter, and the linoleum floor were spattered with blood. Her left forearm and sleeve were streaked with red smears. Garlands of white paper towel hung from the counter to the floor.

There the sound of a key in the door. When it opened, her boyfriend, Joaquim, entered, hair wet and mussed, wearing only a swimsuit and a smile on his handsome face.

"You wouldn't believe how nice the water is," he said. "Just the way I remember it as a kid—"

His eyes found her on the floor of the kitchen. His eyes moved from her hand to the cutting board to the floor, taking in the devastation.

"Jesus," he said, "did you slaughter an animal in here?"

"I cut myself," she replied.

He crouched beside Ainsley, unrolled more paper towels, and gently replaced the one around her finger. "Take this," he said, "squeeze it tightly, and don't let go."

"I was trying to make you lunch," she said.

"You didn't have to do that," he said.

"But I wanted to surprise you. I never cook for you at home because we're both so busy. Now I've ruined our vacation."

"No, you haven't—"

"Yes, I have. We were supposed to go scuba diving tomorrow."

"We'll find something else to do."

Joaquim helped Ainsley to her feet, then brushed her hair away from her eyes and wiped a tear off her cheek. She looked up at him. He was three inches taller than her, a fact for which she was eternally grateful.

"I'm sorry," she said.

"It's okay."

"Really?"

"Of course," he replied, smirking. "You can still pour me a beer with the other hand when I finish scuba diving tomorrow."

Ainsley smacked him across the shoulder.

"Careful now," he said. "Think how stupid you'll feel if you injure *both* hands."

"Shut up."

His eyes found the cutting board. "I'm going to eat the cheese that you bled on."

"Don't you *dare*."

"What? I can wash it."

"If you eat that cheese, I am never kissing you again."

"That's bullshit. You can't keep your hands off me."

Her eyes flashing, Ainsley laughed despite herself. Joaquim was so cocky, the way he expected the world to fall at his feet. The infuriating part was that, very often, it *worked* —he had a successful import business, charisma to burn, and women flinging themselves at him.

In fact, deep down, she wondered why their relationship seemed to be working at all. She, Ainsley Walker, self-styled international gemstone detective, had little to offer any man except a spotty work history, lots of international trips, and a glamorous wardrobe. Only one of those could even remotely be said to draw potential suitors.

Then she hit the brakes on that train of thought. Here they were, a happy couple not even at the ninety-day mark, and already Ainsley was overanalyzing. She needed to let it ride, for once.

In the meantime, Joaquim had gone to the bathroom and returned with a small first aid kit. She watched as he carefully cleaned the blood from her finger, squirted antiseptic, and wrapped it in a bandage. Then he helped her stand and gave her a kiss on the cheek.

"It's really cute," he said, "that you wanted to make lunch for me."

She dropped her face. "I wanted to surprise you."

"You did. Now go change your shirt. We'll go order a pig's ear or something."

"Did you forget?"

His face didn't register. "Forget what?"

"I don't eat meat anymore."

He grinned. "Oh, right. Yes, I'd forgotten."

"You didn't forget. You just don't agree with it."

"Ainsley, you've been vegetarian for less than a month," he said. "And here in Spain, *everybody* eats meat. It's what they do."

"Good for them," she replied. "I'm different."

"For now."

"I'm serious about this."

"Okay," he said, smiling.

Ainsley gave him a withering glance as she went into the bedroom. Joaquim waited until the bedroom door closed. Then he took a piece of cheese from the cutting board, washed off the blood in the sink, and put it into his mouth.

COSTA DEL SOL

CHAPTER TWO

That afternoon, beach bag thrown over her shoulder, Ainsley pushed the red flag into the sand next to the chaise lounge.

These chairs rented by the hour. Having reserved two with the concierge, she'd been handed the flag by the beach concierge and told to place it between the chairs, and that the monitor would charge the hours to the room.

She had moved across the dark brown sand, feeling it squelch between her toes and abrade the soles of her feet, through the neat perpendicular rows of lounge chairs, until she had arrived at the front row. Before them an unbroken view of the wide Mediterranean, its waters starting to roil in the afternoon chop.

Ainsley sat down and arranged her belongings—book, lotion, floppy hat, shirt, camera, phone, all the accoutrements of the modern beachgoer. Then she looked around. A hundred meters to her left, giant chunks of broken rocks marked the end of the beach. To her right was the seemingly endless line of charmless condo towers. They resembled office buildings.

Joaquim returned from the water. He was wearing his

tight blue trunks, and his skin was glistening with beads of ocean water. She admired him for a quick moment.

"How was it the second time?" she said.

"Even better."

She squinted at the sea. "It looks rocky all the way out. And kind of brown."

"Oh yeah, it's almost unswimmable. Just like when I was a kid." He sighed. "I love it."

Ainsley watched a seagull eating trash from an overflowing trash can. Then she turned around, looking at the sparse palm trees, at the angry traffic thundering by on the nearby highway. The scent of diesel exhaust floated on the air. Towering over the scene was a brownish-black mountain that looked as burnt as a cheek that had been pressed against a sauté pan.

"Joaquim," she said.

He lay down next to her, his forearm cast over his eyes. "What?"

"I don't think I like it here."

Her boyfriend uncovered his eyes, squinted at her. "It's our first day, Ainsley. We have a front row seat at the Mediterranean. What's wrong?"

"I don't know ... it's just, kind of gross. And back home we don't have to pay for a chair on the beach."

Joaquim sighed. "I spent my childhood on this coast, little spoon. This was the best place I could find on short notice."

That was true. It'd been a last-minute trip, arranged to fill an unexpected gap in his busy schedule. Ainsley looked at the row of large white yachts that had been docked in a private harbor. "It just doesn't feel like the real Spain."

"Oh, it's not." Joaquim sat up. "Look around at the faces. It's mostly British people here on holiday."

She looked at a pale-skinned family nearby, dragging

inflatable water toys across the dark sand, the children flinging handfuls of mud at one another.

"Why so many tourists?"

"Because Franco encouraged it."

"He did?"

"Yeah."

Ainsley thought about the irony. The fascist dictator of Spain, Francisco Franco, who'd ruled from the nineteen-thirties to the nineteen-seventies from high atop his perch in Madrid, had encouraged foreign visitors. Today the entire Spanish economy is partly driven by tourism.

"I mean, it's not like I'm *unhappy*—" she said.

He interrupted her. "I know what you need."

"A drink?"

Joaquim reached down into her bag and removed his wallet. "I'm guessing a gin and tonic."

"It's an easy guess."

He grinned. "Don't go anywhere."

She watched him stride off across the sand, nodding at passersby, tossing off quips, leaving an ocean of charm in his wake. Ainsley wished she could have that same talent. Instead, she was a plodder, a grinder, an investigator with the tenacity of a bloodhound.

She recrossed her legs, her fingers picking at the bandage on her left hand. Nothing to do except sit on a chair on this muddy beach underneath a high-rise tower, but it'd never been easy for her to do nothing. This wasn't to denigrate those who enjoyed quiet vacations. Ainsley understood that women with demanding jobs, screaming children, elderly parents, and hectic lives needed a facedown holiday on a poolside deck chair once in a while.

But her life wasn't nearly that full. Ainsley wondered how she was going to make it through a week on the beach without swimming.

Joaquim returned with a tray bearing two tall cups. "Unfortunately I had to order premium gin. I hope that might be acceptable to the lady."

"She might survive. And you?"

"Her unbelievably attractive companion ordered a beer."

"I hope he shows up," said Ainsley.

Laughing, Joaquim dropped onto the chair. "You keep me on my toes, little spoon." He watched her closely. "What's wrong?"

Ainsley shrugged. "It just doesn't feel like Spain. I couldn't even order paella last night at the restaurant."

"That's because you tried to order it alone."

"So what?"

"There's no such thing as paella for one. They only make it for two."

"That's stupid." Ainsley could feel her mood worsening by the second.

"Then tell me, Miss Walker—what exactly is Spain supposed to feel like?"

"I don't know."

"Name three things."

Ainsley thought about it. "Bullfights, tapas bars, and Moorish architecture."

"No, that's Andalucía," said Joaquim.

"We're not in Andalucía?"

He shook his head. "Thanks to Hemingway and other writers, that's the Spain that the world knows best. But this country has seventeen different autonomous regions. Each one has a unique flavor."

"So can we go somewhere else?"

Joaquim leaned back in his chair and closed his eyes. "I work seven days a week, little spoon. I have one week until the New Jersey deal gets going. I'd like to just relax, if that's okay."

Ainsley watched him for a moment, saying nothing.

His eyes flew open. "You're quiet. What's wrong?"

"Nothing."

"You're upset."

She turned and faced forward again. "It's fine. We'll stay here."

Joaquim watched her. "Are you sure you're okay with it?"

"Yes."

Ainsley gazed at the Mediterranean. The afternoon sun had pushed through the clouds, and the brown waves were sparkling as they crashed onto the shore. At least she had this view, if nothing else.

She heard the sound of sand squeaking and turned her head. The beach monitor had approached them.

"Pardon me," she said in a British accent, "but you're going to have to change seats."

"Why?" said Ainsley.

She pointed at the red flag. "That's meant for the red seats behind you. These are blue seats."

"We can't keep them?"

"No, the blue seats are reserved for members of the VIP club." The beach monitor gestured to an older couple nearby, towels tucked under their arms, waiting patiently. "If you gather your things, I'll lead you to the appropriate seats."

She turned to Joaquim. "We're being booted to the back row of paradise."

"I guess so," he said.

The beach monitor stood sternly between them and the Mediterranean while Ainsley slowly packed her belongings.

"This way," said the beach monitor.

They followed her towards the back row of chairs. When Ainsley sat down in her new spot, she was staring at the back of a canvas seat.

"This is *not* going to work," she said.

CHAPTER THREE

Later that afternoon, wearing an off-the-shoulder white t-shirt, blue sarong, and black flip-flops, Ainsley strolled down the only shopping lane in the seaside Spanish village. Joaquim strolled alongside her, holding her hand.

Their goal was simple—to find a decent bottle of wine for happy hour on their balcony.

Its whitewashed design mimicked the old Moorish architecture, but the plaster walls and flimsy doors were new. She saw novelty shops offering backscratchers, cafés offering hamburgers, and t-shirt shops presenting the usual array of hyperbolic and raunchy silkscreened offerings. Add a taffy machine and some chubsters wearing fanny packs, and she could've been in any American beach resort town.

Joaquim strolled alongside her, a small bottle of soda swinging from his hand. "God, I used to love running down this arcade."

Ainsley wasn't listening. "What's that?"

She pointed at a man standing outside a café. He was dressed in a red-and-white felt suit and had a white beard and was ringing a bell.

Joaquim sucked his teeth. "That's Santa Claus."

"In a Spanish beach town?"

"Sure, why not?"

Ainsley rolled her eyes. "That's wrong in so many ways."

Nearby, a church bell rang twice. It was two o'clock. The aluminum fronts of several tourist shops began to roll down.

"The church bell tells the people when to take the siesta," said Joaquim.

"Even here?"

"This is a Catholic country," he replied. "The birthplace of Opus Dei."

"I don't use drugs, Joaquim."

"It's not a drug. Opus Dei is a secret Catholic society. They're very conservative, even live in secret communities. During the day, they work regular jobs like everybody else. At night, they punish themselves."

"I'd like to meet one of them."

He shook his head. "Opus Dei doesn't advertise itself."

Ainsley thought about that. "I'd like to meet a matador too."

Joaquim's ears pricked up. "I didn't know you liked to watch the bullfights."

"I don't, but anything would be better than looking at Santa Claus."

Her boyfriend remained diplomatically quiet. Ainsley knew that she was acting out because she was upset. Maybe a better person would choose to keep her mouth shut, accept the holiday, and give it her best shot. But very little so far seemed legitimately Spanish, and Ainsley always craved authenticity in all its forms.

"I bet that place sells wine," said Joaquim.

He was pointing straight ahead to a small market, no more than five meters wide. An arctic blast of air conditioning hit Ainsley's head as she stepped through the door.

Inside, the shelving was packed with all the usual suspects —beer, wine, liquor. The proprietor sat on a high stool behind the counter, one arm propped under his chin. On the counter before him was a small tablet playing a video. As he watched, a smile decorated his face. Ainsley listened. From the device came the small, weird sound of a penny whistle singing over a small woodwind orchestra playing in 6/8 time.

"*Buen dia*," said Ainsley.

"*Buen dia*," he replied. "This music makes me so happy."

While Joaquim busied himself at the wine section, Ainsley approached the owner. "What are you watching?"

"The *sardana*."

Ainsley peered at the screen. A group of people were dancing in a public square, in front the steps of a cathedral. They were circled together, holding hands in alternating sexes, and performing a slow but intricate series of steps with their feet. In the middle of the circle was a stack of bags.

Ainsley tilted her head. "What is that?"

"A dance from my homeland."

My homeland. That was odd, since his accent sounded Spanish. "Where are you from?"

"Barcelona."

Ainsley nodded. "Well, that's not too far away."

"Oh, it's completely different."

"But it's still Spain, correct?"

The shopkeeper lifted his eyes towards Ainsley, a flinty seriousness shining in them. He lifted a warning finger. "No, Barcelona is *not* Spain. It's Catalunya."

Ainsley paused, wondering if she'd just committed a *faux pas*. Last she'd heard, Barcelona was indeed part of Spain, but it seemed as though she were accidentally crossing some ancient cultural rivalry.

Joaquim returned with a bottle of red. "This is our victim," he said. "We can't go wrong with a good *garnacha*."

The shopkeeper looked displeased. "I can suggest a better one."

"Show me," said Joaquim.

The man reached behind him slowly, as if it aggrieved him to move, towards the shelving behind him. He selected one and handed it to Ainsley. "You will love this one."

Ainsley looked at the bottle. It was labeled *Denominacio de Origen: Priorat*.

"From Catalunya," he said.

"Which is *not* Spain," replied Ainsley.

"Exactly." A broad grin crept across the shopkeeper's face.

"We'll take both," said Joaquim.

The shopkeeper rubbed his hands together and began to ring them up. "Excellent. Be sure to drink the Catalan one first."

"Why?"

"So you can't taste that other shit afterwards."

He bagged their bottles and bade them goodbye. At the door, Ainsley looked back. The shopkeeper had returned his attention to the video of the *sardana*. He was holding his arms out and bouncing his shoulders, as if he were part of the circle.

"Joaquim?" she said.

"What?"

"You weren't kidding about those seventeen autonomous regions."

CHAPTER FOUR

With one terrycloth towel wrapped around her torso and a second bunned around her hair, Ainsley plunked her hands on either side of the sink and stared deeply into the fogged bathroom mirror.

She was plumbing the depths of her soul. Trying to understand the reason for her dissatisfaction.

Ainsley had no real reason for it. Their happy hour on the balcony had been delightful. The wine had been good, the view from the third-floor balcony better, the tussle in the sheets afterwards best of all.

But something in her was yearning for *more*.

The problem wasn't Joaquim. He was nearly as perfect a boyfriend as could be. They were still flush with new love, and Ainsley was dearly hoping that this wouldn't be another one of the three-month relationships that had littered her life before she'd met ... *him* ... the one whose name she dare not speak.

The Legal Weasel.

Ainsley hated thinking about him, especially about the

fact that she was legally, but in no other way, still married to the shirker. Supported by Ainsley throughout law school, he'd suddenly, over a year ago, disappeared—out of the apartment, out of the city, out of her life. No warning, no explanation. She hadn't divorced him yet, either, because in her state it was difficult to divorce somebody that you couldn't find. There were apparently sympathetic laws about the abandonment of spouse, though. She needed to look into that when she returned.

A knock at the bathroom door. "Little spoon, are you almost ready?" said Joaquim.

"Just doing my makeup."

"I'm going downstairs to the lobby bar. Hurry up before a local woman throws me over her shoulder and carries me back to her village."

"You said there were no locals here."

"Hurry up anyways."

Ainsley smiled and shook her head. Joaquim was always going on about his millions of other options, and the truth was, he wasn't exactly lying. He *was* a prize—and Ainsley was acutely aware that she wouldn't be young forever, that there were only so many such prizes she could win during a single life.

"Can you give me ten minutes?"

"Okay. But I have something I want to give you."

"What is it?"

"A gift."

She flung open the bathroom door and caught a glimpse of the door closing. She laughed to herself. The cheeky bastard had dropped his little teaser, and then fled. He certainly knew how to motivate a woman.

Ainsley kept the bathroom door open to defog the mirror. She laid out the contents of her makeup case on the counter and quickly did her face. Then she went to her suitcase on the rack and rummaged through it. Most of her clothing was beachwear, but she had remembered to pack one good night-time outfit—a red blouse, sexy jeans with appliqué on the back pockets, and a pair of silver heels. She donned the clothing, slung her black leather coat over her shoulders, then looked across the room.

There, on the desk, sat her white bag, the one with killer hardware. It had accompanied her on all her gemstone adventures. Seeing it here, crumpled and forlorn, was disappointing.

She wrestled her emotions down and pinned them to the mat. Ainsley *wasn't* chasing any missing gemstones. She *wasn't*. She'd come here to southern Spain for a vacation, not for an assignment. She needed to nurture her relationship with her boyfriend.

Ainsley turned her back on the white bag and sighed, feeling as though she were leaving behind a small piece of herself. She slid her key into her back pocket and left the room.

In the elevator, she checked her lipstick again in the mirror, and when the doors opened, she stepped out into the lobby. As her legs carried her across the public area, her heels clacking on the tile, she felt several pairs of eyes tracking her across the lobby. Ainsley knew she wasn't a great beauty, but she did know how to attract male attention, and one of the simplest tricks was taking long strides in a pair of heels on a hard surface. It was the same long stride that, many moons ago, had carried her to the state tournament in track-and-field.

Joaquim was sitting alone at the lobby bar. He had a small glass of beer in front of him and was busy thumbing his phone. Ainsley approached from behind and threw her arms around him.

"Not a woman in sight," she said, "you must be losing your touch."

He whirled around, scanning the lobby. "No, it's just that they mopped up the blood from the catfight."

"I see," replied Ainsley. "So how many were there vying for your attention?"

"I don't know. It was all claws and fur."

"I'm surprised anybody survived."

He shrugged. "It wasn't that bad. I mean, you know how weak women can be, especially when they *really* want something."

Ainsley punched him in the shoulder. "You are *obnoxious*."

Joaquim grinned as Ainsley sat down on the stool next to him. She noticed his eyes roving up and down her body.

"What?" she said.

"You clean up nicely."

"Am I pretty enough to get my present?"

"Not quite. Do you want to go back upstairs and try again?"

Ainsley punched him in the shoulder again. "Sometimes I don't know why I'm with you."

"Because nobody else challenges you." He leaned over and kissed her cheek. "Seriously, though, I bought something very special for us."

"What?"

He fished around in his coat pocket, then pulled out two small slips of paper.

Ainsley tilted her head. "Are those tickets?"

"Yes."

"To what?"

A mysterious expression came on Joaquim's face. "You said that you felt like you weren't seeing the true Spain. So tomorrow afternoon, we're going to see it."

Ainsley read the tickets. She saw the words *Corrida de Málaga, 1300 horas*.

"You're taking me to a *corrida*?"

"Indeed."

"What's that?"

He caught her eyes. "A bullfight."

Ainsley stared at the tickets, then back at him. "Are you *kidding* me?"

"No."

"I don't want to go to a *bullfight*."

"Why not?"

"Because it's *horrible*."

Joaquim looked confused. "Why is it so horrible?"

"The killing, the blood, the ... *everything*. My God." Ainsley felt herself starting to get angry.

He nodded understandingly. "I can understand why you think that, Ainsley. But you never know until you see a *corrida* for yourself."

Ainsley slid the tickets back towards him across the bar counter. "Thank you, sweetheart, but I don't want to go."

Joaquim looked at the tickets but didn't touch them. "The *corrida* is a major part of Spanish heritage. It doesn't get any more Spanish than this."

She ignored the comment, partly because he was right. "Look, I was talking about old castles and cathedrals and stuff. Not *public murder*."

Joaquim turned to her. She could see that he was trying to be sensitive. "I've been to a few bullfights," he said, "and it's not as bad as you think."

"Yes it is. I've read about it."

"Where?"

"In a magazine."

"An American one?"

"Yes."

He nodded. "American media doesn't understand the first thing about bullfighting. But yes, you're right—in Portugal, they don't kill the bulls in the ring." He paused. "They do it *outside* the ring, away from public sight."

"Well," said Ainsley, wrapping her coat around herself more tightly, "it's inhumane."

"Of course it's inhumane. Bulls aren't humans."

"But they should have the same rights."

"Should they?" He lifted an eyebrow.

"Yes."

Shrugging, Joaquim picked up the tickets and put them into his coat pocket. "I understand your position. It's common for Western women to feel the way you do."

"Thank you."

"I just thought you might be curious to see a bullfight because of your comment earlier today."

Ainsley grew alarmed. "What comment?"

"At the beach. You mentioned bullfights, remember? Tapas and Moorish architecture and bullfights?"

Ainsley remembered saying that, and she was flooded with guilt. He'd actually been listening to her, which was more than she could say for most of her previous boyfriends. "Baby, I don't want to upset you—"

He waved his hand. "I'm not upset, Ainsley, don't worry—"

"I really appreciate that you were thinking of me—"

"Always—"

"—but this is just too much to handle. I mean, I would need to prepare myself mentally."

He arched an eyebrow. "How much time would you need?"

"It's just not going to happen."

"Really?"

"Really."

"Swear it."

She lifted a palm in the air. "I swear that I will never attend a *corrida*. Ever."

She could see that Joaquim was trying to hide his disappointment. "Then I'll return the tickets," he said.

Ainsley chewed on her lip. "Listen—why don't you go by yourself? I'm not going to stop you. I can stay here and make dinner for us."

He paused, staring at her.

"What?" she said.

"I'm not sure that's so wise."

"Why?"

"Because you made a bloody mess this morning."

Now it was Ainsley's turn to look at him, stunned, feeling as though an enormous gulf had suddenly yawned between them.

"Are you saying that I'm a bad cook?"

"No, it's just that—"

His voice disappeared to a thin whine. She looked at Joaquim, understanding that he hadn't yet grasped the fact that, yes, she *could* cook. In fact, after her husband had disappeared, her therapist had recommended baking to ground herself. She'd listened to the advice and found it therapeutic. Every evening she'd basted, broiled, sautéed, and seared. She'd bought an immersion blender, an expensive mixer. She'd developed skills.

Ainsley balled up his shirt in her right fist and brought his face close to her own. "Listen up. I'm going to prove to you that I can cook. While you go to the bullfight tomorrow, I will make you the best home-cooked dinner ever."

"That's a promise?"

"You bet."

They leaned in for a kiss, and their lips met briefly. Then

Joaquim pulled back and regarded her skeptically, a smile curling the edge of his mouth.

"What?" she said.

"Do you feel better about Spain now?"

"I do." Ainsley stood up. "And I'll feel even better once you see that I can cook."

CHAPTER FIVE

The next evening, as the Mediterranean breeze wafted around her legs, Ainsley balanced two grocery bags in her arms and wobbled across the condominium lobby.

In the elevator, she'd pressed the button with her knee, then thought about the evening's meal as the elevator car rose into the air. Despite the efforts of some radical feminists, Ainsley was aware of an inescapable truth—men loved women who knew their way around a sauté pan. In fact, many of Ainsley's girlfriends, particularly the married ones, had already rediscovered the pleasures of cooking, canning, pickling, and freezing, all the culinary arts that their great-grandmothers had known. It was a basic part of being a couple.

The doors opened, and walking down the corridor, Ainsley found her mind drifting towards the *corrida*. She'd talked a good game yesterday, but the truth was that she didn't know much about bullfighting, not even how it looked. She imagined it as an ultra-masculine, violent male fantasy. She pictured Joaquim sitting in a small arena, a cup of beer in his hand, shirtless, a primal scream erupting from his throat as dots of bull's blood splattered across his chest.

It was disgusting.

And yet she couldn't stop thinking about it.

She opened the door to her unit, dropped the groceries onto the counter, and set a pot of water to boil. Then she began to empty the groceries, one by one—a can of stewed tomatoes, a bottle of red, two potatoes, four slabs of tempeh, rosemary, sage. It would be a dependable standby vegetarian meal.

Ainsley opened the bottle of red, poured herself a glass, and went out onto the balcony to watch the end of the day. Across the water, the orange sinking sun was bathing the beach in a beautiful orange glow. Forty kilometers to the west lay the city of Málaga, where Joaquim had gone to the bull-fight. Up until the very second that he'd left, he'd tried to persuade her to join him. *Please, trust me, it's civilized, I'll cover your eyes for the killing.* He'd even written down the name of a nearby shuttle that left for Málaga every hour, in case she changed her mind.

She hadn't. But now she found her mind thinking about the *corrida*.

Were the bulls really tortured before the *corrida*? How much did they suffer at the end? Were they ever loved? What happened to the bodies afterwards? Furthermore, how did the matadors feel about killing? Did it warp their souls? Ainsley didn't have any answers to these questions. She suspected nobody found them by simply buying a ticket, either. Bullfighting was probably an insular culture, a world unto itself, one that allowed very few to learn its innermost secrets.

The secrets of Spain.

She stuffed her curiosity deep down into her soul, sealed it shut, and checked her watch. Already six pm, and no sign of Joaquim. She felt the worry rising within her. They were in a foreign country. He couldn't just disappear like this.

From inside the condo, her telephone rang. She slid open the screen door and ran to it. His name lit up the caller ID.

She picked up quickly. "Where *are* you?"

"Having a good time," came Joaquim's voice. It sounded a little wobbly.

"You're supposed to be back by now."

"I know, but I met ... some friends ..."

Her antenna extended. "What type of friends?"

"New ones." He hiccupped loudly.

"At the bullfight?"

"It's a *corrida*."

"Whatever. Where *are* you?"

"An *aficionado's* bar. Everyone here loves the *corrida*." He began to sing. "Everyone, everyone, *everyone* loves the *corrida*—"

Ainsley rolled her eyes. Joaquim sounded full-on drunk, despite her dinner plans. "So when are you going to be back? I've already started dinner."

He groaned. "Ainsley, I can't drive."

Ainsley's fingers massaged her forehead. This is what happened when she let someone as gregarious as Joaquim out of her sight for a single afternoon. He got drunk and made thousands of new friends. Part of her felt a little jealous.

"Oh, come on."

"These guys have been pouring me sherry all afternoon."

"Can you sober up somewhere?"

"I want you to come get me," he said, slurring.

She let the comment hang there. Yes, that was a possibility, one that would require finding the free shuttle from the nearby hotel. Including stops at other hotels, it would be an hour to Málaga, maybe more. Then it would take another hour to find him and the rental car. By that time it would already be eight o'clock. They wouldn't even arrive back at the condo until nine pm.

"Joaquim—" she said.

"Little spoon," he said, "please come. We'll make a night out of it. Tapas, dancing, fun."

"You've already made a day out of it, big spoon."

"I'm on vacation."

"So am I, and I spent the afternoon figuring out dinner here."

"Can you make it tomorrow?"

"Maybe."

The conversation stopped there. It'd reached an impasse.

"I love you," he said.

Ainsley sunk her head into the crook of her arm. Why *now*? He couldn't say those words *now*. He was drunk and she was upset. They hadn't even been together for three months. Furthermore, since the person who cares the least controls the relationship, the first person to utter the *one-four-three* puts himself at a severe disadvantage. Didn't he care about that? Either Joaquim was that reckless, that in love, or just that stinking drunk.

Ainsley sighed. "Well, you're going to love me even more in a few minutes," she said, reaching for her keys.

MÁLAGA

CHAPTER SIX

An hour and a half later, Ainsley stepped out into the cool night breeze of central Málaga, happy to be free of the shuttle.

The bus had been overheated, cramped, and smelly. She'd been seated next to a very drunken British tourist. He was a Manchester City supporter who'd shared his conviction, for nearly an hour, that the management of the English Premier League favored Manchester United, their rival, in ways that were undetectable to the average football fan, which he was most definitely not. As he listed the league's bureaucratic offenses, Ainsley had wearily thunked her head against the window glass and held her hand over her ear.

Now, standing at the intersection of Paseo Parque and Paseo Reding, just east of the Centro, Ainsley inhaled deeply and looked up.

She was staring at the Plaza de Toros de Málaga, or, as it's commonly known, La Malagueta.

It was a bullring.

Almost a century and a half old, this was one of the most famous in the entire world. She gazed at its circular walls,

Mudéjar horseshoe arches, brick ornamentation, and red tile roof. The architect had a real eye for design.

She pressed a button and waited to cross the street. That's when she noticed fourteen copies of the same flyer stapled to the side of a building wall. She strolled over to study it. The flyer read *La vuelta de la espada de Pepe*. It featured the image of a matador preparing to plunge a sword into the back of a bull. His face was screwed up into a ferocious expression. A beautiful blood-red gemstone decorated the hilt of the sword. Beneath the photo was the caption *Pepito vengará su padre, este sabado a Real Maestranza, Seville*.

Ainsley paused to admire the gemstone. Even though it had been mounted on a sword, which was an instrument of murder, it was an outstanding specimen. She wondered what type of stone it was.

Then, from inside the bullring, an enormous roar erupted, followed by prolonged applause.

The sound of slaughter.

Ainsley felt disgusted. She turned her back on the flyers and crossed the street, going west, towards the old town.

Now she was here, in Calle Strachan, the heart of the Málaga party district. She looked at the slip of paper in her hand. It read *La Cumbriata*. She didn't know how to translate that.

Jostled by the crowds, Ainsley headed down the narrow street, beneath the four floors of balconies, the yellow painted walls.

Then Ainsley spotted it.

A sleazy bar, squeezed between a narrow grocery and a narrow newsstand. Its dirty windows stared out defiantly at the street, daring somebody to come inside. An etching of an angry bull hung from an iron hook over the door. The words La Cumbriata were painted above the etching.

She stood outside, squinching her nose. This wasn't the

type of place that Joaquim normally frequented. In fact, on his downtime, he was usually a bit of a homebody, since he travelled so much for his business.

But something had drawn him here, and Ainsley was going to find out what.

She drew a deep breath, slung her bag tightly underneath her arm, and entered.

CHAPTER SEVEN

Ainsley stood in the doorway, the acrid scent of tobacco filling her nostrils. She studied the place.

A dirty white marble bar dominated the left side of room, a few metal napkin dispensers stationed along the way. Over the bar hung a row of fifteen legs of classic Spanish ham, each with a white paper cone affixed to the bottom to catch any oil that might dribble out. Behind the bar was a small antique scale that looked like it had weighed *jamón* for the past hundred years. And all around the room, hammered into the walls, hung framed photos of bullfighters from generations past, swooping, standing proudly in their suits of lights.

Circled around the tables were small groups of men, each swigging from small glasses of beer, their eyes fixed on a television mounted in the corner of the bar. On the screen, a team of mules was dragging the carcass of a dead bull off the sandy floor of a bullring. A smear of deep red blood followed the corpse.

Ainsley glanced away from that. It was too raw. Then she spotted, flattened on the floor, the same flyer that she'd seen posted outside the bullring, the one advertising *La vuelta de la espada de Pepe*. The same matador, the same ferocious facial expression, the same beautiful blood-red gemstone. The same caption: *Pepito vengará su padre, este sabado a Real Maestranza, Seville*.

Behind the counter, a man in an apron was washing a glass in a sink. He wore a knowing grin on his face.

"Are you here to meet someone?" he said.

Ainsley cocked her head. "How did you know?"

"We don't get many women here."

"I'm looking for Joaquim."

"Who?"

"He's Portuguese."

"Ah," he said, grinning, "that dog."

The bartender whistled. In the sea of black mops of hair, she saw Joaquim lift his head. His eyes found Ainsley and, smiling, he shot to his feet, struggling to extricate himself from the knot of men at his table. Meaty hands pushed at him as he tripped over their chair legs.

At last, he greeted Ainsley with a cheek kiss. It was sloppy and smelled like beer.

"You are the best," he said.

"I know."

"Here." He handed over the keys to the rental car. "Do you want to have a beer?"

"No."

"I know you don't want *jamón*."

She frowned and clutched her bag more tightly. "Can we just leave?"

"But this is a fun place." He nodded towards the bartender. "Jose is a dependable man. I've known him since I was eighteen."

"I don't like bullfighting."

Joaquim dropped his head. "Okay."

The bartender edged in closer to their conversation. Then he said, "Joaquim, is this the one you were describing?"

"This is her."

Ainsley looked at Joaquim. "You were talking about me?"

"Only good things, little spoon."

The bartender nodded. "He said that you find gemstones."

"I do."

"Where do you go?"

"Anywhere. Usually it requires international travel."

The bartender glanced her up and down. "I don't believe it."

"Why not?"

"A detective needs to be very smart, very persistent, very sensitive to culture—"

Before Ainsley could open her mouth, Joaquim answered. "She is all of those things, Jose. Did I tell you what she did for me in Portugal?"

"No, you didn't," said Jose.

Ainsley listened, embarrassed and self-conscious, as her boyfriend described her previous gemstone adventure, how she'd risked every last one of her dollars to pursue a sapphire *azulejo* across the neighboring Iberian country. Joaquim grew louder and more animated as he told the story.

Then Ainsley noticed somebody. An older man smoking a *cigarillo* was sitting in a nearby chair, very still, and seemed to be listening closely. A tuft of white hair stuck out from beneath a black beret and a black patch was slung over his left eye.

And his right eye was fixed upon Ainsley.

It wasn't a creepy gaze, and it wasn't malicious either. It was the gaze of a breeder gauging the quality and potential of a new animal. Ainsley returned his stare for a moment, then looked away.

"If even half of his story is true," the bartender said, "then I take back everything I just said."

Ainsley tore her attention away from the character in the corner. "Thank you," Ainsley said. Then, to Joaquim: "I'm ready to go."

"Okay."

The man with the eyepatch suddenly hoisted himself to his feet. He checked his watch, which hung from a fob on a chain. The other patrons around him grew oddly quiet, averting their eyes. A few scooted their chairs aside as he began moving forward.

A tingling sensation zinged down Ainsley's spine. He was coming towards *her*—and all signs pointed towards the fact that he was somebody important.

The man with the eyepatch hobbled across the tile floor, leaning heavily upon a wooden cane, until he stopped directly in front of her.

"Hello," said Joaquim.

"*Buenas noches*," he replied. His manner was courtly and respectful. Then he turned to Ainsley. She noticed that he had an unfortunate pair of buck teeth.

"*Usted busca las piedras preciosas?*"

Ainsley felt something stirring deep within her. "*Cuando una persona me paga*," she replied.

He nodded softly. She saw his gnarled hand softly squeeze the knob of his cane. "*Nos vemos en la estación de tren de Seville esta noche.*"

Ainsley tilted her head. She couldn't have heard that right. *Meet me at the train station in Seville tonight.*

"*Seville? Esta noche?*"

"*Sí.*"

She started to laugh, then abruptly stopped. The man looked stricken.

"*Que no es una broma*," he said. *It's not a joke.*

"*Mia culpa*—"

He interrupted her apology. "*Hay una tarea para ti.*"

Ainsley's mouth fell open. She knew what that meant, had heard it perfectly, and felt something tingle deep inside.

There is a job for you.

She stepped back from the man, studied his black beret, the odd tuft of white hair, the eyepatch. He was quite a character. "*Quién es usted?*"

"*Puede llamarme Zamorano.*"

His name was Zamorano. Ainsley grew suspicious. "*Cuál es la misión?*"

"*No puedo decirse.*"

I can't tell you.

He drew a circle on the ceiling with a finger. In Spanish, he said, "I am leaving on the nine o'clock train. There is another train leaving at eleven o'clock. I will be waiting at the Seville train station. If you are interested, you will join me."

The old man shook her hand. It felt thick, firm, calloused. Then he kissed her on the cheek. "*Hasta que llegas.*"

She noticed that the entire bar had gone silent. Thirty pairs of male eyes were watching them. Zamorano swung a hand around the bar in a sign of farewell, benediction, or both. Then he adjusted his beret, limped out of the pub, and disappeared into the crowded street.

Ainsley watched him, her fingertips touching the hollow of her throat. She felt hypnotized.

"Are you okay?" said Joaquim.

She shook her head. "Who the hell *was* that?"

He shrugged. "Zamorano, I guess."

"It felt like he was trying to pick me up."

"No," said Joaquim, "not with me here. This was something else. It felt like an authentic offer."

Ainsley felt fingers encircle her upper arm. It was the

bartender, reaching across the marble counter. His eyes were intense.

"You should go to him," he said.

"Who is he?"

The bartender's eyes grew serious. "Zamorano knows everybody. He connects people."

"Well, I don't know him."

The bartender grew serious. "Zamorano is a little unusual but he doesn't bullshit. His offer is serious."

Ainsley chewed on her lip. "I don't know."

"Go to him. You will not regret it."

The bartender released her arm and returned to washing glasses. Ainsley stared at him, feeling confused, as Joaquim pulled her out the door.

CHAPTER EIGHT

Driving their rental sedan back to the condo, Ainsley found the A-45 smooth, free of potholes, and empty of traffic, at least heading out of the city. Joaquim was dozing beside her.

Her mind was fixated on a single thought.

Zamorano.

She kept replaying their short conversation in her mind. His image was burned indelibly into her mind—the black beret, the white tuft of hair, the unfortunate pair of buck teeth, the eyepatch, the cane. She'd never seen so many props on a single human.

And now, an hour later, meeting him felt like a hazy dream, except there was no doubt that he'd been right there at La Cumbriata. She remembered the way the other men had shown him their quiet respect. The bartender had vouched for him, and Joaquim had vouched for the bartender. And she, of course, could vouch for Joaquim.

Beside her, her boyfriend stirred, yawned, and sat his seat up. He stared at her, groggy.

"You," he said, "have a secret."

"I have a thousand secrets," said Ainsley. "Which one were you referring to?"

"The one about Zamorano."

"That weirdo? I have no secrets about him."

"You're thinking about him."

Ainsley didn't say anything.

"I don't know who he is," Joaquim continued, "but I was watching him all evening, before you arrived. He listened to everybody's arguments but didn't speak. That's how you know he's smart. They asked his opinion only when there was a serious disagreement."

"It sounds he's got a lot of experience in the world of bull-fighting."

"Apparently. And the bartender sent him drinks all night."

Ainsley's fingers drummed on the steering wheel as she chewed over the odd characters. Then Joaquim broke the silence.

"I can't wait to wash my face," he said.

She laughed. "You say the oddest things."

"Washing my face always sobers me up."

"You don't have to do that."

"Of course I do," he replied. "Who else is going to drive you to the train station?"

Ainsley looked at him, astonished. "You think I should do this?"

Her boyfriend nodded. "You're made for this type of adventure. It's in your nature. And you said you wanted to see Andalucía anyways."

"But we never have time together, and I don't want to ruin our vacation—"

Joaquim waved it off. "I can't expect a fish to be happy on land. It needs to be in the water."

"I'm not a fish."

He rolled his eyes. "Or someone who loves metaphors."

Ainsley thought about the offer. "Look, chances are, this guy was a bullshitter and it won't work out. I'll probably be back by the morning."

"Probably."

"You know how careful I have to be. I don't accept assignments from just anybody."

"True," he said. "Lots of questionable people hire you."

Joaquim squeezed her hand. Ainsley pulled into the parking garage beneath their condo, into their assigned spot, and turned the motor off. She turned to face him. "Are you seriously okay with this?"

"Yes," said Joaquim.

"Are you *positive?*"

"If you love something, set it free," he said. "And if it doesn't come back to you, hunt it down and kill it."

"You can keep those rifles in the closet," she said. "I'm coming back right away."

"So you think," he said.

"I am."

He opened the car door. "Hurry up and get packed, little spoon. You have ninety minutes until you have to be at the train station."

CHAPTER NINE

After enduring two hours of kicks, Ainsley finally closed the book in her lap and thunked her head against the cool glass of the train's window.

She was on the eleven pm express train to Seville, which, despite its name, was a slow, clacking ride. She'd barely caught the thing, having leapt onboard with less a minute before departure. The attendant had already yanked away the footstool from the steps.

On her back had been a lightweight knapsack, borrowed from Joaquim. Inside had been a change of clothing, some makeup, a pair of heels, her phone, and not much else. Ainsley was travelling light.

After all, she wouldn't be gone long.

The more she thought about it, the more Ainsley was sure that Zamorano had been bullshitting her. No person in his right mind would offer a job to a total stranger based on overhearing a story told by her boyfriend. Maybe he wasn't in his right mind. After all, Zamorano had been drinking all evening. She imagined him slumbering peacefully on the nine o'clock train, having missed his stop and now safely on his way towards the Pyrenees, towards France, towards points beyond.

Or maybe not.

What Ainsley *did* know was that the seat-kicking had started as soon as she'd sat down. A small girl, no more than five years old, was self-destructing in the row behind her. Ainsley was sympathetic, since it was almost midnight.

Instead, she'd concentrated on reading her book, a history of Andalucía she'd found on the bookshelf of the condo association's common room. Turning the pages, she realized that everything she thought she'd known about Spain was wrong.

Andalucía, for example, had been controlled by a group of Muslims for eight hundred years. They were called Moors, and they spent those centuries worshipping Allah, praying five times a day, making architecture and design that focused exclusively on geometric patterns. Even the word *Andalucía* itself had actually derived from an Arabic word, *Al-Andalus*. Today, many English words beginning with *al-* (such as *algebra*, *alcove*, *alchemy*, and *alcohol*) have their roots in Moorish culture.

In fact, if you consider Latin to have five grandchildren—French, Italian, Romanian, Portuguese, and Spanish—it's the last one that has travelled the farthest from the family home. That's largely because of the Arabic conquerors. Their influence is heard today in many bits of Spanish pronunciation, particularly the soft, throaty "j" sound heard in words such as *jefe* or *Jorge*.

An extremely strong kick jolted Ainsley out of the book. Then came an unearthly shriek.

Ainsley fumbled in her bag until she found a small plastic sack of caramels. This sweet was her greatest weakness, and she liked to carry them everywhere.

She sat up, turned around on her knees, put her forearms on the back of her chair, and looked down at the offender. It was a little dark-haired moppet with a mischievous scowl on her little mug. Next to her sat a harried mother, rosary beads wrapped in her hands.

"We have a problem," said Ainsley.

"Yes," replied the mother, "she is a child of the devil. The angels turned their backs upon her years ago."

"Maybe she should just go to sleep. It's very late."

"Marta never sleeps," said the mother. "She only shuts her eyes while she plots more evil." The woman shook her daughter's knee and berated her. "Now look what you've done. This woman wants to know why you behave like an animal."

The girl shrieked again, and her mother buried her face in her hands. "The whole world is embarrassed by you."

Ainsley held out a caramel. "Marta, this is for you."

"Don't," said her mother.

"But she can't scream while she's eating. And caramels take a long time to swallow."

Her mother thought about it. "That's a good point."

Ainsley handed the caramel to the little girl. She grabbed the candy, unwrapped it with uncoordinated fingers, and stuck it into her mouth.

"Blessed silence," said her mother, making the sign of the cross.

"Here," said Ainsley, handing her the sack, "take the rest. It'll make the ride much easier on all of us."

The woman accepted the gift. "You're an angel. You must be coming to Semana Santa to hand out blessings."

"What is Semana Santa?" said Ainsley.

"Holy Week. It's the seven days before Easter Sunday."

"It's this week?" she said.

"Of course," said the mother. Her finger circled around the travelers in the car. "That's why everybody is on this train. Me, I'm going to ask the Virgin to give Marta relief from her affliction."

"What affliction?"

"I already told you—she is a child of the devil."

The mother said it with a straight face. Ainsley had thought she'd been kidding. In the United States, child psychologists would explain that little Marta was exhibiting oppositional defiance disorder, or suffering from an attention deficit hyperactive disorder, or seeking attention from a distant mother. She would probably be prescribed a mood stabilizing drug, patted on her back, and sent on her way.

Here, the girl was simply possessed by the devil.

"Do you have a place to stay?" said the mother.

"No," said Ainsley.

"The whole city is booked up. There are no rooms."

"Really?"

"It's true. But don't worry. The parties go on all night long. You can sleep in the park in the morning."

That sounded like no fun whatsoever. Over the intercom, a man's voice announced the next stop: Seville, the San Bernardo station.

"Good luck with her," said Ainsley.

"Let me know if I can help you somehow," replied the mother.

———

As the train pulled into the station, Ainsley felt a little disappointed. She'd been expecting a massive cathedral of transportation, like Grand Central Station in New York or Shinjuku in Tokyo. After all, this is the city from which countless *conquistadores* had launched countless explorations.

But the San Bernardo station had a grand total of two platforms, a pair of escalators, and a vending machine.

At least this would make it easier to find Zamorano. And yet, as the train slowed down, and as her eyes scanned the few people waiting on the platform ... the black beret, the white tuft of hair, the buck teeth were nowhere to be found.

A sudden jerk told her that the train had come to a halt. She heard the hiss of some unseen mechanical system underfoot. The passengers rose from their seats, hoisted their luggage from the overhead bins, and filed towards the exit. As they walked, Ainsley heard Marta shrieking behind her. Squirting her with a vial of holy water suddenly didn't seem such an outlandish choice of discipline.

A moment later Ainsley found herself disgorged on the platform, the tiles hard underfoot, the sodium lights buzzing overhead. A mass of fellow passengers had disembarked and were streaming past her, families, couples, children, old people—all headed towards the escalators, towards the festivities above.

Towards *Semana Santa*. Holy Week.

Ainsley stood behind a pillar, waiting until the rush had passed. Her eyes fell upon the same flyer on the pillar. *La vuelta de la espada de Pepe*. The matador with the fierce facial expression, the blood-red gemstone.

When the crowd had passed, she hoisted her knapsack around her shoulder, her white bag around the other, and moved towards the escalators, which slid up a long tunnel towards the surface.

At the base of the escalator, she stopped.

A silhouette was descending towards her. It wore a beret and carried a cane.

When the figure reached the lip of the platform, and stepped out into the light, she recognized the face. It was Zamorano.

Her heart bolted out of her chest like a greyhound out of a gate.

As the man's eyes found Ainsley, a knowing smile crept along the side of his face.

"*Señorita*," he said.

"*Señor*."

"You have courage."

Ainsley nodded. "And you know someone who wants to find a gemstone."

"Indeed," said Zamorano, "so let's hurry along. He's waiting."

"Who?"

"The man."

"What's his name?"

A glint shone in his eye. "You will find out shortly."

Then Zamorano turned and stepped onto the up escalator. Rising into the darkness, he checked his watch.

"Oh dear," he said, "we're going to be late. He's going to be angry."

"Who is he?" said Ainsley.

Rising out of sight, Zamorano's voice came down like a dream: "Are you coming?"

Taking a deep breath, Ainsley stepped onto the escalator and began rising with him.

SEVILLE

CHAPTER TEN

Ainsley hadn't known what to expect of Holy Week in Seville, but she was pretty sure it wasn't supposed to look like a Ku Klux Klan rally.

The escalator had deposited her directly into a street in the center of the historical center of Seville. The street was swarming with hundreds of festivalgoers.

Momentarily confused, Ainsley struggled to orient herself. Elaborate Mudejar buildings lined each side of the narrow cobblestones, each five floors high, each decorated with narrow wrought-iron balconies. She gaped, marveling at the medieval urban design that concentrated all human activity into a single ground-level strip of frenetic festivity.

Then Ainsley'd realized that she was standing alone. Panicking, she'd scanned the heads. There, twenty meters away, was the black beret, bobbing up and down as it scampered away through the crowd.

Zamorano was a slippery bugger. She was going to have to keep an eye on him.

A quick little sprint, slipping sideways through the knots of people, and Ainsley'd pulled up behind him. He was hopping along in a three-step pattern. *Foot foot cane*, *foot foot cane*. It looked like compensation for an injury.

Ainsley had sidled up alongside him.

"We can't stop," he'd been muttering. "We're going to be late—"

"Late for what?"

"Very late—oh no."

He'd stopped next to a lamppost and pointed at the intersection ahead. It'd been clogged with a thick knot of people, at least a thousand, police officers standing at the barricades.

"What's happening?" Ainsley had said.

He'd lifted a finger to his lips. A hush had fallen over the people—and then Ainsley had heard the trumpet blast.

It was a bright yet somber melody, in a minor key, that had sent shivers from the crown of her head to the toes of her feet. Then she'd seen the cross arrive. The *Cruz de Guía*, nearly five meters high. Tall enough for thousands of spectators to see. It'd moved solemnly above the heads of the procession.

Semana Santa. Holy Week.

Next came what appeared to be the Ku Klux Klan rally, if that group had relocated to the other side of the ocean, converted to Catholicism, and discovered colors. The resemblance was eerie. A phalanx of figures, cloaked in purple penitential robes and tall purple pointed hoods, was moving slowly down the street. Each figure struggled under the weight of a large brown wooden crucifix.

The spectators had fallen utterly silent. Ainsley felt a chill in her legs.

"Zamorano," she whispered, "what is this?"

"The *cofradía*," he answered. "It's a brotherhood. Those are the *nazarenos*, and they have been walking for six hours from their home church. Many are barefoot. Some whip themselves."

"Why?"

"They are reenacting the way of the cross."

"But why?"

"Tradition."

"Is this the only *cofradía*?"

He shook his head. "There are almost a hundred in these streets this week. And even more throughout Andalucía. But to me, this is one of the most special."

"Why?"

"My father belonged to it." He dabbed his eyes with a handkerchief, then stowed it away. "I was trying to cross this street before it was scheduled to arrive. It's too emotional for me. Now we have to wait." He shook his head. "He's going to be angry that we're late."

"Late for what?" Ainsley said. "I still don't know where you're taking me."

"Shh," he replied, "here comes the *paso*."

Zamorano crossed himself and kissed the back of his thumb. Ainsley swung her eyes back to the parade.

Swaying above the heads of the crowd was the grand finale—a float, draped in red and gold fabric, nearly as wide as the street itself. Atop the swaying platform, forty silver candlesticks, each as high as a man, lit up the night. Behind them, beneath an elaborate wooden canopy, stood a golden sculpture of a weeping Virgin Mary. She was covered in garlands of fresh flowers.

She leaned over to Zamorano. "How is the float moving?" she whispered.

"Go and look."

"Where?"

"Up front. You will see."

He gently pushed her forward. Ainsley threaded her way through the packed crowd, apologizing, *con permiso*, over and over, until she had nearly reached the barricade. From here, she could see the penitents tipping their candles towards the small children lining the curbs of the street, who formed multicolored balls of wax from the drippings.

The trumpets blared the melody again—and this time, women in the crowd began singing out loud, at the top of their lungs, arms flung out towards the *paso*, rosary beads dangling, tears streaking down their cheeks. Soon the women were joined by other women crowding the narrow balconies above. The melodies were arrows of pain flying towards the virgin sculpture, wrenched from the very souls of the people.

As the float drew closer, Ainsley gazed up at the Virgin's tearful face, heard the anguished melodies, saw the tearful faces of the people—

—and suddenly, she understood. This was catharsis. A release of whatever fear, angst, and frustration was felt by the Andalucían people. All in a socially sanctioned manner.

Ainsley thought hard. In the United States, there were very few public practices like this. Football games, maybe. Or, in the old days, fundamentalist preachers performing the laying-on of hands in revival tents.

Then she remembered to look for the method of propulsion. Scanning the float, she saw that the elaborate red-and-gold drapery hanging along the sides stopped just short of the ground. Ainsley looked down.

Moving beneath the edge of curtain was the left edge of a bare foot.

It was a human foot, and it was shuffling along at no more than one centimeter at a time. Scanning the length of the float's curtain, she counted twelve more such feet. This meant at least twelve more people on the other side of the giant float, plus probably another row in the middle.

That meant nearly *forty* people heaving and sweating and grunting in the darkness beneath that wooden dirge, carrying what amounted to a yacht on their backs.

Ainsley stood in respectful silence as the float trudged past her, the candles swaying. Then the parade route faced a corner, and she watched the feet shuffle sideways as it turned perpendicularly, the Virgin sculpture rocking on its stand.

Then, the maneuver accomplished, the *paso* slowly disappeared down the next block. In front of her, the municipal police removed the temporary barricades. The crowd began to rush into the open space.

Turning, Ainsley swam against the human tide, back to the lamppost where Zamorano had been standing.

He was gone.

Cursing, Ainsley whirled around, scanning the heads. Finding him would be nearly impossible in the dimness and the crowd.

Then she spotted him. The black beret, the tuft of white hair, hopping away through the crowd.

"That," said Ainsley, starting after him, "is a very strange creature."

CHAPTER ELEVEN

As she trailed Zamorano through the darkened streets, Ainsley discovered the sensual side of Seville.

The brisk night breeze tickling her cheeks. The scent of orange blossom. The food carts on the streetcorners, offering *churros con chocolate*. The drunken revelers spilling out of crowded tapas bars onto the cobblestones.

Semana Santa. Holy Week.

She followed him through the Plaza Espana, a huge semi-circular public space filled with glazed tiles, fountains, bridges, and art deco design. Then she followed him out of the historic center, across the illuminated Triana Bridge, to the neighborhood of the same name on the other side.

Ainsley regretted the fact that she had nearly written off this city. In her mind, she compared Seville with her own hometown, a grim, humorless place where dutiful obedience was demanded, where bedroom lights were turned off by nine o'clock every night. It was like comparing a pair of sexy heels with a pair of sturdy black nurse's shoes.

Ahead of her, Zamorano was scampering along a row of residential buildings. *Foot foot cane*. Then she he disappeared down an outdoor staircase. This was the place. She looked up at the structure. It was a centuries-old building, walls painted the color of old blood, scabbed with wrought-iron.

Without pausing, Ainsley ran down the outdoor staircase and pushed through a heavy coffered door. She plunged into a dark passageway. At the far end was a single overhead light illuminating a residential door.

Behind her, the heavy coffered door clicked shut.

As she plunged further into the darkness, hearing her own shoes clacking on the floor, Ainsley felt her heart hammering against her sternum. Ahead, Zamorano was a mere shadow scampering in the darkness.

As she drew closer to the spiral staircase, she saw a splash of red and black paint on the residential door. She squinted and peered.

It was a silhouette of a bull being murdered.

She could see the white *picas* sticking out of its hump, the fur drenched in blood, the lifeless stare as the eyes rolled backwards in its skull.

Ainsley felt a sudden wave of revulsion. This place was overwhelming, suffocating, claustrophobic. Coming here had been a mistake.

She stopped. "I can't go any further," she said.

"Why?"

"I don't know you, I don't know this city, and I hate the *corrida*. I'm going back to my boyfriend—"

Before Ainsley could turn back, she heard the *thock* of Zamorano's cane grow louder on the floor as he drew closer. Then she felt his fingers catch her by the arm.

"I want to show you something," he said.

She heard him unrolling a paper. Then she heard a match striking. An orange flame illuminated half of Zamorano's face, the buck teeth, the pink eyes. It was a good face, ugly but kind.

He slowly lifted something up to the light. She recognized it.

It was the flyer. The one that read *La vuelta de la espada de Pepe*. The matador with the ferocious facial expression, the blood-red gemstone decorated the hilt of the sword.

"You have seen this?" he said.

"Of course."

The man fell silent. His eyes intensely searched Ainsley's face. Spanish people had stares that seemed to spring from their very souls.

"You must choose," said Zamorano. "Either come with me or leave. But if the answer is yes, you cannot turn back."

Ainsley looked towards the door with the painting of the murdered bull. Then she looked at the bullfighter on the flyer. Zamorano gave her a knowing tilt of his head. He was letting her put two and two together.

"If that's the case," she said, "then I want to leave."

Ainsley backed away from the small man, from the painting—then turned and fled down the hallway, back towards the heavy wooden door that had clicked shut behind her. In the darkness, she fluttered her hands across the coffered door, trying to find the way out. When she found the knob, squarely in the middle, she grabbed it with both hands and yanked hard.

It didn't budge.

"You need a key," said Zamorano's voice.

"To get out?"

"Yes."

"Can I have it?"

"I don't have one."

"Why not?"

"I don't live here. But he does."

"Who?"

"Him."

Ainsley slowly turned around. At the far end of the hall-way, the painted door had been opened. In the doorway stood the silhouette of a stocky man, his arms held away from his sides.

"Who are you?" she croaked.

"I am called Pepito," said the man in a booming voice, "and you must be the one who finds gemstones."

CHAPTER TWELVE

Ainsley felt powerless to resist. The figure's voice was too commanding, the heavy coffered door behind her too immovable. She felt her legs carrying her forward again, towards the silhouetted man at the end of the hallway.

"Come into the light," said the man.

She stepped into the circle of light formed by the single overhead bulb, with Zamorano staying safely behind her. Ainsley lifted her chin. Though Pepito was still nothing more than an outline, she could feel him studying her.

"Why do you want to leave?" he said.

"I don't know," she replied.

"Are you afraid?"

"No."

His voice deepened. "I said, are you afraid?"

She gulped. "A little."

"I would be, in your position. A beautiful Anglo woman following a stranger into the basement of a building. Then the door locks behind me." He paused. "You must be a little crazy."

Ainsley bristled. "So what if I am?"

"I like that."

The man stepped into the light, and Ainsley felt her knees go a little weak. Not from attraction, but from his sheer undeniable presence.

It was Pepito.

The matador on the flyer.

A squat bull of a man, Pepito looked to be about fifty years old. Everything about him screamed mesomorph. His body was laden with muscle—not the highly defined, isolated groups of sculptured muscle fiber built in an artifical weight room. He had real muscle, outdoors muscle. Work muscle.

She studied the rest of him. The short, beefy forearms. The invisible neck. The skull that sat atop his shoulders like a dropped anvil. The jaw as square as a coffee table.

His clothing was unusual too. Wrapped around his head was a piece of white fabric, in Arabic fashion, and flowed down the back of his shoulders. Around his stocky chest was a white V-neck t-shirt, soaked in sweat. His loose black pants rode high, revealing his bare feet and ankles, which were edged with gray dust and caked in dried blood.

The matador noticed Ainsley noticing his feet. "Do you know what my feet signify?"

"That you're a *nazareno*," she answered, remembering the term.

He lifted a finger. "But not a member of a *cofradía*. The brotherhood from Santa Eustacia asked me for help."

"Because Pepito is very strong," added Zamorano, "he's a popular substitute when someone gets sick. Every year at least one *cofradía* calls him."

"I imagine," said Ainsley. She gestured at his feet. "Does it hurt?"

The matador looked confused. "I don't understand."

"Walking barefoot over these streets, carrying a float on your back, doesn't hurt you?"

He shrugged. "I don't feel pain."

"Never?"

"Never."

He held her eyes, as if to underline his point. Ainsley regarded him with skepticism, but he made no attempt to clarify the statement any further. It was simply a fact.

She finally broke the silence. "Pepito, I need to leave, so if you have the key—"

The matador crossed his arms. They looked like a pair of heavy tree trunks fallen across a wooded path. "But we have only just begun to talk."

"About what?" she said.

"My problem."

"Zamorano said that you're missing a gemstone," she said, "but I don't really feel comfortable talking to you."

"Why not?"

"Because I don't trust you."

The matador snorted at the idea. "You can trust me to pay you, if that's what you're worried about. But the real question, *extranjera*"—he pushed a finger into her shoulder—"is whether I can trust *you*."

Ainsley stumbled backwards from the force of the finger, then recovered, feeling her pride wounded.

"Of course you can," she said.

"*Señor*," interrupted Zamorano, "remember that José in Malagá vouches for her."

"That's very good," replied Pepito, "but I would prefer to look into her eyes and judge for myself."

The matador took two steps towards her. She lifted her gaze. He'd had drawn uncomfortably close to her face. As his eyes found her own, she instinctively averted his gaze. His two meaty hands clapped either side of her head and snapped her face forward again. Ainsley felt her heartbeat accelerate, her breathing quicken, her muscles tense. The fight-or-flight instinct. She willed herself to stay calm and looked into the matador's eyes. His dark pupils were burning into her own, flicking left, right, left, right.

Suddenly he released her and stepped back. A small cry escaped her lips as her breath rushed back into her body and she collapsed onto the floor.

"Good," said Pepito, "there is no lying in your face."

Ainsley rubbed her jaw and glared at him. "What does that mean?"

"It means I can trust you." He extended his hand. "I invite you into my home."

Ainsley sized him up. "Only if you have red wine."

"I have tempranillo. Unless you prefer something else."

"Garnacha."

He nodded. "I will pour it."

Ainsley felt her defenses lower. This man was speaking her language. Pepito stepped aside, held the door open, and gestured for her to enter. Rising to her feet, she took a deep breath.

This was the real Spain.

CHAPTER THIRTEEN

The matador's living room displayed the memorabilia of someone who'd spent many years inside a bullring.

Ainsley studied the room. A pair of large bull heads mounted on the red walls spoke of past victories. A shelf of half-empty whiskey bottles pointed towards a fondness for Scotland's finest. In the corner, an old turntable spun a passionate flamenco piece. And overhead, the muscular arms of a chandelier flung yellow bits of light onto the floor.

Pepito emerged from the kitchen with two glasses of red wine. He handed her one and held aloft his glass. "*Salud, señorita.*"

"*Salud, señor.*"

They both drank. Ainsley tasted the dry red wine coursing down her throat. It was a delicious vintage and she felt her body begin to relax.

A large dog with a heavy bone structure padded into the room behind the matador. Ainsley recognized the breed—it was an *alano español*, sometimes called a Spanish bulldog, a member of the molosser family. The animal was a meter high at the head, and its broad nose and black mask were pulled back in a snarl as it looked at its visitor. The wrinkles on its short neck bunched up as it reared back, and a low growl escaped its throat. Its ears were laid flat. Ainsley felt a little shiver of fear.

Pepito barked a short command, and the animal lay down with its head on its paws.

"How do you call it?" she said.

"He doesn't have a name," said Pepito, "but I take him everywhere with me. He is my enforcer." The matador drained his glass of wine and poured himself another. "What about you? How are you called?"

"Ainsley Walker," she replied.

"Ainsley Walker," he said, rolling her name around his mouth.

She walked behind a club chair, running a hand along its back, feeling the aged leather beneath her fingertips. Then she sat down on the edge of the cushion, keeping her spine erect, and crossed her legs.

"I'm a gemstone detective," she said.

"The job is pleasing to you?"

"It's never boring."

"You have many clients?"

Ainsley nodded. "Gemstones have been valuable to people for thousands of years in thousands of cultures. Some people will do almost anything to recover them."

Pepito looked sad. "When I face a bull, I feel powerful. When I face another problem, I don't feel powerful. This is why you are here."

"Tell me about this problem."

He held up a finger. "Not yet."

"Why?"

"It's very sensitive."

"Okay."

"You need to be discreet."

Ainsley nodded. "I am."

"I cannot tell you until you are committed."

Ainsley drew back a little, smoothed her clothing. "Money certainly commits me. Show me some money."

The matador ignored the request and eyed her curiously for a moment. "Do you like the *corrida*?"

Ainsley was grateful that Joaquim had taught her that word. "My opinion doesn't matter," she replied.

"But do you *like* it?"

"I'm irrelevant. This is about you."

"No," he corrected her, "it's about *you*."

"Why?"

"Because this assignment will send you into the world of the bulls."

Ainsley felt her stomach hit her shoes. She'd been aware, in the back of her mind, that this adventure was heading towards the violent, murderous side of the Iberian pastime. Now that fear had been confirmed.

Ainsley mentally reviewed her options. One, she could continue dodging the question, but Pepito was getting impatient. Two, she could lie and profess a lifelong love of public animal slaughter. Or, three, she could tell the truth.

"I honestly don't know much about the *corrida*," she said, "but I'm open to learning."

There: It wasn't too far from the truth. The matador narrowed his eyes, leaned back, crossed his meaty arms, and held a single finger to his lips in deep contemplation. Then he nodded and slapped his hands on his thighs.

"It's good," he said.

"Thank you."

"Now, Miss Walker," he said, "Before I explain my problem to you, I have to wash the sweat off my body and change my clothing so we can go out."

"But we just got here."

He swung his arms in a pantomime of stretching. "I need more room. This house is so small."

"Why don't you buy another one? Maybe in the country?"

He shook his head. "I can't afford it."

"All right. Where do you want to go?"

"A bar. It's where I always do my business."

Ainsley played hard-to-get. "I don't know, Pepito. I might get bored waiting for you. I might just leave."

The matador smirked. "No, you're not going anywhere." He crouched and tapped his dog on the head. "*Chato—la puerta.*"

Like a colossus rumbling to life, the *alano español* lifted its head from its paws, drew itself to its feet, padded over to the front door, and sat down, facing Ainsley. She could smell its thick, wet odor.

It was watching her.

"Ten minutes," said Pepito.

As the matador disappeared into the rear of the home, Ainsley leaned forward and reached for her phone in her bag on the floor. Before she could find it, a low, intimidating growl emanated from the dog's throat.

Ainsley stopped, her hand hanging in the air. Then she slowly withdrew her hand, leaned back in the chair, and began to wait.

She didn't have a choice.

CHAPTER FOURTEEN

A half hour later, Pepito was sauntering down the cobblestones of Triana with the casual dominance of a lion moving across the savannah.

Dressed in a red polo shirt and blue jeans, the matador strolled down the middle of the gaslit street. Passersby whispered, casting nods towards him. Vehicles swung around, giving him wide berth. He didn't seem to notice any of it.

Ainsley walked a safe distance away and watched the matador. His vitality was astonishing. He didn't seem like a man who'd just spent six hours barefoot carrying what amounted to a large boat on his back.

"It feels better out here in the street," he said, swinging his arms. "I don't like feeling so constricted."

"Like I said, you could move to the country," Ainsley replied.

"No, I travel too much for the *corridas*. Maybe when I retire." He paused. "Now, the business."

"Yes."

"Miss Walker, I am missing a gemstone. It's a valuable one."

"How valuable?"

"One of the most unusual you've ever seen."

"Try me."

"It's inlaid in a sword."

Ainsley remembered seeing it, on the poster for the upcoming bullfight—a blood-red gemstone embedded in the handle of the weapon. In the back of her mind, she'd assumed that it was merely a piece of colored glass. After all, the world had stopped producing jewel-encrusted swords back in the medieval era, and almost everything that old and that valuable was safely ensconced inside a fancy museum, behind thick glass, protected by motion sensors and other forms of top-level security. She didn't have the resources needed for those types of recoveries.

"I saw it on the poster," she said.

He nodded. "It's called the sword of Pepe. Pepe was my father. He was one of the best matadors of the nineteen sixties and seventies."

"How did he lose it?"

"He didn't lose it. He died forty years ago." Pepito lifted his barrel chest and thrust out his jaw. "He was gored in the ring by a Miura. He bled to death in the hospital."

"You were young."

"I was twelve."

From deep, unfortunate experience, Ainsley knew what it was like to lose a parent. Since then, she'd instinctively known how to speak to people about death.

"I lost my father at the same age," she said.

Pepito looked at her with new eyes. "So you understand the pain."

"I do."

He nodded. "You lose a parent that young, it makes you want to take over the entire world. To see everything, learn everything, do everything. So you can know *why* it happened."

Ainsley thought about that. She'd never had much interest in navel-gazing, preferring instead to look at the world around her. In fact, she'd always been inspired by that fanciful nineteenth-century drawing of an enormous transparent eyeball on two long legs, high-stepping over the countryside, gazing at everything. That was her attitude. The world was far more interesting than she could ever be.

By now they'd arrived at the Guadalquivir River. Down the road she could see the Moorish Revival chapel, the Triana bridge lit up blue in the darkness, the crowds milling everywhere.

She produced a small steno pad from her bag and swung the conversation back to the task at hand. "So who lost the sword?"

"I did," he said, "last week."

"What type of gemstone is it?"

"A tourmaline. The color of blood."

Ainsley jotted it down. She knew the tourmaline very well. They were semi-precious stones with vitreous luster that were found across the globe, from Maine to Madagascar, in almost every color of the rainbow. The tourmaline group includes a whopping twenty-nine different subvarieties, including schorl. Certain specimens were even used by early physicists to polarize light. Ainsley herself owned a watermelon tourmaline, so called because it was green on the outside and pink on the inside.

"When was the last time you saw the sword?" she asked.

"At my last *corrida*, in Córdoba. I always have it with me, in the sword case, but I never use it." He flashed his small pebbly teeth, grinning. "There is no need at that *corrida*. The *impresario* only purchases Saltillos, a cowardly animal. I almost fell asleep waiting for it to charge."

Ainsley tried to imagine dozing as a wild creature weighing half a ton snorted at her across the sand. She couldn't. Her imagination failed.

"So what happened?"

"The usual. After the *corrida*, the *mozo* cleaned all the weapons and put them away in the bag."

Mozo. Ainsley knew that word meant "waiter" in some countries, but she suspected it had a different connotation here.

The matador noticed her confusion. "*Mozo de espadas*. He carries my swords."

Ainsley made a note on that. "So how did he lose your father's sword?"

"He didn't lose it," said Pepito, "somebody *stole* it."

Ainsley tapped her pen against her teeth. "Just like that."

"I know what you're thinking."

"What?"

"You're thinking that the *mozo* stole my sword. That he betrayed me."

Ainsley lifted a questioning eyebrow. "It's not out of the question, right?"

The matador's eyes flashed. "This *mozo* has been with me for thirty years. He is as loyal as any human being."

Despite his protests, Ainsley could tell that Pepito had been mulling this scenario for quite some time. She'd touched a nerve.

"And it would be too obvious," she said.

Pepito gave her a clever look. "You are a wolf who knows."

Ainsley didn't understand exactly what that meant, but she took it as a compliment. They arrived at a street corner, and on a pole was stapled Pepito's flyer. Her eyes fell upon the caption at the bottom.

Ainsley looked up. "You're going to kill the bull using your father's sword?"

The matador nodded.

"Why?"

"Because it's good marketing. Everybody loves revenge."

"Revenge on a bull?"

A fire flashed in his eyes. "Of course. Plus, it's a Miura."

He waited for that to sink in. It didn't.

"What's a Miura?" she said.

He rolled his eyes. "It's the most dangerous breed. It's large and fast and very smart. It's the same breed that gored my father and kicked him as he bled to death on the floor of Maestanza. In fact, it's a direct descendant."

Ainsley looked again at Pepito's face on the flyer. Then she looked into Pepito's real face next to her.

"The event is sold out," he said. "Fourteen thousand tickets. The people are expecting a comeback."

Ainsley glanced back at the flyer, at the caption along the bottom.

Pepito vengará su padre, este sabado a Real Maestranza, Seville.

She squinted, reading again.

Este sabado.

She turned to the matador. "Pepito, the *corrida* is this Saturday."

He placed two burly hands on his hips. "It is."

"That's only one week away."

"I know," came his reply, "which is why you have to start right away. I have more to tell you." He pointed straight ahead. "There is my favorite place. We can get more food and talk."

CHAPTER FIFTEEN

As Ainsley followed Pepito into the tapas bar, she wondered how they were going to cram themselves inside, much less continue the conversation.

The room was smoky and crowded, shoulders and elbows jostling for room at the counter. Nearly thirty legs of *jabuco* ham hung from hooks on the ceiling, white paper cones affixed to the end to catch the grease drippings. Ainsley felt her stomach turn at the sight, and the volume of shouted conversation made her nearly cover her ears.

Then someone noticed Pepito—

—a few elbows were thrown—

—and, slowly, the crowd began to part.

The matador strode down the middle of the room, swagger made flesh, with Ainsley following close on his heels. At the bar, the other patrons shuffled to the left and right, until there was enough room for the two of them to squeeze up against the wooden counter. Ainsley was close enough to the matador to catch the scent of his aftershave. It smelled like old leather and horse sweat.

"See," said Pepito, "the people like me here."

"Or they're afraid of you."

"Fear or love, it doesn't matter. Either way, they respect me."

The tapas bar owner came over, a flat, affectionless smile drawn onto his skull. He gripped Pepito's hand at the wrist and greeted him with a swift yank. It looked like an attempt to pull the matador across the counter. The two men leaned forward and exchanged some quick words.

Then the owner turned to Ainsley. "What would you like?"

"*Patatas bravas.*"

Pepito looked at her oddly. "No *jamón*?"

"I already had some today," she lied.

"This is the best *jamón* in Seville."

Ainsley smiled nicely. "No, thank you."

Ignoring her, Pepito turned to the owner. "*Jamón por los dos.*"

Ainsley watched as the owner approach the enormous animal leg. It was at the rear of the bar, propped sideways on a special stand. The owner picked up a special knife and drew it gently lengthwise along the top of the leg. Razor-thin slivers of pink meat curled up from the leg.

The plate arrived a few seconds later. Ainsley studied the meat, the way that each thin slice boasted a deep, rich reddish-brown color and was marbled with delicate lines of white fat.

Ainsley watched Pepito as he slowly devoured the meat. Between bites, fuelled by a never-ending series of small *finos*, the matador described the small slices of rich *jamón* in ways that were usually reserved for the bedroom. He talked about the history of *jamón ibérico*, how the suckling pigs were raised on a diet of nothing but acorns, how their food troughs were kept a quarter mile away from their water troughs to force them to build muscle. He discussed the aging process, the extra tangy flavor that the legs developed by hanging in a room of tobacco smoke. He described, in excruciating detail, the precise reasons that *jamón serrano* and *jamón bellota* were both inferior.

Ainsley finally interrupted the lecture. "Tell me about the tourmaline sword."

"The sword of Pepe," he corrected her.

"Yes, the sword of Pepe. If you don't have it by the time of the *corrida* this Saturday, what will happen?"

"My reputation will be finished. I mean, it's on the advertisement. I will be seen as a clown. Someone who promised everything and delivered nothing." He sighed. "It's already my last chance. I'm not as famous as my father was, and he died forty years ago. Soon there won't be anybody who remembers him."

Thinking, Ainsley drummed her fingers on the counter. "So who do you think stole it? Who could've wanted to hurt you?"

His eyes were a pair of bullets, staring through the wall to an unseen enemy in the distance. "There are people who ... suffer from jealousy," he said.

"Of your success?"

Pepito shook his head. "I don't have that much success."

"Then what are people jealous of?"

He shrugged. "Maybe my body."

She doubted that. Pepito was a thick slab of meat, no doubt, but few people wanted to be shaped like the guy you hire to hang drywall.

"It's possible," she said, "but would that make somebody jealous enough to sabotage your comeback? Who are your real enemies, Pepito?"

Ainsley pulled out her steno pad, placed it upon the countertop, and uncapped a pen. She looked at him, prepared to take notes. But Pepito had been struck dumb.

"I don't know," he said.

"You don't have *any* enemies?"

"No," he said.

"Maybe other matadors?"

"No," he said, "they respect me."

She had a sudden brainstorm. "What about the animal rights' groups? Could they have done this?"

"Maybe," he said. "Equanimal is very irrational. I tried to talk to them once, telling them that it's more sensitive to the animal to watch a *corrida* than to order a steak. They wouldn't listen to me."

Ainsley wrote down the word *Equanimal* in her notebook.

"But honestly," he said, "I'm not famous enough for them. Equanimal goes after the most famous matadors. To make a statement."

Ainsley had followed the radical actions of animal rights' groups in the U.S., and it was possible that Pepito didn't understand the depth of the anger against him. She underlined the word *Equanimal*.

"Anybody else?"

He shrugged. "Maybe my ex-wife."

"Why?"

"She says that I owe her money."

"Do you?"

"No."

He left it at that. Ainsley considered the possibility. If she really wanted money, it wouldn't make sense that Pepito's ex-wife would sabotage the one project that would earn him money. But people sometimes do irrational things in the name of anger, so she wrote down the woman's name anyways.

"That's everyone," he said.

She closed the notebook. "There's something else we need to talk about."

"What?"

"Money, Pepito."

An odd look spread across his face. "You expect money."

"Yes."

The way he said it frustrated Ainsley. She wasn't a local. She couldn't be paid with a bag of onions, or a song, or promises of future reciprocation. Ainsley needed cash to work, no exceptions.

To her surprise, Pepito pulled an envelope from his pocket and placed it on the counter. Then covered it with a plate.

"What is that?" she said.

"In this envelope is the first half of your payment."

That was distressing. He hadn't even presumed a negotiation, or that Ainsley had a standard rate. Implied was that this assignment was his way or the highway. She decided to play along. It was possible, after all, that his way would be adequate.

"How much is inside?"

"You can look. But be discreet."

Ainsley lifted the plate, slid the envelope beneath the counter, and unsealed it. It was packed with clean, crisp bills. She counted off the money. There were one thousand euros.

"That's the first half," he said.

"The other half upon delivery?" she replied.

He nodded.

She did the math. If she succeeded, that would be two thousand euros for a job that was guaranteed not to extend past Saturday. That was very good money. Even if she failed, one thousand euros wasn't anything to turn her nose up at either.

"It's a deal," she said.

"Now," said the matador, "I need two more things from you."

"What are they?"

His beefy hand suddenly sprang down onto her own with the strength of a bear trap snapping shut. Ainsley found her hand pinned to the counter.

"Give me your passport," he said.

"Excuse me?"

"I want your passport. You won't need it until you leave the country."

Ainsley grew very still, feeling his thick, calloused hand on her own. Travelling around a foreign country without a passport was possible, of course, but it was also asking for trouble. "Don't you think—"

Pepito shushed her with a wave of his hand. "No questions. I have been burned by too many *impresarios*. Give it to me."

She had to admit that this paranoia was understandable. He was giving her a large amount of cash on nothing more than her word. This was a way to guarantee that she wouldn't leave him in the lurch. Ainsley reached into her bag, fumbled around for her passport, and handed it to Pepito. He pocketed it quickly.

"Good," he said.

"You said there were two things. What was the other?"

He slid the plate of *jamón ibérico* directly in front of her. "Eat."

"I'm not hungry."

"I don't care. You have to show me that you aren't one of those vegetarians." He paused. "Or you don't get the job."

Ainsley looked down at the thin reddish-brown slices of cured meat. She'd only been vegetarian for a few weeks now, but she'd really intended to follow through this time. If she stuck to her guns, however, she'd lose the job.

Taking a deep breath, steeling herself, she picked up a small slice in her fingers. It felt slippery. She carefully laid it on her tongue. Then she closed her eyes and concentrated on the flavor. It came in waves—first salty and oily, then meaty and rich, then a nutty finish. She could feel the fat literally melting on her tongue.

It was like nothing she'd ever tasted before.

Ainsley's eyes popped open. As much as she wanted to dislike it, there was no denying that her body had missed the taste of well-cured pig. She thought about Joaquim and his gentle needling of her vegetarian diet. She wondered what he would say now, if he could see her.

"What do you think?" said Pepito, watching her.

"I feel," she replied carefully, "like I've been reborn."

The matador lifted a glass. "To mutual trust."

She lifted her own glass and managed to croak a response. "To mutual trust."

They clinked their drinks and swallowed quickly.

"Tell me how you are going to approach this problem," said the matador.

Ainsley wiped her mouth. "To begin," said Ainsley, "I'd like to meet your *mozo de espadas*. He may be able to tell me information that he cannot even tell you."

"He is called Gabriel," said Pepito, "and he is more worried than I am. This weight is on his shoulders."

"Can I meet him tomorrow?"

"You can meet him right now," replied Pepito.

Ainsley checked her watch. It was three o'clock am. "If he's awake."

"Of course he's awake. It's *Semana Santa*."

"Do you know where he is?"

Pepito shook his head. "He isn't answering his phone. We will have to hunt for him."

"Where?"

"We ask at his favorite tapas bars. If he isn't there, then I know where to look."

He motioned for the check. Ainsley looked down at her hands. A tiny moist ball of white paper lay crumpled in her palm. She was feeling terrible. Not even five hours had elapsed since kissing Joaquim goodbye, and she had already begun to betray her own principles.

She wondered how far this job was going to take her.

CHAPTER SIXTEEN

Three hours later, as the first fingers of a pink dawn crept over the rooftops, Ainsley and Pepito wended their way towards the hulking mass of the Seville Cathedral.

They'd walked the streets of Seville all night, visiting a multitude of tapas bars, inquiring with the owner of each. None had seen Gabriel, but Ainsley had been obliged to take a sherry at each. By five o'clock am, she'd become a little drunk and switched over to espresso. She would last longer on caffeine than on alcohol, and it was nearly morning anyways.

Now, outside the cathedral, Ainsley tilted her head and studied the massive building. A Gothic structure that had taken more than a century to construct, it represented the Christian reconquest of formerly Moorish land. It lay in the center of the old town like the fallen carcass of a mastodon.

"Are you sure this guy is inside?" said Ainsley.

"I know Gabriel like a brother. When he's not working for me, he's either taking *tapas* or asking God's forgiveness for being alive. He does nothing else."

They circled the cathedral, which was empty, for the

moment, of arriving *pasos*. Later in the day, when the parades started again, Pepito said it would be impossible to get near the cathedral.

"I'm ready," said Ainsley. "How do we get inside?"

"There are fourteen different entrances," said Pepito. "I only enter through the Puerta de la Asunción."

"Why?"

"Because it's the biggest."

They circled the structure until they found it—an enormous pair of iron doors framed within four layers of archivolts. Passing inside, Ainsley waited for her eyes to adjust to the dimness. When they did, she was stunned by what stood before her.

It was an enormous *retablo* altarpiece, twenty meters high, featuring thirty-six different scenes of the life of Christ—all in relief, and all of it in *gold*. She'd never seen anything remotely like it. A thick set of forged iron bars separated the crowd from the treasure.

Pepito shrugged. "Everybody says oh, it's so beautiful, blah blah blah. I have no use for it." He picked his teeth with a fingernail.

"I think it's amazing," Ainsley said.

Then the matador grew excited. "Ah—I see him. Look, there he is."

Ainsley tore herself away from the magisterial altarpiece and followed his finger. It was pointing towards a thin, slouched figure sitting miserably alone in a row of pews, his head buried between his arms.

"That's Gabriel?" she said. "Your *mozo de espadas*?"

"Yes," he replied, "and he doesn't want to talk to me. See how he avoids looking this way? You will have to introduce yourself."

"I can do that."

The matador suddenly gripped Ainsley by the shoulders.

"He will give you much information. You need to be *confidential*."

"Always," she reassured him.

"Remember, I want you to investigate Gabriel as well."

Ainsley was confused. "I thought you said that you trusted him."

Pepito made a fifty-fifty motion with his hand. "You never know in Andalucía. We're a bunch of lying thieves. Go on."

He slapped Ainsley on the back as though she were an errant cow. She stumbled forward, regained her footing, and shot Pepito a dark look. Then she walked down the aisle of the nave. To her left and right were massive fluted columns; far overhead stretched the vaulted ceilings. It felt like she was headed to the fifty-yard line of the biggest football stadium in the world.

She turned into Gabriel's pew, shuffled sideways, and sat down next to him. A lanky man, he wore a thin black sweater over a white collar shirt and a pair of orange loafers under his navy blue slacks. He'd dropped his head between his arms, and his lips moved silently. A string of rosary beads dangled from his hands.

Ainsley cleared her throat. He didn't look up.

"Gabriel," she finally said.

The man slowly lifted his head up. His face was long and thin and haunted. His eyes peered out from the dark recesses of their sockets like exhausted mice from a peephole.

"How do you know my name?" he said.

"I'm Ainsley Walker," she said, presenting her hand, "and we have something in common."

"What is that?"

"We both work for Pepito."

Gabriel looked confused. Ainsley's eyes flicked over his shoulder. Noticing this, the *mozo de espadas* quickly twisted around. He spotted Pepito, standing near the door. The matador waved once, then left the cathedral.

Sighing, Gabriel buried his face again in his arms. "I knew he would find me," he said. "The man is an animal when he's on the scent."

"He knows that you don't want to talk to him," she said. "He knows you feel bad. That's why I'm here. I'm going to help find the sword of Pepe."

The *mozo de espadas* lifted his agonized face to the ceiling. "I have betrayed his trust. My carelessness is going to ruin his career."

"We're going to make sure that doesn't happen," she said. "I need you to tell me everything about how the sword of Pepe disappeared."

He said nothing.

"Can you help me?" she said.

The response finally came. "Yes," he said, "but I need to walk. Let's do the circuit together."

CHAPTER SEVENTEEN

"The job of a *mozo de espada*," explained Gabriel, "is more than just cleaning swords."

The thin man was stooped over, the weight of worry sagging his bony shoulders, his orange loafers trudging softly over the floor. He and Ainsley were on a slow loop around the interior of the massive cathedral. Underfoot was the black-and-white checkerboard tile floor. Around them were more fluted columns, more decorations, open spaces leading to even grander open spaces. And overhead, eighty distant meters above, the domed Renaissance vault looked down upon them like the eye of God.

It was the type of gargantuan architectural blockbuster that was impossible to photograph. Ainsley recalled reading on the train that this cathedral, when it was finished, had displaced the Hagia Sophia as the largest religious building in the world. Even today, depending on how you measure interior space, its sheer volume still challenges St. Peter's in Rome and St. Paul's in London.

"What else do you do?" said Ainsley.

Gabriel ticked off the responsibilities on his fingers. "I'm the driver who takes Pepito to the *corridas*. I'm the valet who cleans and organized his capes and his suit of lights. I'm the manager who delivers the official documents for the Guardia Civil and demands the money from the *impresarios*. I'm the travel agent who books the right hotels."

"What kind of hotels?"

He shrugged. "The ones that will accept the blood, sand, and parties."

Ainsley nodded. "So you have a lot of responsibility."

"Without me, Pepito is nothing. Oh, *and* the swords."

"Where do you keep them?"

"In a big green case."

"How many are there?"

"Seven. Three caping swords, three killing swords, and one *descabello*."

"What's that?"

Gabriel made a snipping gesture with his fingers. "It cuts the spine if the bull is suffering."

"And the sword of Pepe—"

"—is a killing sword. He rarely ever uses it. In fact, last year I asked him if we can leave it at home, but he said that he wanted it with him."

"And now it's gone."

"Can you believe it? The easiest part of my job—carrying the swords. And I *lose* one." He laughed bitterly at himself.

"Did you leave the sword at a bullring?"

"No. I never take it out of the case except for cleaning, maybe once a season."

Ainsley tapped her teeth with her pen. "So somebody stole it."

He sighed heavily. "That's right."

"Did you leave the case out of your sight?"

"On the day it went missing, yes."

"Why?"

"Because I had a family emergency."

That sounded suspicious. "Can I ask what happened?"

"Maybe." The *mozo de espadas* suddenly changed the subject. "Look, that will be beautiful as soon as the sun rises high enough."

He was pointing at a massive circular stained-glass window. It depicted a pair of people on either side of a path to a large cathedral.

"Come this way," he said.

Ainsley followed him into a side chapel, which itself was the size of a typical church. She'd counted at least twenty such spaces, in styles ranging from Gothic to Baroque to Mudejar. This one featured a rack of red votive candles and fifteen rows of pews. Ainsley watched Gabriel light one of the votive candles, make the sign of the cross over himself, and lower himself down onto the kneeler. He closed his eyes and clasped his hands over his heart.

She followed suit. Kneeling beside him, Ainsley clasped her hands and studied the altar ahead of her. It consisted of a white altar cloth draped over three slabs of stone. A silver chalice rested on the fabric next to a small paten, a silver disk used to catch tiny crumbs of the host. A clothbound hardcover missal had been placed behind the chalice. To either side of the altar stood a pair of stands that held an explosion of white lilies.

It was an arresting tableau. Ainsley admitted to herself that Catholics knew the power of interior décor. Back in the medieval era, designing anything for the church had been the equivalent of getting hired today to design handbags for Hermès.

"My brother," said Gabriel wearily, "is a drug addict."

Ainsley said nothing. It was better to keep quiet when someone was exposing his darkest stories.

"I don't usually talk about this," he continued.

"You don't have to," said Ainsley.

"Ah, but that's exactly why I can tell you about this. I'll never see you again." He grinned.

"What's your brother's name?" she said.

"Isaac," he said. "So on the morning of the theft, I receive a desperate text message from him. It says that he wants to end his life." A tear appeared in his eye. "I can't ignore him. He's overdosed before."

Ainsley jotted everything down.

"So I leave Pepito at the hotel," continued Gabriel.

"Which hotel?"

"The Hotel Maghrebi," he said. "It's in Córdoba. We had a local *corrida* that afternoon. A pitiful event, the attendance less than five hundred. It's the only type of work Pepito has been able to book for the last year. Anyways, I leave him at the hotel and come back to Seville to find Isaac. I arrive at the shop—"

"What shop?"

"My brother's shop. It's in the Barrio Santa Cruz, near the flamenco museum."

"What does he sell?"

"Tourist shit."

"Like what?"

"T-shirts, mugs, little ceramic bulls. He isn't religious. So I arrive at the shop and find Isaac passed out upstairs in his *tearoom*."

The *mozo* snorted, and Ainsley understood his insinuation. "It's not really a tearoom."

"It's a flophouse. *Drogados* passed out everywhere. This is the dark side of Seville that the tourists don't see. So Isaac says he doesn't remember texting me. I open his phone and show him the sent message. He doesn't remember doing it."

Ainsley crinkled her forehead. "Do you think he was high when he sent you the message?"

"Maybe, I don't know. But that exact moment is when the sword of Pepe disappeared from my case in Córdoba. I had left it in the storage closet of the hotel under the care of the bellman and God.

"Was it locked?"

"I don't know."

"What did the hotel say?"

"They claim nobody touched the bag."

"Who did you talk to?"

"The manager, Hugo. We have known each other for decades. He suggested it was stolen when Pepito went to the bullring, since there was nobody with him to watch the bag."

"But you seem skeptical."

The *mozo de espadas* nodded. "It's not likely. At the bullring, Pepito put the bag in the *callejon*, the viewing area, because it was empty that day. And he was fetching his own swords and capes, so the bag wasn't unattended for very long anyways."

"But there were times when he was busy with the bull."

"Of course."

"Which do you think was more likely?"

"The hotel."

"Then I'm going to talk to the hotel owner."

"He's not going to help you. He'll see you as an outsider."

They were passing a crowd gathered around a tall sculpture of four men carrying a coffin. "What is that?" said Ainsley.

"Somebody's tomb."

"Who?"

"Nobody. Go see for yourself."

Curious, Ainsley walked over. A small plaque read *Cristóbal Colón*. That was the Spanish name of Christopher Columbus, and this was his tomb, right here in the heart of Seville.

Ainsley remembered learning that he'd left on his famous 1492 voyage from this city, as did so many other *conquistadores*, after securing funds from the Spanish king. In fact, the Portuguese king had turned down his proposed adventure because his terms were too restrictive. Now she was looking at his final resting site.

She returned to Gabriel. "You're funny."

"Why?"

"That's the most famous man in American history. Many people believe Christopher Columbus discovered my continent."

He shook his head. "Here in Seville he was just another Italian hotshot."

Ainsley seriously doubted that, but she decided to let it slide. It wouldn't do to challenge him right now.

By now they'd reached the Puerta de la Asunción, the door through which Ainsley had entered. A stream of tourists was pouring through it.

"Can I give you some advice?" he said.

"Okay."

"Don't follow this any further. Give Pepito his money back and go home."

She faced him. "Why?"

Gabriel grew impassioned. "There is no happy ending to this story. People will become upset, friendships will be ended. Even Pepito's life will be in danger." He paused. "You know he has chosen to challenge a Miura."

"What is that?"

"The most dangerous breed of bull in Spain. They're intelligent, fast, strong. A wise matador avoids the Miuras as much as possible."

"But not Pepito."

Gabriel shook his head. "It's the same breed that killed his father."

"So he doesn't care about his safety?"

"Not at all. I tried to persuade him to choose a different bull, but he isn't afraid to die. All matadors are like that. They face death every day."

"If he doesn't care about his own life," said Ainsley, "then I won't either. I'm not here to save Pepito from himself. He's just paying me to find a tourmaline sword. That's all I want to do."

"He doesn't know what he's getting himself into. Neither do you."

Ainsley shrugged. "Maybe, but if we don't try, we'll never know." She kissed him on the cheek, in the Spanish way. "Thank you for your help, Gabriel. You've given me some good starting points."

She turned and walked towards the massive entrance of the cathedral. Gabriel stared at her. "I know Pepito gave you my phone number," he said. "Don't try calling me. I won't help you. I don't want him killing himself in the ring."

"I'm not asking for your help," said Ainsley.

"Good. I'm not giving it to you."

"Okay."

"Do you hear me?" he repeated. "I'm *not* helping."

"I understand."

As she left the cathedral, Ainsley saw Gabriel staring at her. Behind him, the bits of stained glass began to glow on the distant wall of the cathedral.

CHAPTER EIGHTEEN

Standing outside the Museo del Baile Flamenco, Ainsley cursed softly under her breath.

There were seven tourist shops on this block alone.

Around her wandered the prey—thousands of tourists, chatting happily in German, French, Italian, English, Russian, and other unrecognizable tongues. All had been drawn to Andalucía by the power of the religious holiday.

Semana Santa. Holy Week.

Leaving the cathedral, Ainsley had decided on her next move: She would try to find Isaac, Gabriel's drug addict brother. To chat with him, to maybe discover what had impelled him to call his brother away from a *corrida* on the same day that the theft occurred. It was possible that Pepito's paranoia was just that, mere paranoia. That Isaac had been deep in the throes of a drug-addled depression. That the threat of an overdose merely coincided with the theft of the sword.

Or there could be more to the story.

Gabriel had been ashamed of his brother Isaac's condition, however, and Ainsley hadn't wanted to push the subject by asking any more questions about which tourist shop he owned. Now she began checking all of them, at least on this street.

She strolled the pedestrian avenue, scanning the tourist shops for an upstairs tearoom. Most of them appeared to be simple one-room novelty shops, replete with matador figurines, castanets, and *mantillas*. The owners stared out from behind cash registers with dark, wary eyes.

Ten minutes later, Ainsley had arrived at the end of the block, so she returned on the other side of the street, passing restaurants, bars, more shops. Nothing. She explored the cross street too, but it was fruitless.

There was no tearoom within sight.

She felt a twinge of exhaustion creeping into her bones. It was time for caffeine.

Ainsley chose a café with a streetside patio for people-watching. She sat at a small round table that had been inlaid with colorful mosaic tiles. She set her bag onto the seat and felt her skull erupt in a massive yawn. Staying up all night was something that young people did. While she was still technically young, at age twenty-nine, her body was telling a very different story right now.

A waitress arrived, black hair pulled into a rough ponytail. She had one of those severe Spanish faces that always looked as if it had just discovered a cockroach on a piece of birthday cake.

"Good morning," she said, "what would you like today?"

"One coffee," replied Ainsley.

"What kind?"

"I don't know. What is there?"

The waitress grew impatient. "You can have a *solo*. Or a *cortado*. Or a *corto de café*. Or *largo de agua*, *Nescafe*, *café helado*, *café con hielo*, *carajillo*—"

Ainsley rubbed her eyelids with her thumb and a forefinger as the list continued. She was too tired to remember what any of those words meant.

"I'll just have some tea," she said.

"We're out of tea," said the waitress.

"Really?"

The girl scowled. "No, but I don't want to explain those to you too."

That was rude. Ainsley stared at the waitress, beginning to remember that the phrase *customer service* had been an American innovation, and that service employees everywhere else in the world usually regarded humans as unnecessary intrusions into otherwise happy workdays.

"Bring me a cappuccino," she said.

The waitress disappeared and returned shortly with the drink. Ainsley sat quietly, sipping the coffee, feeling the morning sun warming her face. Then, from a table behind her, she heard a familiar shriek.

It was little Marta from the train.

She turned. There she was, the wicked dark-haired moppet, her mother frantically praying over her, an untouched cup of warm milk steaming on the table.

"Marta," said Ainsley, "did you like the caramels?"

The mother saw Ainsley, and a smile flashed over her face. "My angel from the train," she said. "Do you know that those caramels kept her quiet all night long? I can't thank you enough. But now the devil has returned." Her eyes noted Ainsley's haggard appearance. "Did you sleep in the park?"

"No. I didn't sleep anywhere."

She nodded. "A true Semana Santa."

Then Ainsley remembered the woman's offer of help, back on the train. "Can I ask you a question?"

"Of course."

"I'm looking for a tearoom in a tourist shop."

The mother dipped a napkin into her water glass and scrubbed her daughter's mouth. "This is a tearoom."

Ainsley's finger drew on the mosaic tile. "No, I was told that there is a special tourist shop ... with a staircase ... that leads to a tearoom. On the second floor."

The mother's mouth fell open slightly. "You want to go *there*?"

"You know it?"

"Yes, but it's not for tourists."

"I don't care. I'm investigating somebody."

"All right, here's what you do." The mother pointed down the street. "Go to the *panadería* at the far end of the concourse and turn down the tiny alley. You will see it down there, on the left."

"Thank you."

Marta started to shriek again. Ainsley finished her cappuccino and reached for the bill.

"No," said the mother, taking it away from her.

"Are you sure?" said Ainsley.

"Of course," she said. "Thanks to you, I was able to sleep."

Ainsley laughed. That was fair.

On her way out, Ainsley tousled the little girl's hair. She immediately stopped shrieking.

"My angel," said the mother, "you have the power to eject the devil."

"From what you just said about this tearoom," said Ainsley, slinging her bag over her shoulder, "it sounds like I'm going to need it."

CHAPTER NINETEEN

Even in the cold yellow sunlight of an early spring morning, the alley still smelled of dampness and mold.

Ainsley walked slowly over the stones, as though she were wading through heavy soup. Her hips were starting to ache from her sleepless night. Behind her, the hubbub of the pedestrian street faded in the distance until the only sound that remained was the insistent clicking of her boots.

Then she spotted it.

Above an open door, a hand-stencilled sign that read *Recuerdos de alta calidad*. The doorway was barely wide enough for a pair of shoulders.

Ainsley squeezed her way into the shop and looked around.

A few desultory shelves held a smattering of tourist memorabilia—posters of bullfights, miniature Virgin Marys, replicas of the cathedral. A clothing rack held several red-and-white polka-dotted dresses, each with three layers of flounce plus a white fringed shawl. These were Sevillana dresses, Ainsley remembered, that were intended to be worn during the *feria* that always took place a few days after the conclusion of Semana Santa.

Otherwise, the shop was empty. There wasn't even a cash register.

And then she saw the staircase.

It was a rickety spiral number, made of rusted iron. A simple cardboard sign read *Salón de té*. A redundant upward arrow pointed the way.

Ainsley placed her hand on the railing, felt the cool iron in her palm, and began to slowly climb the staircase. She kept her face pointed upwards.

Circling twice, she emerged into the tearoom and surveyed the space. It was filled with brown tufted sofas, green silk throw pillows, and low tables. A silver Moroccan tea set sitting atop a hexagonal filigreed bronze cart waited in the center of the floor. A hazy yellow light fogged the thick air, illuminating tiny motes of dust. In the corner was a beaded curtain that led to a side room.

And there was a man.

He was spread out lazily on a sofa, his long legs arrayed uselessly from beneath his long-sleeved white shirt, a hookah dangling from his lips. His narrow-set eyes gazed sadly out from beneath his eyebrows like children peering out of an orphanage window.

Ainsley guessed that this was Isaac, the brother. He looked like Gabriel, but with a few more kilometers on the odometer.

The man's misty eyes floated towards his visitor. "Are you here for shopping?"

"No," said Ainsley, "I came for some tea."

That was a partial truth; she needed caffeine and sugar to stay awake. Of course, that wasn't the only truth.

A knowing look appeared on the man's face. He hoisted

himself up to a sitting position. "I am the proprietor. Please, join me."

"Thank you."

Ainsley sat cross-legged on a silk pillow, keeping the handles of her bag wound around her hand. The man tilted his head back and shut his eyes. "Hamza," he said loudly.

"Coming," said a voice from behind the beaded curtain.

"What is your name?" said Ainsley.

"Isaac," he said.

There it was: the positive identification. She watched his shoulders glide dreamily to the music inside his head.

He opened his eyes. "So you are an American?"

Ainsley wasn't surprised that he'd guessed that. She'd learned that foreigners could usually spot Americans by mannerisms alone, even those who weren't wearing baseball caps, dressed in white athletic shoes, or chewing gum.

"Yes," she said, "just visiting."

"It's the best city in Spain," said Isaac. "Place of dreams. Happiness. Anger. Death."

Isaac's eyes turned glassy and a weird smile smeared across his face. Then Ainsley heard the click of plastic beads. A swarthy Arabic man in a beige linen suit had emerged from the curtain. He was carrying a silver circular tray, on which were two glasses and a silver filigreed teapot.

This was Hamza. First he slid the tray onto the table. Then he took a glass in his left hand, the teapot in his right, moved back two steps, and lifted the pot high into the air. He proceeded to pour the tea into the cup from more than a meter. Ainsley watched the long, thin stream of liquid course down through the air. Then she looked at Hamza's swarthy face. She noticed a scar in the small cleft between his lower lip and his chin.

He set the glass before her. She lifted it to her lips and

tasted. The tea was warm, minty, and very sweet. He repeated the process for Isaac.

"It's good?" said Isaac.

"Very."

Hamza disappeared and returned with a small dish, which he placed on the table. It held a mound of gooey brown candy. It appeared to be a mix of dried fruits, nuts, and honey.

"This is *majoun*," said Isaac. "Try some."

"Thank you."

Ainsley pulled off a clump of the candy and placed it on her tongue. It tasted sweet and savory, soft and crunchy, all at once.

"Is it pleasing to you?" he said.

Ainsley nodded, her mouth full.

"So how did you discover my shop?" Isaac asked.

"It was recommended to me," said Ainsley.

"By who?"

"Someone I met. In a tapas bar."

"Ah."

He fell into silence. Her mouth full of the sweetly weird confection, Ainsley found herself at another loss for words. This conversation was going nowhere. Isaac began humming a melody.

Ainsley listened. She vaguely recognized it. She couldn't remember the title or artist, but it was a hippie classic from the trippy sixties.

"I know that song," she said, "but I can't remember the words."

"That's too bad."

It was becoming harder to focus her eyes. She felt her mouth loosen. "Okay, so that thing I just told you," she said.

"Yes."

"It was a lie."

"You remember the words."

"No, before that. About the recommendation in the tapas bar."

Ainsley was feeling oddly dizzy.

"So what's the truth?" he said.

She lifted her hand to her face and stared at it. The veins were moving, squirming, trying to break out of the skin—

"Gabriel told me to come here," she blurted.

Isaac's eyes sprang towards her. His body stiffened. "My *brother* recommended my shop?"

"No, but he just—"

"Then what did he say?"

Ainsley's head felt like it'd been jammed inside a salad spinner. The walls were flashing past, whirling. Her hand clutched the edge of the table for balance. *And you've just had some kind of mushroom and your mind is moving low*—

"He said ... that you ... texted him ... and then it was stolen..."

Isaac crinkled his nose. "Are you talking about the sword? Is he still talking about that stupid *sword*?"

"Pepito wants it—"

He rolled his eyes. "*Que me jode.* Yes, I know that shit-eater wants his sword back. And I know what they think of me. But I tell you, I didn't have anything to do with that theft."

"There was a text message—"

"Somebody used my phone. Many people come in here all the time. My phone is always on the table." Isaac paused, looking at Ainsley. "You don't look too good."

A gaseous cloud of vapor had inflated inside of Ainsley's head. Her mouth had fallen open. It felt as though she were having an out-of-body experience. *Go ask Alice, I think she'll know*—

She tried to focus on Isaac. "What did you *give* me?"

"I didn't give you anything. You took for yourself." His eyes glanced at the mound of *majoun*.

The White Knight is talking backwards—

Isaac grasped the hookah, inhaled deeply, and blew a cloud of smoke out of his mouth into Ainsley's face. A dopey grin spread over his face. "Remember what the dormouse said—"

"What ... did it ... say ..."

"*Feed your head.*" Isaac slid the dish of *majoun* towards Ainsley.

He replaced the hookah on its stand. "What's your name, American?"

There was no response.

He looked over. Ainsley had slumped over on the pillows, unconscious.

CHAPTER TWENTY

A hand gripped Ainsley's shoulder. She felt it shaking her. Then the shaking grew more insistent.

"Anglo, wake up," she heard a man's voice saying.

As she swam to the surface of consciousness, one eyelid slowly fluttered open. Hazy yellow sunlight. Green silk pillows. The silver hexagonal Moroccan tea set.

Slowly the memory came back to her. The tearoom. The weird conversation.

The strange candy.

Ainsley lifted her head, one eye still squinched shut, and looked around. The room was empty except for the man standing over her. She looked at his feet. It was a pair of orange loafers. Her eyes tracked upwards. Navy blue pants. Black sweater.

It was Gabriel.

The *mozo de espadas* was looking down on her with an unreadable expression.

"You found me," she said.

"And you found the tearoom," he answered. "It's not easy to find."

"I couldn't stay awake," she said, yawning.

"Isaac said you ate the *majoun*."

"That was the candy with the nuts and dried fruit and honey?"

"Yes."

She nodded. "It was really good."

Gabriel looked sternly at her. "It was *hashish*."

"You're lying."

"No."

Ainsley struggled to sit up, but her arms buckled. She fell backwards onto the sofa. Gabriel extended his hand and helped her to sit.

"That was made of—"

"The resin of a plant. It sends you into outer space." He glanced at her. "Then it causes sleep."

That described her perfectly. Ainsley rubbed her eyes and looked at the place on the table where the candy had been. The stuff had walloped her, with almost no notice. She'd never used drugs, which might explain why. So might the fact that she'd been up all night running through the streets of Seville.

"So you came over here to find your brother," she said.

"He texted me. Someone had passed out in his tea shop and he couldn't wake her up. He said it was a tall American girl."

"And you knew it was me."

"I guessed."

Gabriel offered his elbow. "Let me help you downstairs. I want to talk to you about something."

Ainsley slowly rose to her feet, her temples throbbing with the exertion. She clutched Gabriel's arm. He guided her down the steep spiral staircase into the tourist shop on the main floor.

Isaac was perched on a stool, an enigmatic expression on his face.

"You should put a warning label on the *majoun*," she said.

"Why?" came the reply.

"Because it really screwed me up."

"Do you hear that?" said Gabriel. "You really screwed her up."

Isaac shrugged. "She took the candy."

"And you put it in front of her."

"So what? She's not my sister."

"She," said Gabriel, "is working for Pepito."

Isaac stiffened. "Doing what?"

"Trying to find the sword of Pepe."

Isaac clutched his head and spun around on the stool. "I don't know *anything* about that sword. I beg you, stop talking about it."

"It's time for me to go," said Gabriel. "My brother is making me angry."

He steered Ainsley out of the tourist shop, into the alley that smelled of dampness and mold, and walked her over the cobblestones back up to the pedestrian street. There, far from his brother's tearoom, Gabriel drew a deep breath, held it, then released.

"Thank you," she said.

"I have something for you," he replied.

The *mozo de espadas* reached into his coat pocket and produced a debit card. He handed it to her. She looked at the name.

Ainsley Walker.

It was her card.

Her jaw fell open. "How did you—"

"My brother stole it from your bag. Here."

He reached into the same pocket and produced a roll of

money. He handed it to her. "He took this too. Count it and make sure it's all there."

Eyes wide, Ainsley rummaged through her bag and found her wallet. It was empty. She'd had nearly two hundred euros.

She took the bills and counted them. "One hundred ninety-four. It's all there. Why did he—"

Gabriel interrupted. "Because my brother is drug addict. He is a bad guy. He will rob from his own mother." He paused, feeling great pain. "He *has* robbed from his own mother."

Ainsley started to go back down the alley, but Gabriel caught her by the arm. "No, don't bother."

"But—"

"He cannot be saved. He will face his judgment in heaven."

Frustrated, Ainsley stopped. "Okay," she said.

"Now do you see why I think he was involved with the theft?"

"Yes."

Then Gabriel ran a nervous hand across the back of his head, ruffling his hair. "Also ... he didn't text me about you."

"But you just said that he did."

He grew frustrated. "I didn't want to start a fight in the shop. Miss Walker, I guessed that you would be persistent and find the tearoom. So I waited two hours, then showed up. When I arrived, he was going through your bag. We had a fight. He tried to choke me."

Ainsley looked at his neck. There was a red mark on the left side of Gabriel's throat.

"He's a disaster," she said.

"Now," replied Gabriel, "it's time for you to admit something, Miss Walker."

"What?"

"That you are going to need a guide."

She dropped her head. "Maybe."

"You are persistent but possibly stupid."

Ainsley sighed. "Now wait a minute—"

He lifted a finger. "And if this is how you investigate, the sword of Pepe will stay safely hidden until the end of time."

"That's not fair—"

Gabriel didn't crack. "Tell me that you need a guide."

It pained her to admit this to herself. On previous cases, she'd managed to make do without much help at all. But it was the sign of an egotist to refuse assistance from people who were willing and able to do so.

"I need a guide," she said.

"Good, but let me make one thing clear."

"What?"

"I'm not helping you."

Ainsley smiled, remembering how he'd said that a couple of hours earlier in the cathedral. "Okay, then what are you going to do?"

"As I just said, I'm merely going to *guide* you."

She was puzzled. "What's the difference between *help* and *guide*?"

"It's very complicated," he said, "and I don't think your Spanish is good enough to understand."

"I see," said Ainsley. "*Tu eres un caballero,* Gabriel."

He held up a serious finger. "*Usted, por favor.*"

Ainsley lowered her head. She'd used the second-person familiar many times in Latin America with no problem, but things were different here in Spain. There were walls between strangers here.

"Of course."

He brushed the sleeves of his sportcoat. "Now, it's time for us to go."

"To where?"

"Córdoba. You're going to figure out a way to make that devil of a hotel owner talk. And I have an idea how to do it." He crooked a finger. "Follow me."

Ainsley followed him.

CORDOBA

CHAPTER TWENTY-ONE

The local train that Ainsley had taken from Málaga felt like a kiddie train at a zoo compared with the smooth, powerful ride she was experiencing right now.

She was onboard the AVE, Spain's sprawling monster of a high-speed train network. It allowed bullet trains to hurtle at speeds up to three hundred kilometers per hour across the country. Sitting beside her was Gabriel, quietly reading a small Bible. They were headed from Seville to Córdoba. The trip would take twenty-five minutes. In a car, given the difficulty of navigating and parking, it would've taken at least three hours.

Ainsley wondered at the pace of change in Spain. Such a modern rail network had been unthinkable in the early nineteen-eighties, when the nation was still struggling to escape the shadow of forty years of dictatorship. Now it was taken as an article of faith by Spanish youth.

She cleared her throat. "Gabriel, I have a question."

"Of course."

"Is Pepito considered a great matador?"

"He is very brave," he replied, closing the book, "and

there is an old saying that only two things will make a coward out of a matador."

"What are they?"

"A serious goring and a happy marriage."

Ainsley laughed. "He said he was divorced."

"Correct. And he has never been gored." Pepito made a quick sign of the cross and kissed his own thumb.

"So is he a great matador?"

"It is difficult to define," he said, "and there are always many opinions. Is he great like Manolete? No, that man was a genius. Is he flamboyant like Jesús Janeiro? No, but that's because he's smarter."

"What do you mean?"

"Pepito actually *thinks* like a bull. He *becomes* the bull. I've been with him for decades, and it still amazes me." An admiring sigh escaped his throat. "If I were a spectator, I would like his style the most."

"Why?"

"There are no tricks. He's very sympathetic with the animal."

Ainsley wondered about that. It struck her as difficult to believe that a matador could remain sympathetic with the bull he'd been hired to publicly slaughter.

A voice announced the next stop: *Córdoba*. As the train slowed to a stop, Ainsley and Gabriel gathered their items and exited down the steps. They moved off the platform, through the small station, and out into the streets of the medieval quarter. Ainsley felt the sunshine on her shoulders, the stones under her feet.

This was Córdoba.

She remembered what she'd read about this city the previous night. The capital of the ancient Islamic caliphate, Córdoba had boasted three hundred thousand people in 1000 C.E. In fact, it had been the largest city in Europe at that time, bigger than London, Paris, or Rome. The city had held palaces, mosques, synagogues, public baths, fountains, running water, and the largest library in Europe. More impressively, its Moorish rulers, the Almoravides, had acted generously towards their Sephardic Jewish and Christian minorities, whom they called *dhimmi*. For nearly three hundred years, the city had served as a model of religious diversity, with even famed Jewish philosopher Maimonides claiming it as his home.

Córdoba became known as the Jewel of the World.

But it didn't last long.

Slowly, over the ensuing decades, Christians began descending from the north, attacking its borderlands, pushing the caliphate further south, even penetrating Granada (where they provoked a Jewish massacre in 1066) and finally capturing Toledo in 1085. The ruling Almoravides withdrew to Africa and were replaced by a far stricter Islamic group, the Almohads, who treated the *dhimmi* much worse. They expelled the Jews completely sometime near the end of the twelfth century.

That had been news to Ainsley. She'd assumed that the famous expulsion of the Jews—the one committed by Queen Isabella and King Ferdinand three centuries later—had been the first of its kind on the peninsula. But that wasn't true. In fact, this earlier expulsion had been far more damaging, because in the eleventh century the Jews represented a much greater part of the wealth and knowledge of the caliphate than they did later.

The result: As Jews trudged away to the Christian north, or moved to other lands, Córdoba entered a long, slow decline.

Gabriel interrupted her reverie. "Up ahead, Ainsley, we will take some lunch."

"Excellent."

He led her to the side of a famous *taberna*, where they stood along a very narrow slat of wood that had been hammered into the outside wall of the building. The waiter had brought them two *cazuelas* filled with pork and fresh tomatoes. Ainsley noticed that it was exactly as wide as the slat of wood.

Ainsley stood there in the alley, shoveling food into her mouth, too hungry to savor the intense flavors. Neither did she notice the tourists walking back and forth a few steps behind her back.

Gabriel watched her devour the food. "You eat like a man," he said.

"And you talk like a woman," she answered.

Gabriel laughed. That itself was a minor miracle. After all, earlier this morning, in the cathedral, he had seemed about two Hail Marys away from slitting his wrists. Of course, it didn't matter that her insult wasn't even remotely true; Ainsley needed to prove herself to this man after the disgrace of the druggy tearoom. The fact that the insult came from a woman carried even more weight.

"The Mezquita is down there," he said, waving down the alley, "where all the tourists are going, but the Hotel Maghrebi is the other way."

Ainsley finished her pork and tomatoes and went for the basket. She swabbed a hunk of crunchy bread in the plate of olive oil. The flavor of the oil nearly burst in her mouth—it was bright and grassy, with notes of citrus.

"The manager's name was Hugo, right?" she said.

Gabriel sipped his water and nodded. Then his eyes creeped sideways, over to her sweaty shirt and plain pants. She'd worn them through the night and now through the morning as well.

"What?" she said.

"You need to change your clothes," she said.

"Why?"

"I thought maybe you want to attract men."

"I don't want to do that. I have a boyfriend."

Gabriel chose his words carefully. "You should do whatever you can to get Hugo and these people at the hotel to talk to you."

Ainsley smiled. "Then buy me some new clothing."

"Why?"

"Because this is all I have."

He looked horrified. She guessed that he was the type of man who always wore crisp, clean outfits. "I can't do that," he said.

"Why not?"

"I just can't. It's too worldly."

Ainsley rolled her eyes. "I have an idea. Do you have Pepito's credit card?"

"Yes."

"Give it to me and I'll go shopping."

He looked skeptical. Ainsley sought to reassure him. "This is strictly business," she said. "Besides, he has my passport, so I can't use my own card."

"I will have to explain the charges to Pepito."

"Of course."

Shrugging, he reached for his wallet. "Okay, but I'm not helping."

"Gabriel," said Ainsley, accepting Pepito's credit card, "a woman never needs help shopping for clothing."

CHAPTER TWENTY-TWO

An hour later, Ainsley emerged from a branch of El Corte Inglés, Spain's most famous department store, wearing a new outfit. She saw Gabriel waiting quietly on a bench outside.

"What do you think?" she said.

He cast his eyes downward, embarrassed. "It's pretty."

Ainsley frowned. The outfit *was* pretty, but he hadn't even glanced at her. She was wearing a low-cut red silk top with flouncy sleeves, a jet-black pencil skirt, and a pair of Roman sandal-inspired flats. These were trendy, and though Ainsley didn't care much for them, she'd deliberately chosen to err on the side of caution. Wearing a pair of heels with this flashy ensemble could've pushed it over the edge, and the last thing she needed was to be mistaken for a streetwalker.

"I know," she said. "It feels like a cape."

"Are you trying to anger a bull?"

"Maybe. Do you notice anything else different?"

Gabriel looked up, his brow furrowed. It felt as though he were viewing her from a great distance.

"Did you put on makeup?" he said.

Ainsley laughed. That was the understatement of the

century. For what felt like an eternity she'd sat in a cushioned chair at the makeup counter while a young woman stood over her, cleaning her face, blotting out the cheeks, creating two very smoky eyes, and using an arsenal of unfamiliar powders, blushes, and applicators. Looking in the mirror afterwards, Ainsley had barely recognized herself. That was a good thing, based on how she'd looked beforehand.

"Yes," she replied, "it was a makeover."

He shrugged. "Can I have the card?"

Ainsley cocked her head. She couldn't tell if Gabriel was being serious, or if he merely possessed the driest sense of humor in the world. She decided on the former. He was, after all, unmarried and a devout worshiper. In her experience, such cluelessness seemed to be typical of devoutly religious men.

Together they walked a few more streets to the Hotel Maghrebi. It was a whitewashed structure, with rows of Moorish arches across its three arches. Two neatly trimmed squares of green hedges welcomed the visitor through a single stone latticework arch. The structure wasn't enormous, but Ainsley still sensed hidden depths that unfolded within. It was the type of labyrinthine place in whose twisting hallways you could easily lose yourself.

Gabriel stopped just before of the arch. Ainsley noticed that he was trembling.

"What's the matter?" she said.

"I am so angry at Hugo. I feel that I cannot enter his hotel."

"Really?"

"Yes." His arms were shaking, and his fists were clenching themselves. "We had a big fight about the sword. A week ago."

Ainsley nodded. "Then I'll go inside alone." If that were true, she'd find out more on her own anyways.

"And do what inside?"

"Get a room."

"No," he said, "absolutely not, that is—"

"—a smart thing to do?" finished Ainsley. "Somebody in this place conspired to steal the tourmaline sword. There's no doubt."

"Yes, and—"

"Listen, they're not going to talk to an outsider about this. But they might talk to a guest."

"Then you should return the clothing."

Ainsley shook her head firmly. "I'm still going to need it. Plus it makes me feel pretty." She pointed at his coat pocket. "Give me the card again."

Gabriel looked miffed. "I have to explain all these expenditures to Pepito."

"If you let me do my job," she said, "you will also be explaining to him how you found the tourmaline sword."

At the thought, Gabriel smiled in spite of himself. He lifted his chin and looked at a faraway building.

"What is it?" she said.

He handed her the credit card. "Go inside and get a room. I will go to church to pray."

Ainsley smiled and dropped it into her purse. "Fine. I'll call you when I know something."

He shuffled away, and she walked into the hotel. A small room with impeccably polished floors, the lobby boasted a few artfully placed red candles that burned steadily against the white walls. Overhead, a row of dark wooden beams ribbed the ceiling. A young man in a crisp white collared shirt was standing behind a polished wooden front desk.

"Can I help you?" he said.

"Do you have any rooms available?"

"For tonight?"

"Yes."

"Are you here for the *fiesta de los patios*?"

Ainsley didn't know what that was, but it was always advisable to keep the conversation moving. "Of course."

He clicked on his mouse and studied the results on an invisible screen. "We have one room," he said. "Our Royal Suite."

"I'll take it."

"Good." He thumped his hands together. "I will need a credit card and a passport."

Ainsley froze. She had the credit card, but Pepito had confiscated her passport. Allowing him to do that had been extraordinarily stupid.

"Here's a photo ID," she said, laying her U.S. driver's license across the counter, "and this is ten euros for being nice."

"You don't have a passport?"

"Can I get it to you later?"

He cleared his throat, adjusted his collar, and smiled wanly. "I'm really not supposed to allow that."

Ainsley slid another ten euros across the counter, then flipped her hair. "Of course you can."

The front desk clerk relented. "When will you get the passport?"

She scrambled for a cover story. "My asshole brother put it in his suitcase when he left for London," she said, "but he says he is sending it to us tonight."

"Tell me when you can."

She watched him slide her credit card and print out her agreement. "Sign here."

She did so and slid the paper back to him.

Ainsley smiled nicely, then pulled the club back for the twenty-meter putt. "And if I needed to safely store my luggage someplace, maybe for a day, who would I talk to about that?"

"That would be Javier," he said, "but he's not here today."

"When will he be in?"

"Not until tomorrow. He's preparing his mother's home for the *fiesta*."

That word again. Ainsley moistened her lips. "Do you have any information about the *fiesta de los patios*?"

The clerk looked stunned. "It's your first time here?"

"Yes."

He reached beneath the desk and produced a pamphlet. "This will tell you everything you need to know. The homes open to the public all day, and all night."

Ainsley looked at the pamphlet. It was a map of the city, with six different walking courses marked in different colors.

"Thank you," she said.

"It's nothing."

"Just out of curiosity—where is Javier's mother's house?"

The clerk looked at her oddly, then pointed to the western side of the map. "In the Zona Juderia. It's called Reñopedes."

Ainsley nodded. She guessed that he most likely wouldn't have answered that question if she hadn't been a paying guest.

"Thank you," she answered.

He handed her an iron skeleton key. "The Royal Suite is the third floor. You will take the stairs to the left. We have a breakfast available beginning at six thirty am."

"It's on the third floor?"

"No, it *is* the third floor."

Alarmed, she looked at the bill for the room. It read €499.00.

"Thank you," she said, gasping.

As Ainsley ascended the inner staircase of the Hotel Maghrebi, she thought about the size of the eruption that would occur when Pepito saw his credit card statement.

CHAPTER TWENTY-THREE

In the depths of sleep, her hair floating like a nimbus around her head, Ainsley heard a strange noise in the distance. It sounded like a *muezzin* shouting a call-to-prayer.

The ringing had been occurring for quite a while. Stretching her limbs, she kicked her way back to the surface of consciousness, then sat up.

Momentarily confused, she rubbed the sleep from her eyes, trying to recall where she was, where she'd been, where she'd gone. Ever since she'd chosen to follow the enigmatic Zamorano, everything'd felt like a dream, a vague shadow of existence, far removed from ordinary life. It had all started less than a day ago.

Around her was a large suite, meticulously decorated in an Islamic manner. Gauzy window treatments, gilt-edged furniture, geometric tiles laid in the wall. She was sitting in a four-poster bed, wearing only her underwear. Through a window to her left were the silhouettes of several rooftops silhouetted against a flaming red ball.

The fierce sunset.

Then she remembered: the Hotel Maghrebi.

She had booked the Royal Suite earlier that afternoon. She'd arrived in the room, stripped off her clothes, and fallen onto the bed for a long, well-deserved *siesta*. It was a local tradition; over the centuries, the people of Andalucía and southern Spain had bifurcated their workdays to better avoid the scorching heat of midday. Ainsley knew that the *siesta* was a dying tradition, but after the sleepless night spent scurrying around Seville, it'd been exactly what she needed.

That distant sound called her again. This time, she recognized it.

Her phone.

She pushed off the covers and scrambled on all fours across the bed to her purse, which was on the floor. She leaned down, plunged her hand inside, and retrieved the phone.

The caller ID read Joaquim. It took a second for her to recognize the name. Her boyfriend.

She cursed herself softly, then picked up. "I was wondering when you might call," she said.

"I was waiting for a distress signal," came the reply.

"Not necessary," she said, "at least not yet."

"Give it time. I'm sure you'll screw up at some point."

"I kind of already did. Would you like to hear my confession?"

"Unburden your soul, my child."

She paused. "I'm not a vegetarian anymore."

The peals of laughter were so loud that she held the phone away from her ear. "Why are you laughing?" she said.

"I *knew* it was going to happen."

"Yes, and you were right."

"Let me guess," he said. "You tasted *jamón ibérico*."

Ainsley sank back onto the bed. "How did you know?"

"It's impossible to resist. Especially when they wrap it

around melon. I know Muslims who've renounced their entire religion just for *jamón*."

"It was *so* good—"

"Tell me what else has been happening."

"I don't know where to start."

"Start at the beginning."

Ainsley described all the events of the last twenty-four hours, the Semana Santa processions, meeting Pepito, accepting the job, finding Gabriel in the cathedral, hunting out his brother in the scuzzy tearoom, getting high on *majoun*, passing out, being rescued by Gabriel, the train to Córdoba, the new outfit.

"So, just another day at the office," he said.

"Yep. This is work."

"Sure, whatever you say." He cleared his throat. "Well, I'm doing fine, thanks for asking."

"I'm sorry, I was about to—"

"No, don't apologize. Today, I sat in the seventh row on a crowded beach, swam in murky salt water, swallowed a soggy lunch of fish and chips, and then passed out in bed for two hours. Oh, and I did it all alone."

Ainsley felt guilt wrench her stomach. "Come and join me," she said.

"No."

"I'm serious."

"We're too goofy together, little spoon. Besides, in a traditional Mediterranean country, you'll get further as a damsel-in-distress. I would slow you down."

Ainsley sighed.

"Betcha I can get you to say something mushy," he said.

She rolled her eyes. This was a running joke between them. "Never."

"What's your favorite breakfast?"

"Toast."

"Liar."

Ainsley laughed. "It's *oatmeal*."

"There, mush-ion accomplished."

Ainsley felt a choke in her throat at his bad joke. "You know, I'm still going to cook for you when I get back."

"As long as it's not oatmeal."

She laughed. "I'll call you soon."

"If I don't call you first. Oh, and no steaks tonight, Walker. You've got to work up to that."

They disconnected, and Ainsley sat looking at her phone for a long time, feeling a familiar type of heartache, painful but pleasant.

It had a name, but she couldn't make herself say it.

CHAPTER TWENTY-FOUR

Later that night, Ainsley strolled through the darkened streets of Córdoba, map in hand, her white bag slung beneath her arm. She was trying to find her way to the Zona Judaria.

The Jewish quarter.

Centuries ago, it'd been a ghetto, in the original sense of the word; today it was a lovely neighborhood, built on a two-thirds scale. The sidewalks were barely wide enough to park a scooter, the doorways narrow enough to scrape shoulders. Each of the buildings was an orderly mess of gray concrete, white paint, and stone doorframes. Into the sides of the houses were laid small plaques bearing images of menorahs and the names of medieval Jewish philosophers who'd once lived at those addresses.

Ainsley was heading for one place.

Reñopedes.

She'd never met this man Javier, in charge of the luggage at the hotel, never even seen a photo. But she knew from the map that Reñopedes was located on a street called Samuel de los Santos Geiner.

Through the twisting alleyways she moved, feeling herself

drawn down further into the rabbit hole, down towards an ancient crossroads of cultures that was neither Spanish European nor Moorish African, neither Muslim, Jewish, nor Christian. It was a mysterious mélange of all those spirits who'd trodden these streets over the centuries.

Then she saw it.

Reñopedes.

Five uplights spotlighted the craggy surface of its exterior plaster wall, twice the height of a person. A thick wooden gate with horizontal studded copper bands had been propped open, a sign of welcome to the public. The murmur of a crowd could be heard over its walls.

The *fiesta de los patios* was an annual event whose purpose was exactly that—to celebrate their patios. The locals opened the doors of their private homes for neighbors to enter and admire. Ainsley guessed that such gestures carried a lot of weight, given the Spanish tradition for secrecy, protection, and family lineage.

Then she glimpsed the patio, and her heart leaped in her chest.

Hundreds of small candles inside of glass globes lit the place. To her left, an entire wall had been decorated with a geometric pattern of plants whose containers had been bolted into the side. An elderly man was using a watering can on a three-meter-long pole to reach the highest ones.

The center of the patio boasted a large fountain shaped like a date palm. A thick layer of dark fuzz coating the pedestal told Ainsley that this fountain was probably centuries old. And throughout the space were thousands of flowers—red geraniums in stands, green ferns in hanging pots, bright bougainvillea hanging from windowsills.

It was the image of Spain.

As Ainsley moved through the open gate, she discovered herself inside a crowd of people milling about the patio, some holding glasses of *fino*, others holding cups of tea. Most were older and were murmuring softly, luxuriating in the softness of a night filled with accent lighting and succulent leaves. A few women even wore the traditional *mantilla*.

Ainsley looked around for a conversational foothold. She momentarily regretted not inviting Gabriel tonight, but he'd mentioned a heated argument with the hotel staff. His presence could hurt her efforts to learn something from Javier.

She felt a hand at her elbow. It was a kindly old man, very short, wearing a rumpled brown suit. He was holding out a glass of red wine.

"A beautiful woman needs a beautiful drink," he said.

Ainsley's eyes lit up. "Why thank you!"

"It's from my vineyard."

She sipped the wine. It tasted cold and bright in her mouth.

The elderly man wrung his hands nervously. "Do you like the patio?"

"I do."

"It won the award last year."

"Are you the owner?" she asked.

"No, that's Dolores. She's over there."

He gestured to a tiny elderly woman wearing a black widow's ensemble. She was standing with one gnarled hand wrapped around the knob of her cane, the other around a railing.

"She takes care of this patio by herself?" said Ainsley.

"No, she has a son who helps."

"Who?"

The old man pointed to a fiftyish man slouching next to Dolores. He wore a corduroy vest and a smirk. A *cigarillo* was burning between the tips of his tobacco-stained fingers.

"That's Javier. The *pasota*." The old man shook his head sadly.

Ainsley didn't know that word. "What is a *pasota*?"

"You don't want to know," said the old man. "Where are you from?"

"The United States."

"Are you married?"

"It's complicated."

"Why are you visiting?"

"For work."

The old man seemed to accept that answer. Suddenly he reached for Ainsley's hand. Then, to her surprise, pulled her face down and kissed her on the cheek. She felt his gray stubble scrape her skin.

"*Bienvenido*," he said.

"Thank you," she replied, a little breathless.

He turned and hobbled away. Ainsley was surprised by the friendliness, always delivered in a serious manner, of the Spaniards.

It was time.

Drawing a deep breath, she turned towards Javier and his mother, who were momentarily standing alone. Her next move was going to require the sensitivity of a counselor, the improvisation of an actor, and the brassiness of a street-walker. She was going to have to thread the needle.

Ainsley approached them. "Are you Dolores?"

The elderly woman blinked. "Yes."

"Your patio is the most beautiful in the whole world."

The elderly woman's rheumy eyes were encased in the sadness of age, but at these words, they began to glow. Her body straightened up. "It's my passion," she said, "and it keeps me alive."

"I can see why," said Ainsley. She turned to Javier. "What about you? Do you help?"

Her greasy son took a drag from his cigarette. "No."

The old woman jabbed Javier in the ribcage with an elbow,

and a sneer landed on her face. "My son believes in nothing except himself."

Javier shrugged. "It doesn't matter."

"What doesn't matter?" said Ainsley.

"Everything."

Ainsley was starting to get a better sense of him. He was a passive-aggressive, a guy who shrugged off everything in life. He wasn't going to deter her. She stuck her hand out. "I'm called Ainsley."

Javier looked at her hand, then looked back to her eyes. "Javier," he said, making no move to shake her hand. Then he took another drag and looked away.

"Are you the Javier who works at the Hotel Maghrebi?" she said.

He shrugged. "When I feel like it."

"I'm staying there," said Ainsley. "It's a beautiful place. In fact, I was looking for you earlier today."

Javier looked alarmed. "Why?"

"Because I love the *corrida* and they said that you do too."

A cynical smirk reappeared on his face. "You love the *corrida*?"

"Absolutely."

"Who is your favorite matador?"

Ainsley tried to recall the names of the famous bull-fighters that she'd learned. "Manolete was the best, of course." She paused. "But I like Pepito the most. I have tickets to his big return this weekend."

She watched Javier's face closely. A flicker of alarm passed across it, but he said nothing.

"You know," she continued, "I heard someone at the hotel say that he might not appear."

"Who said that?"

"I forgot. They said that the sword of Pepe was stolen from the Hotel Maghrebi last week. Can you believe that?"

"I hadn't heard about that," he said.

"Pepito promised the *aficionados* and the world that he would use it. It's terrible." Ainsley paused, choosing her next words carefully. "What do *you* do at the hotel?"

His eyelids lowered halfway. It looked nearly reptilian. "I ... watch ... the closet."

"The storage closet?"

Javier nodded.

His mother leaned over and interrupted. "Javier knows all the matadors. They always stay at the hotel when they come to Córdoba."

"So you must know Pepito?" said Ainsley.

He shrugged. "A little."

Ainsley plastered fake excitement across her face. "Oh, I would *love* to meet him."

Javier shrugged. "Matadors are all the same."

His mother rapped him in the ribcage with the cane again. "You see people at your hotel. Maybe you can find out who stole that sword?"

"Mama," said the bellhop, "I don't know anything. And I don't care."

"But you're in charge of the storage," said Ainsley. "You must've heard something about that."

Dolores interrupted. "Javier, that man who came to the door last week—"

"It was nothing, mama—"

"The tall Catalan with the big chin—"

"Mama, he was *nobody*. It was nothing. Now that's enough."

His mother fell quiet. Ainsley found herself holding her breath. *The tall Catalan with the big chin.*

"Who is she talking about?" said Ainsley.

Javier stepped between her and his mother. "My mother is suspicious of everybody. It was just a friend."

He took a drag from his *cigarillo* and blew the smoke into Ainsley's face. She coughed and waved the air. This was an undeniable sign that she'd crossed the line.

"A pleasure," she said to Dolores.

"Equally," came the reply.

Ainsley retreated to the opposite side of the patio and found an open bench beneath a manicured branch. The drooping tendrils of a red flower gently brushed her arm like an ancient trader imploring her to try his wares. Ainsley didn't notice. She was thinking.

The Catalan with the big chin. True, that could've been a friend, or someone from the hotel, but from what Ainsley had been learning, the Catalans didn't have friendly relations with the rest of Spain. Joaquim had said that many Catalans would rather fly to New York City a hundred times before visiting Madrid once. Ainsley thought back to the Catalan owner of the liquor store on the Costa Brava, and his defense of his region.

Across the patio, Ainsley caught sight of Javier. She noticed the way that his cheek was twitching, the way that his fingers were fidgeting with the buttons on the sleeve of his shirt.

And she noticed the way that he was returning her gaze.

Intently.

She felt a primitive alarm zipping through her spine. This might be a good time to leave. Ainsley finished her red wine, set the glass down, stood up, and walked out of the patio of Reñopedes.

CHAPTER TWENTY-FIVE

As she walked through the neighborhood of San Basilio, Ainsley found her phone and dialed Gabriel. He picked up on the first ring.

"I've found Javier," she said.

"That *pasota*. He's impossible."

Ainsley thought back to the old man who'd used that word too. "What's a *pasota*?"

"A young person who did a lot of drugs in the seventies. They passed on joining society."

From what she'd seen of Javier's personality, Ainsley admitted that made sense. "Well, I talked to him."

"He probably told you nothing."

"Correct," said Ainsley, "but his mother mentioned something interesting."

"You met his mother?"

"At their family home. It's called Reñopedes. It won the *fiesta de los patios* last year."

"You are kidding me," he said.

"No, really."

"What did his mother say?"

Ainsley didn't answer right away. The hair on the back of her neck had pricked at the sound of a heavy pair of boot-steps behind her. She turned and spotted a dark figure, shuf-fling along, head down. The orange tip of a cigarillo was burning between his fingers.

It was Javier.

"I have to call you back," she said.

Gabriel sounded concerned. "Are you in danger?"

Ainsley ended the phone call. Then she slipped into an alley, barely wide enough for two people to walk abreast, and pressed herself against the wall. She held her breath, clutched her bag tightly against her side, and felt the darkness of centuries wrap itself around her. Her phone rang again, but she put it on silent.

The bootsteps grew louder, and Ainsley braced herself, prepared to run even further into the darkness. A sliver of light shone white along the curved edge of her eye and cheek.

He didn't seem to be pursuing her, or anybody else. But it was interesting that he had left his mother's patio on such an important night—and that he was headed in the same direc-tion as Ainsley.

Every muscle in her body was tensed, and she turned her face towards the wall. She heard his bootsteps grow louder as he approached the entrance to the alley.

Then they stopped.

She cracked open an eye. Javier was standing in her field of vision, muttering to himself. His head was hanging down.

Ainsley closed her eye and prayed to herself, not even daring to breathe.

Then the bootsteps started again, growing lower and fainter as he travelled further down the street.

Eventually there was no sound at all except for the drip-ping of water from a nearby spout.

Ainsley waited another five minutes, just to be sure, her

face pressed against the alley wall, breathing in the scent of wet stone. Then she peeled herself away, stepped out into the narrow street, and returned the way she'd come.

Just in case.

Using the map for the *fiesta de los patios*, Ainsley navigated the long, covoluted path back to the hotel, through the Zona Judaria, the Santiago San Pedro *barrio*, the Regina Magdalene *barrio*, and others.

An hour later, she staggered into the Hotel Maghrebi. In the lobby, the desk clerk looked up from behind the front desk. When he saw her, a dark cloud appeared on his face.

"Miss Walker," he said, "we have a serious problem."

"What is it?"

"You cannot stay here any longer. Not without a passport."

"I told you that my brother would be here with the passport tomorrow."

"You must leave."

Ainsley stepped backwards and lifted her hands. "No. You have my credit card. It's authorized."

The clerk hit a small bell on his desk. Ainsley heard boot-steps behind her, and the hairs on her neck pricked up. She turned.

It was Javier.

"You," she said.

His face was a mask.

"Follow me," he said.

"Why?"

"We have your goods in the storage unit by the pool."

She turned to the clerk. "You took my things out of the room?"

The clerk nodded. "They're in storage for safekeeping."

There was nothing she could do. Ainsley followed Javier through a short hallway, out a heavy door, and onto the pool deck. Its waters were illuminated a cerulean blue by underwater lighting.

Javier moved towards a smaller door just to the left. Ainsley studied him as he pulled out a set of keys from his pocket, swiftly opened the lock, popped open the hasp, and swung the storage closet open. She wondered how many times he'd performed this exact motion.

And whether he was ever accompanied by a Catalan with a big chin.

"Here," he said.

He produced Ainsley's lightweight knapsack and handed it to her. She looked inside and counted the items. Nothing seemed missing.

Ainsley looked at Javier. His eyes were regarding her through a wreath of cigarette smoke. "You don't have to do this," she said.

"Who are you?" he replied.

"I'm Ainsley."

"Who are you *really*?"

"I just told you."

"You are working for somebody."

"Nobody. I'm a tourist."

He snorted. "Tourists don't talk like you."

"Bellhops aren't rude like you."

He stepped forward, took a drag from his *cigarillo*, and prepared to blow it in her face again. This time, Ainsley snatched the cigarette out of his mouth and flicked it aside. At the same time, she pressed her hand against his shoulder and gave him a firm shove. Caught off balance, Javier stumbled backwards.

"My name is Ainsley," she said, "and your mother should be ashamed of you."

"My mother is nothing," he spat.

"I thought all Spaniards worshipped their mothers."

Another smirk darkened his face. "Stereotypes."

Ainsley turned, walked back down the hall, and crossed the lobby, and left the Hotel Maghrebi.

Out in the street, in the darkness, she spotted a thin figure heading towards her. As he walked beneath a gaslamp, she recognized Gabriel. His eyes spotted her bag over her shoulder, her distraught face.

"What happened?" he said.

"The hotel just kicked me out for not having a passport. But I think I have a lead."

Gabriel looked excited. "So do I. There is a swordsmith in Toledo who was just approached about buying a tourmaline sword."

"Toledo?" said Ainsley.

"Yes."

"So we're going to another city?"

"Yes."

She felt her body beginning to sag with exhaustion. "Can't we find a different hotel here? I need sleep."

The *mozo de espadas* wagged a stern finger. "This is urgent. The swordsmith keeps unusual hours. Now let's hurry—the next train leaves in twenty minutes."

Ainsley inhaled and began to follow him back towards the train station, despairing that she would never see a full night's sleep again.

TOLEDO

CHAPTER TWENTY-SIX

Rubbing the weariness from her eyelids, Ainsley took a second look at the canvas above the altar, just to make sure that her eyes weren't deceiving her.

They weren't.

She had followed Gabriel onto the last AVE train out of Córdoba that evening, ridden into Madrid, switched trains at Atocha, and thirty minutes later had stepped out into the train station at Toledo.

Gabriel had checked his watch. "We need to wait another hour."

"Why?"

"It's only eleven o'clock. Samson doesn't start working until midnight."

"That's weird."

"That's because he is insane."

"Really?"

Gabriel's face was serious. "Yes, he's clinically insane. And he's going to try to force me to buy a sword. He does it to everybody."

Ainsley's ears perked up in alarm. "Is there anything I

can do?"

"Yes. Don't speak."

That, Ainsley thought, was going to be harder than he suspected. "So what should we do until then?"

"I'm going to look at my favorite painting. I do it whenever I visit Toledo."

"Can I come?"

"If my friend will let you in. He's quite strict."

"Even stricter than you?" Ainsley said.

"Much."

Thirty minutes later, that friend, a somber-looking deacon, had met them at the heavy front door of the Church of Santo Tomé. After a formal embrace with Gabriel, he took a long look at Ainsley. He grunted approval and produced a heavy iron key ring.

"Good," said Gabriel, "you passed."

"Passed what?"

"The clothing test. If you hadn't been dressed appropriately, he wouldn't have let you in."

The deacon ushered them into the small church. He'd flicked on the lights, accompanied them past an empty ticket booth, and around a turn—

—at which point Ainsley had found herself standing at a small altar. Behind the table, on the wall, stretched a wide canvas. A small card read Burial of the Count of Orgaz, but Ainsley hadn't needed to read it. She'd recognized the painting immediately.

It was El Greco's masterpiece.

"You could've told me what we were seeing," she said.

"I did," he replied. "It's my favorite painting. I visit it every time I come to Toledo."

While Ainsley's eyes roved the canvas, Gabriel described the content of the painting. How the Count of Orgaz was being buried by the burghers of the town. How the accurate depiction of the faces had insured that the painting had become an absolute sensation when it was unveiled, as the locals tried to identify themselves or their family members. Gabriel was most enthused by its Catholic theology, especially the muddled earthly mess at the bottom in contrast with the miraculous celestial unity in the heaven overhead.

"That is the truth of life," he said. "Ordinary life leading to eternal salvation. The universal call to holiness."

Soon Ainsley found herself so absorbed by the two-tiered composition, by the lean, elongated figures, that she didn't notice the gentle tugging at her elbow.

"It's midnight," said Gabriel, "and Samson is at work now."

Outside the church, the deacon locked the door. Ainsley noticed the two men mutter a quick prayer, make a quick sign of the cross, then embrace before pulling away. It seemed smooth enough to have been rehearsed. She wondered if Catholics practiced this stuff.

Soon Ainsley and Gabriel were hiking up a sloping medieval alleyway. Above their heads, the full white moon hung in the sky like a communion wafer. Behind them, at the bottom of the hill, lay the River Tagus, the ruins of Roman bridges standing in the swirling waters.

As they walked, Gabriel explained the history of Toledo, how it'd been the first city reconquered from the Moors in 1085, how it'd been the seat of the royal family until before they'd relocated to Madrid, how it'd been the official home of the Spanish Inquisition.

He described the torture devices—the thumbscrews, the iron maiden, the Black Maria, the rack.

Gabriel led her imagination into some very dark places, and as he spoke, Ainsley began to look at him with new eyes. The *mozo de espadas* was proving to be surprisingly sadistic guide, dragging her through Seville, Córdoba, now Toledo—a trio of immensely historical cities, in just over twenty-four hours. It amused her to think that, only two days ago, she'd been complaining to Joaquim that she hadn't been seeing the real Spain.

"Tell me about Samson," she said.

"Toledo's most infamous swordsmith," he replied. "I've met him on several occasions and have always been surprised."

"Why?"

"I already told you. He's insane."

"How delightful."

Gabriel looked at her, shocked.

"Delightful? I just told you he was insane."

Ainsley realized that she'd used sarcasm with a stranger. Unlike Americans, especially young ones, most Spanish people took a dim view of anyone who didn't say what she meant.

"It was a joke," she said, trying to recover. "I was saying the opposite of my true feelings."

"Why would you do that?" he said. His eyes accused her of treachery.

"Because my culture teaches me to," she replied.

He thought about that. "America is a very strange place."

Ainsley smiled. "You might be right," she said. "Now, tell me why we're visiting Samson."

"Because he will probably know something that can help us."

"Who says?"

"In the sword community, all roads eventually lead to Samson. He hears everything."

Ainsley thought about that. "What should I say to him?"

"Nothing," replied Gabriel. "He's a very difficult person, even for me. I will do the talking."

"Okay."

They'd found their way into the more obscure streets of this ancient hilltop city. Straight ahead, between a garbage bin and a boarded-up restaurant, was a storefront. The front was nothing more than a rolled-up garage door. A wicked orange glow emanated from the bowels of the place. The sound of a slow, heavy clanging filled the air.

"That," said Gabriel, "is Samson's forge."

Ainsley felt a twinge of fear, but she forced it down as they stepped inside the open storefront. The walls were lined with a thieves' ransom of swords—at least a hundred, by Ainsley's count—short ones, long ones, wide, narrow, sculpted, filigreed, and more. There were rapiers, training swords, curved katanas, medieval belts, even letter openers. Some had cloths draped over them, some were laying across whetstones, some piled in discard heaps on the floor. On the walls were circular metal coats-of-arms with three swords mounted behind it.

Then she caught sight of a figure.

At the other end of the room, a muscular, shirtless man was standing before a massive forge that was glowing a deep orange. He lifted a hammer and brought it down with a clang onto a sword, bellowing with each blow.

"And that," whispered Gabriel, "is Samson."

CHAPTER TWENTY-SEVEN

Ainsley looked more closely at him. The sweat was glistening on his chest. He was wearing a pair of heavy gloves and a protective mask. The sword had been heated so that its tip was glowing red-orange.

"Isn't it dangerous," said Ainsley, "to do that work shirtless?"

"Probably."

The figure raised his hammer again. Gabriel cupped his hands around his mouth. "Samson."

The swordsman looked up, his arm paused for the next blow. Then he lowered his hammer and ripped the mask off his face.

"Who are you?"

"Gabriel. *El mozo de Pepito.*"

"Ah."

He stuck the sword into a bath of water. It sizzled, and a cloud of steam enveloped the handle.

Then Samson walked over. As he drew closer, Ainsley got a good look at his face. His eyeballs were huge and wild and he didn't seem to have any eyelids, which gave him a perpetual air of surprise.

"You come to buy a sword," he said.

Ainsley noticed that it was a statement, not a question.

"I have a question," answered Gabriel.

"I have one too?" said Samson. "Do you know what sword to use against the Saracens when they attack?"

"No," said Gabriel.

"This one."

He yanked out a long, curved scimitar. It was a Turkish blade. "Because it looks like a woman, it distracts the barbarians. They can be distracted because they lack discipline." He run a finger along the blade, admiring his own handiwork. "It has the power of a Christian God."

Ainsley was confused. Had Samson used the present tense to discuss an ethnic rivalry that had ended seven hundred years ago?

"Your words have strength," said Gabriel. Ainsley saw that he was trying to soothe the madman.

"If they are holding steel such as mine," Samson replied, "all men become powerful."

Samson drew his arm back and threw the scimitar across the room like a javelin. It landed into a wall and stuck there, quivering. His eyes blazed red in the reflection of the forge. Feeling a stab of terror, Ainsley quietly moved closer to her guide.

"I have a problem," said Gabriel. "I lost a sword."

"Which one?"

"The sword of Pepe."

"Where did you lose it?"

"In Córdoba. It was stolen."

Samson lifted a squeeze bottle, opened his mouth, and pushed a blast of water down his throat. He had the delicacy of an anvil falling through a sunroof.

"That is a shame," he said, "especially because of its honorable history."

Glancing at Ainsley, Gabriel quickly changed the subject. "What's important, Samson, is that we recover the sword. This week."

Suddenly Samson looked over their shoulders. Ainsley turned. A pair of fat tourists had poked their head into the reddened forge. "I don't know," said one in English, "I don't think there's a bathroom here—"

"*Vete*," growled the shirtless sword maker. He grabbed a sword and lunged for them. The tourists disappeared back into the darkened street, whimpering.

"Cockroaches," Samson said.

Gabriel maintained his calm. "Have you heard anything about the sword of Pepe?"

"What do I get out of this?"

"I will buy a new *descabello* for Pepito."

"He doesn't need a *descabello*. He is a talented matador."

"Ours is damaged, and you never know."

Samson stroked his jaw, studying Gabriel. Then his eyes flicked to Ainsley.

"Who is she?"

"You can trust her."

A low rumble issued from the swordsmith's throat. "She looks like ... an *activist*."

He spat the word with such vehemence that Ainsley now fully cowered behind Gabriel, but he stood his ground.

"She is not an activist. She is an investigator hired by Pepito."

"A woman," replied Samson, "should be at *home*."

Suddenly he thrust a thick arm around Gabriel and grabbed Ainsley by the upper arm.

"Samson, *por favor*—" said Gabriel.

The sword maker whirled on him. "*Necesito hacerle una prueba.*"

He began to pull Ainsley across the room. She struggled to free herself, but his grip was much too strong. Her instincts told her to slug him with her free hand, but that would be asking for even more trouble. Her only choice was submission. She'd been thrown onto this crazy train, and now she had to ride it to the end of the tracks.

"People say I am mad," said the sword maker, his eyes dancing. "Do you think I am mad?"

Lips tightening, Ainsley tipped her chin and looked him dead in his eyes. "Without a doubt."

He nodded. "I talk to people. People who have been dead for centuries. And they talk back to me. You don't know the chaos inside my head. I cannot get any rest. That's why I am here, beating these swords every night. *Bang bang bang.* The devil's workshop. It's my only relief."

"You could drink whiskey until you pass out," said Ainsley.

He laughed once, a short guttural bark. Then a second time. He released her arm. Ainsley relaxed a little.

Wrong move.

Samson yanked a sword out of a case, stepped back, and pointed it at her. In a flash, Ainsley felt the tip of a rapier pressing into her sternum.

"This is a killing sword," he said.

"They're *all* killing swords," Ainsley replied.

"Tell me you are not an activist."

"I'm an American."

"That doesn't mean anything. *Who are you?*"

The point pressed harder. Ainsley felt her skin beginning to break. Samson's eyes were a pair of red-hot burning coals.

She looked at Gabriel for help. He was beside himself, twisting his hands, chewing on his lip, but there was nothing he could do. He'd warned her that Samson was insane.

Ainsley quickly reviewed her options. She could tell him the truth, that she was a gemstone detective hired by Pepito, but he wouldn't understand that. She needed to concoct a story that would strike close to home.

Then, over the madman's shoulder, she glimpsed a white sheet hanging on the wall. Embroidered onto the sheet was a familiar insignia. It was a red cross with bowed arms. She suddenly recognized it.

It was the symbol of the Knights Templar.

"I'm a scholar," she blurted out, "studying the Knights Templar. I'm here in Spain for research."

Samson erupted in another guttural bark. "*You* ... are a scholar of the Knights Templar?"

"Yes."

"Tell me what you know," he said.

Ainsley struggled for a response. All she remembered about them was what she'd read in a very popular novel about museums, murders, and frantic races around Rome. But she needed to keep the bullshit rolling. It was the only way to get the tip of this rapier off her chest. Plus, she suspected that this wild-eyed shirtless swordsmith had minimal possession of his faculties.

"All the conspiracies," she said. "They still live, you know. I have heard them whisper. At night. You know—the dreams that keep you awake." She paused. "The voices speak to me too."

She arched an eyebrow. Then, slowly, Samson lowered the rapier. Ainsley didn't dare to breathe as she watched the tip trace its way down her abdomen, down her leg, and finally off her body. Samson dropped the sword, and it clattered on the floor.

"You," he said, "are crazy like a fox—"

She held her breath, waiting for the verdict.

"—and I *love* it."

Ainsley exhaled in relief, and then felt the swordsmith fold her in a crushing embrace. He was slick with sweat and his ribcage was twice the breadth of her own body. His skin smelled of iron and lunacy.

Slowly, she disentangled herself. "I'm glad that we could reach an understanding."

Nearby, Gabriel cleared his throat. "I told you that we could trust her."

Ainsley fumbled in her bag for her tissues, then wiped his sweat from her face and arms. She looked down at her beautiful new shirt. It had been stained with dark smudges of iron.

"Now, please, about the sword. Tell us what you know."

"Good," replied Samson, "we can speak openly now. The sword of Pepe has a tourmaline in the handle."

"Yes," said Gabriel.

The swordsmith walked over to his smithy, the muscles of his powerful back fanned out like a manta ray. "I heard something about it. A few days ago."

"Tell me," said Gabriel.

The sword maker crossed the room. He picked up a caping sword, inspected it in the red light of the forge. "Somebody said that the marquesa had been searching for it."

Ainsley felt her heartbeat accelerate. She leaned in to listen even more closely.

"Who?" said Gabriel.

"The Marquesa de Grantruca," said Samson.

"Who is that?"

"You don't know her name?"

"No."

"She is very old. She is an *aficionada*."

"As God watches over us," said Gabriel, "she is a stranger to me. Who is her husband?"

"The *marquès* is long passed. He held the title." Samson met Gabriel's eyes. "He was one of the loyal ones."

Gabriel nodded, as if he knew what that meant. Ainsley was dying to ask, but she didn't want to interrupt the conversation.

"Samson," she said, "what else did you hear?"

"I heard that the marquesa was looking for the sword of Pepe."

"Before it was stolen?" said Gabriel.

"After."

Gabriel's jaw dropped. "So this woman is trying to *help* us?"

"Maybe." Samson lifted a small hammer and pounded it against his palm. "She has an interest. Maybe she is working for herself. You should find her and ask."

"Where does she live?" said Ainsley.

"In Madrid. She has an estate in the country too."

Ainsley was speechless.

"Now," said Samson, "which sword do you want to buy?" His arm swept around the room.

Gabriel glanced at Ainsley, then directed his eyes downward. She followed his gaze. Behind his back, Gabriel's index finger was urgently pointing towards the street. Ainsley took the hint. She casually backed away, out of the shop, into the darkness.

From the street, she heard Samson bellow, an anguished sound like the rending of a soul. Ainsley tensed her muscles. He'd suddenly flipped again. In the U.S., this guy would be held on a seventy-two-hour involuntary psychiatric lockdown. In Spain, he led a happy and fulfilled life building and selling deadly antique weapons.

There was a loud crash. Suddenly Gabriel came sprinting out of the shop. He saw Ainsley and grabbed her arm.

"*Run,*" he hissed.

Ainsley found herself yanked off her feet and into a sprint.

"What are we running for?"

"I didn't buy a sword. He swore to cut my head off."

"Jesus."

They dashed through the maze of alleyways. "The train station is down this way," said Gabriel.

Ainsley stayed on his heels. "We're leaving Toledo?"

"Of course. Time is of the essence."

"That man was insane."

"If you think *he* was crazy," said Gabriel, "just wait until you see how *los gatos* in Madrid spend their nights."

CHAPTER TWENTY-EIGHT

An hour later, packed inside a crowd of late-night commuters, Ainsley moved across the vast, plant-filled plaza of Madrid's Atocha Station.

She looked up. Overhead was a glass-and-wrought-iron ceiling. Around her lay an extensive indoor garden, the planters packed with trees and shrubs. The sound of trickling water caught her ear. To her left, a large indoor pond had been built. An informational panel described the types of frogs and ducks that could be found in the habitat.

It was striking that all of this was in a train station.

Even more striking to Ainsley, who'd been born and raised in the vast, decentralized United States, was how close together major cities could be in Europe. The train ride from Toledo had only taken thirty minutes, and now she was about to enter the vast beating heart of Madrid.

The capital of Spain.

The home of Castellaño.

Gabriel was walking alongside her, placing phone calls in rapid Spanish, trying to find someone who knew the Marquesa de Grantruca. He closed his phone.

"Any luck?" she said.

"No."

"Do you want to wait until tomorrow?"

"We can't," he said, "this is too important. Are you hungry?"

As Ainsley opened her mouth to respond, her stomach growled loudly in response.

"This way," he said. "I know just the place. You will eat and I will make more phone calls."

They climbed into a taxi and drove down to the Plaza del Sol, the heavily trafficked pedestrian area north of the train station. Ainsley felt the difference immediately. Unlike the people of Andalucía, the *madrileños* were quick and modern. Striding, yapping, laughing, the men dressed in modish dark clothing, the women sleek and leonine. Through the taxi window Ainsley saw unfamiliar stores such as La Martina and Hackett slide past, and more familiar global brands such as Valentino and Tag Heuer.

Near the corner of Calle Serrano, a busy artery, Gabriel led her down a small side street. Halfway down the block was an unmarked restaurant with a patio.

"This is Pepito's favorite place," he said. "What day is it?"

Ainsley crinkled her forehead. "It's Tuesday. Why?"

"Good," he replied. "I'm going to order Pepito's favorite dish for you. They only serve it on Tuesdays."

After a quick conversation with the owner, Gabriel and Ainsley were seated on the patio.

A moment later, he returned with a bottle of red wine and poured two glasses.

"No," said Ainsley, "I need coffee."

The owner looked as though she'd just asked him to pour a glass of paint.

"Really?" he said.

"Yes."

He returned a minute later with a ceramic cup of espresso. Ainsley threw it backwards down her throat, then handed it to him. "Another, please."

While Gabriel made phone calls, the owner brought Ainsley three more espressos. They didn't do anything for her. She still felt run over by a truck.

She distracted herself by watching a group of young bucks moping past the table, cigarettes drooping from their mouths, scratchy facial hair, stonewashed jeans clinging tightly to their thin legs.

"What are you looking at?" said Gabriel, scrolling through his contacts list.

"These young guys," she said.

He lifted an eyebrow. "You are attracted to them?"

"No. They look kind of slovenly."

"That's because they're unemployed." He punched another number on his phone. "More than half of the young people in Spain cannot find work."

Then the owner arrived carrying a large pot. "*Cocido madrileño*. There are three *vuelcos*. This is the first."

Ainsley peered inside. It contained *fideuà* noodles in a hot yellow broth. Using a large spoon, she slurped the noodles as fast as her utensil could scoop them. The flavorful broth scalded the inside of her mouth, but she didn't care. The second plate arrived, a fried mixture of chickpeas and vegetables, which she shoveled into her maw. On the final plate was an army of sliced meats, blood sausage, and marrow bones. She wolfed those too, her vegetarianism now a distant memory.

Gabriel touched his phone and set it down. Then he pounded the table with a gentle fist. A look of ecstasy had lit up his face.

"I did it," he said. "José Luis, a very old friend from Ronda, is acquainted with the Marquesa's *mayordomo*. He will call them in the morning to arrange a meeting." He smiled. "It's good to keep old friends."

Ainsley nodded dreamily, her eyes beginning to close.

His eyes glanced at the empty plates. "You finished all that food?"

"I was hungry."

"It was supposed to be for two people."

"Sorry."

The *mozo de espadas* covered his yawn with a hand. "It's no problem. I'm going to the hotel that we customarily stay at. Do you want to share a cab? Spending *un noche en los tilos* doesn't have any attraction for me, but I'll show you the best streets to begin the party."

"Okay," she mumbled.

"Let's go."

Gabriel paid the bill, refusing to let her contribute. They walked to the corner and hailed a different taxi and climbed inside.

"See, on a tapas crawl, what you want to do is keep moving," he said. "At each bar, ask for only their most popular tapa. Order that one dish, and always one drink too, maybe a cider from Asturias, maybe a *txacoli* from Basque country. Eat, pay, and move on. Keep the momentum. Otherwise, you won't last the night. Now, up ahead is the first one you should go to, Casa Revuelta. Here, you only get the deep-fried *bacalao*—"

He stopped talking. The sound of light snoring had begun issuing from Ainsley's mouth.

The taxi stopped. The driver looked in the rearview mirror and said, "Casa Revuelta."

"Never mind," said Gabriel. "To the hotel."

CHAPTER TWENTY-NINE

Standing in the shower, Ainsley spun the water nozzle to ice cold in a final effort to wake herself up.

It was already past noon. She'd been roused by the sound of a fierce pounding on the door of her room. The house-keeping staff had been unaware of the deep exhaustion that lay behind the door.

Ainsley had pushed herself over the last forty-eight hours, and her body was letting her know that. Every muscle on her body ached. Her shoulders were stooped. Her face felt as though it were sliding down off her skull. There were limits to a person's endurance, despite her best efforts to ignore them.

In the shower, she'd washed the shampoo out of her hair, applied conditioner, let it rest, washed that out too. Then she'd used pink facial soap on her cheeks, allowing it to rest for twenty seconds. She'd leaned against the side of the tile to wait. That's when she'd fallen asleep, standing up like a horse.

When the cold water hit her skin, a scream escaped her throat. She leapt out of the shower, wrapped a towel around her face, and shivered.

At last, she was awake.

Ready for the day.

While toweling off, Ainsley's mind wandered to the Marquesa de Grantruca. How did somebody get a title like that? Did she have to purchase it from the government? Did someone bequeath it to her? Or could she simply announce herself to be a marquesa?

A few minutes later, she'd finished her makeup, and rummaged around the drawers until she'd found an iron and ironing board. She filled it with water and steamed the same clothing that she'd worn yesterday, the outfit from the El Corte Inglés. She let it cool for a minute, decided to ignore the iron stains on the front of the blouse, and slipped into the clothing. Then she took her bag, collected her room key, and travelled down the elevator.

Gabriel was already in the lobby, sitting stiffly in a straight-backed chair. Ainsley approached him from behind and placed her hands on his shoulders.

To her surprise, he leaped up and backed away from her, palms up, a look of sheer panic on his face.

"*Don't* do that," he said. "Please, I *don't* like people touching me."

"I'm sorry," she said.

"Please, don't do that."

Ainsley lifted her palms up. "Never again."

Her guide paced the lobby for a moment, hands in his pockets, wracked with some inner torment.

Finally he lifted his face. It was intense. "We have an audience with the marquesa at two o'clock pm."

Ainsley wasn't expecting that. "That's great news. How did you get that?"

"Because of José Luis, she has a high estimation of me. It should run smoothly. I think she will tell us everything we want to know."

Ainsley wondered if things really were going to work like that. In her experience in foreign countries, friends-of-friends were rarely treated with any seriousness.

"It's one o'clock. Let's go find out."

As they stepped outside of the hotel, she noticed a commotion across the street. A group of fifty young people in black t-shirts were standing in a row in a small plaza. They were holding up a large banner. It read *Tauromaquia abolicíon*.

"Activists," said Gabriel, shaking his head. "They stand on this street and protest when a new shipment of bulls is brought to Las Ventas."

Ainsley guessed that Las Ventas was Madrid's bullring. She watched the group closely. They were young, very serious, and very idealistic. None were smiling. Truth be told, it was the type of activist group that some of her friends had tried to form years earlier, except in their case it was to lobby against the removal of rhinoceros tusks in west Africa. Ainsley had known many of the girls very well, and she hadn't doubted their sincerity, but she also wondered why so many activists cared so much about injustices occurring to animals halfway around the world. To Ainsley, there was plenty of human anguish occurring right underneath their own noses.

"Do the people like them?" she asked.

"It depends."

"Here?"

"In Madrid, generally, yes. In Galicia, the activists embar-rass themselves by following the fox hunters with loud air horns. They blow the horns to scare the foxes away before they can be shot."

As if on cue, a volley of airhorns sounded from the lineup of demonstrators. Ainsley whipped her head around. The group of protestors had stepped out into traffic. Cars and buses screeched to a halt. The line of fifty quickly assumed a sideways formation, in three rows. They were fully blocking traffic.

"The bulls must be coming," said Gabriel. "Yes, there they are. Do you see them?"

Ainsley followed his finger. One block down the street was an enormous silver truck. It didn't look like a typical eighteen-wheeler back home, the types carrying loads of beverages. This one looked reinforced, heavy and strong.

Then she heard a massive boom emanate from the truck. Even from this distance, it was the type of deep sound that you didn't forget. It echoed in your body.

She looked at the vehicle. A pair of silver bulges had appeared in the side wall of the truck.

That truck really was carrying a bull. The furious animal had, evidently out of sheer frustration, used its immense power to plant its back hooves into the wall of its prison.

On the sidewalk, various men had begun clapping at the sound. Others shook their fists in the air, grinning. A few were shouting *toro*.

Ainsley looked back at the activists. The first row had laid facedown on the street, spreadeagled. The second row had dropped to their knees. The third row had stayed standing upright.

The drivers were upset. Some had begun to lay on their horns out of sheer frustration. Others had emerged from their vehicles, shouting.

"We should leave," said Gabriel, "before the police arrive. Sometimes these things turn ugly."

Ainsley followed him away from the scene, understanding for the first time just how divisive the *corrida* could be.

CHAPTER THIRTY

The taxicab dropped them off in the expensive neighborhood of Salamanca. Here, the streets were clean and manicured. Expensive women strolled with great pride down the street, wrists dripping with gold and silver, the tawny skin of their faces glossy with makeup.

Using the maps app on her phone, Ainsley easily found the house of the marquesa. From the sidewalk, the edifice looked stolid and conservative. A tall iron fence surrounded the property, and the only way in was through a heavy gate.

Gabriel approached the callbox and pressed the button. Ainsley noticed that he'd dressed exactly the same today as he had yesterday. She admired the way nothing seemed to affect the *mozo de espadas*. He seemed to be propelled by a higher power. Ainsley, by contrast, felt like a piece of roadkill, and it took an hour of heavy prepwork in the bathroom just to reach decent.

A voice squawked from the box.

Gabriel said, "It's Gabriel, sent by José Luis, for the marquesa."

Another squawk, and a buzz sounded. The gate popped open. Gabriel held it open for Ainsley.

They crossed the small yard, the path wandering through some hedges. The branches of a shrub seemed to salute as they passed. A rhododendron stood near the front door like a sentinel, its rubbery leaves thick and shiny. Ainsley noticed how different the vegetation was here, in the colder center of the peninsula, than it had been in Andalucía.

The front door swung open as they approached. A trim man wearing a gray suit stood stiffly inside the doorway, centered. His black hair was quite short, nearly militaristic, his face smooth, his eyes large and sympathetic. His mouth had a serious set.

"Gabriel?" he said, shaking hands.

"Indeed. This is Ainsley Walker."

"A pleasure," said the man, kissing her cheek. "I am called Juan Carlo."

They stood on the porch for an awkward moment. Usually, at times like this, Ainsley reflected, the visitors are invited into the house. But Juan Carlo occupied the center of the doorway, and he didn't seem to want to budge.

Then he grew suddenly sad. "Something unexpected has happened."

"Tell me," said Gabriel.

"The marquesa's mind isn't working as well as it used to."

Alarmed, he straightened up. "Please, go on."

"When the marquesa learned that you, Gabriel, would be visiting today, she confused you with Gabriel Sanlucar."

"Gabriel Sanlucar? The traitorous matador?"

"Yes."

The *mozo de espadas* flared his nostrils. "The one who defected to Equanimal and now gets paid to spout lies about the mistreatment of the bulls."

"Yes."

Gabriel clutched his head, then laughed bitterly. "Did you remind the marquesa that I am not that man? That I am actually Pepito's *mozo de espadas*?"

"Of course," replied Juan Carlo. "But she had already become very angry, and her mind isn't working right. You know, her advanced age." He paused. "I have never seen her become so adamant before."

"So what is the result?" said Ainsley.

"The marquesa has decided not to speak with you," he said.

Ainsley felt her heart drop. They'd come all the way to Madrid to speak to this old woman, only to be stymied by a misfired set of synapses. A senior moment.

"We are looking for an important sword," said Ainsley, "one with a tourmaline set in the handle. Gabriel's job depends on finding it. Pepito's career depends on finding it. And we were told that the marquesa is interested in finding it too. Is there any way to speak to her?"

The *mayordomo* shook his head. "The marquesa is very stubborn. When her mind is made up, it is made up."

Gabriel's shoulders were stooped. Feeling crestfallen herself, Ainsley reached out to comfort him, then remembered his aversion to touch. She lowered her hand.

"This is very disappointing," said Gabriel. "There must be a solution."

"I am sympathetic to your dilemma," replied Juan Carlo, "and I can offer one possibility."

Ainsley perked up. "What do you suggest?"

"The marquesa loves to attend the *corrida*," he said. "Her dear husband taught her to appreciate the artistry, and now it reminds her of their many years together. I accompany her once a week."

"That's very touching," said Gabriel, "but tell us the plan."

"Las Ventas, tomorrow afternoon," he said. "If you attend

the *corrida*, and sit near us, I will point you out to the marquesa. Show your passion. When she sees your commitment to the *corrida*, she may reconsider."

Gabriel clapped his hands. "Excellent. We can do that. Where are your seats?"

"I will show you."

While he and Juan Carlo conferred about the seating chart at Las Ventas, Ainsley stepped off the porch, wandered into the yard, and moodily kicked the grass.

If she wanted to solve this mystery, she was going to have to attend a bullfight.

CHAPTER THIRTY-ONE

At five-thirty the next afternoon, Ainsley reluctantly followed Gabriel into the biggest bullring in the entire world, the epicenter of the *corrida*.

Plaza de Toros de Las Ventas.

They stood in the aisle that wrapped around the midsection of the stadium. Ainsley took in large ring of tan-colored dirt, the two neatly drawn rings of white chalk, the long rings of bleachers around her, the arches ringing the top. About half the seats were filled.

"Today's matadors aren't very famous," said Gabriel. "Otherwise, this entire stadium would be sold out."

"Fortunately for us," said Ainsley.

He looked at her. "You seem upset."

"Me?"

"Yes."

"No, I'm fine. Let's watch some killing." Ainsley tried to punctuate that with a big smile.

"Ah," said Gabriel, "this is your first *corrida*, isn't it?"

Ainsley looked away. "Yes."

The syllable came out clipped and abrupt. Gabriel nodded

sympathetically. "Let's find our seats, and I'll explain everything to you."

As he led her down the stairs, Ainsley felt her stomach beginning to churn. It grew grew worse as Gabriel led them to two empty seats in the front row.

"How did you get these tickets?"

"I have connections," he replied. "But these *barrera* seats aren't as popular as you think. Many people like to sit higher for a better view. Still, we need to sit lower so that the marquesa can see us. Look."

He gestured backwards, and Ainsley twisted around. Seven rows behind them sat Juan Carlo, wearing the same gray suit. He saw Ainsley and nodded.

Next to him was the marquesa.

A shrunken elderly woman with wispy white hair, she was drowning inside a bright red sportcoat that looked like it should've been on a much larger woman. It fit her like a tent. On her face, she wore red lipstick and red earrings and rouged cheeks. Her expression was serious. From this distance, she looked nearly waxen.

Ainsley faced forward again. "Did you see her?" said Gabriel.

"I did."

"Remember, you have to look excited."

"I will."

A wave of revulsion passed over Ainsley. She fixed her gaze upon a cloud in the distance. She decided that talking might help her anxiety.

"Has Pepito performed here?" she said.

"Almost thirty times," answered Gabriel. "Once every year, usually. Las Ventas pays well, and they don't try to cheat you. Plus, matadors usually reserve their best performance for this stadium, so that all the mouths in Madrid start talking. Then word gets around, and they get more contracts. But it's very difficult. Madrileños are the most discerning audience in the country."

That made sense. Ainsley watched the vendors strolling the stairs, selling pastries, sugared almonds, cups of beer. It felt much like the start to any other sporting event.

Then the *corrida* began.

A heroic bugle melody sounded throughout the stadium, and without any other introduction, a large procession entered the ring—men with small swords, men on horses, and finally the six matadors, who strode proudly into the ring. The crowd applauded. Ainsley studied the six men. Each was dressed in satin knee breeches that had been embroidered in gold thread, a short vest, silk hose, and flat shoes that looked like ballet slippers. On each of their heads was a Cordobés cap that looked like a pad ornamented with tassels. And each carried a short cape of embroidered satin, thrown across on his shoulder, in various colors—purple, blue, orange, yellow.

"The entrance is called the *paseíllo*," said Gabriel. "It's always the same."

Ainsley found herself admiring these matadors' physical appearance. Unlike Pepito, they were long, lean, and elegant. One of them, in fact, was downright gorgeous. The costumes helped, of course—they'd been designed to emphasize masculine musculature and create sex appeal, particularly highlighting the legs.

In the center of the ring, they saluted somebody on the other side of the stadium.

"That's the governor," said Gabriel, "and now they're going to get the *toril*."

"What's that?"

One of the matadors walked over to the box, where the governor handed him a large key.

"The key to the bull pen," he said.

Ainsley watched as five of the matadors disappeared into

the narrow protected alley around the bullring. Then she noticed others standing there too, photographers, journalists, carpenters, and medical staff.

She looked back to the ring. Four men on four heavily padded horses had taken up positions in opposite corners of the circle. They held lances. Ainsley noticed that the stirrups were made of iron, and that their legs were protected by iron casts as well.

"The picadors," said Gabriel. "The horses are always old and handicapped, just in case."

"In case of what?"

Gabriel caught her eye. "In case the bull charges them."

"Silence!" said a voice.

It boomed across the arena over the sound system. Ainsley twisted around looking for the source. Gabriel pointed to the left. Two sections to the left, a man was standing over the bull pen, a microphone clipped around his ear. He had his hand on a lever. It led to the gate.

The audience obeyed, falling almost completely silent. Then the man with the microphone gestured to the ring. "A man risks his *life* here today!"

"Always the same phrase," whispered Gabriel. "Now they will lift the gate."

"Where is the matador?"

He smiled. "Look on the ground."

Ainsley craned her neck, trying to see around the other spectators. Five meters in front of the gate, on the ground, was the matador. He was crouching, one knee on the sand, his purple cape held out over his elbow, his eyes staring straight towards the gate.

She felt a flash of panic rip through her body. That young man was going to be killed, instantly, before the *corrida* had even begun. It was like crouching on the median line of a freeway.

"Is he crazy?" she whispered.

"Of course," said Gabriel, "he is a matador. But also remember, this is Madrid. He has to put on a real show to impress the audience."

The man with the key suddenly pulled the lever, and the gate cranked up. Two seconds later, a huge black creature burst out of the gate, already running at full speed. The matador swished his cape to the side, drawing it slightly to the left, and the bull narrowly missed him. It galloped into the center of the ring.

Ainsley found herself applauding with the audience. "He is very brave," said Gabriel, "to crouch in front of the gates of fear. Very brave. Pepito stopped doing it years ago."

"Why?"

"One of his friends was kicked in the face. Now he is in a wheelchair and lives on a liquid diet."

Ainsley looked back at the ring. A group of men carrying scarlet capes were taunting the bull, trying to lead him towards the picadors, who had ridden towards the middle.

"They are called *capeadores*," said Gabriel. He tilted his head, studying the animal. "Oh, this bull is very stupid."

"How can you tell?"

"I've been watching the bulls for thirty years. A smart bull runs lightly and ignores everything except the matador. A smart bull is the kiss of death for a matador." He paused, thinking. "The crowd loves the stupid ones, though. They are overly aggressive and will charge anything. Look, it charges the horse."

The bull had rammed its horns into the heavy drapery on the side of one of the picador's animals. The poor horse staggered sideways but didn't fall. Ainsley clapped a hand over her mouth, stifling a scream. She didn't like riding horses, never had, but she hated to see violence done to them.

Gabriel leaned over and whispered, "You must look excited." His eyes rolled backwards, towards the marquesa.

Ainsley dropped her hand from her mouth, straightened up in her seat, and began to clap vigorously.

"Okay, not that excited," he said.

After a few more rams, and a few more staggered horses, the second part of the *corrida* began.

"The *banderillas*," said Gabriel.

A bugle sound announced the arrival of three men, each holding a pair of tiny steel swords with colored ribbons. They circled the bull, dancing lightly when it swung its horns near them. Whenever the bull was sufficiently distracted, a *banderilla* stuck one of the tiny swords into the hump of muscle mass above the bull's shoulders.

Soon the bull had five small swords sticking out of his back, like a tiny pincushion, and the blood was running down the sides of the animal. It had slowed its prancing.

"Now he's weakened," said Gabriel, "and the matador will finish the performance."

That meant the kill. Ainsley felt her heart thump faster in her chest.

CHAPTER THIRTY-TWO

The matador had appeared in the center of the bullring. This time he was holding the iconic red cape and a different, heavier sword. Ainsley found herself tensing, her palms slick with sweat, wondering what he would do next.

"This is called the third of death," said Gabriel. "He has fifteen minutes to finish the bull. If he doesn't, the bull is removed from the arena and allowed to live the rest of his life."

"I hope the bull survives."

"Whatever happens, you must act appreciative. Just do what I do."

"Okay."

The bull stood below Ainsley, no more than ten meters away. She could almost catch the primal scent of his blood leaking out of his body. In fact, if he turned and decided to make one good jump, she might even find a bull in her lap.

But the matador was skilled, and he was slowly approaching the animal, one arm holding the red *muleta*, the other hand gripping a slim sword. His handsome face had changed too. It now carried an expression of fierce concentration.

"That's the killing sword," said Gabriel.

"Like the sword of Pepe."

"Yes. But the sword of Pepe is beautiful. When the tourmaline flashes, the women love it."

Suddenly the bull reared its head back and let loose a loud bellow. It was eerie and primitive, unlike anything Ainsley had ever heard. She felt goosebumps appearing on her forearms.

"He's hurt," she said.

"No," said Gabriel, "he's alerting the rest of the herd to a new danger."

Ainsley snorted. "How can a bull think a man is dangerous?"

Gabriel gave her a knowing smile. "Because he hasn't seen a man before. You didn't know?"

Ainsley shook her head.

He explained: "It's Spanish law. The bulls may not stand face-to-face with a human until this very moment, here in the arena. Otherwise, the bull will lose its fear of humans, and the fight will never be fair."

Ainsley didn't think the fight was fair anyways, given the lopsided history of which side usually ended up dying.

Suddenly the bull began his charge. The matador quickly twisted sideways, lengthening his body, and swept the cape alongside his left flank. The bull's horns missed him by inches.

"That was a *verónica*," said Gabriel. "It's the most basic pass. Notice he keeps the front of his legs always turned away from the bull. That's to avoid injury to the femoral arteries."

Ainsley was biting her nails as she watched the bull sweep past the matador, again and again, left and right, the man sometimes dancing, stretching, swishing the cape, even drawing semi-circles in the sand.

"This is a slow kill," said Gabriel. "The *madrileños* are getting restless."

"Why is he taking so long?"

"This bull is exceptionally strong and won't tire." He checked his watch. "Only three more minutes. The matador needs to make a move."

At last the bull stopped walking. It stood there in the ring, snorting, sides heaving, looking somewhat defeated. Five brightly colored *picas* stuck out of the hump of its back. Beneath its hoofs, the sandy floor of the bullring was splotched with dark red patches of blood.

The matador stepped closer to the animal, holding his *muleta* up protectively, his other arm drawn back.

"Stand up," said Gabriel, lifting Ainsley by the arm. "Show the marquesa that you appreciate the art of the kill."

Ainsley stood on shaking legs. She wanted to avert her eyes, cover her face, turn her head, flee the arena—anything but applaud the butchery that was about to occur before her.

"Wave this newspaper," he said, "like this."

Ainsley took the paper and swept it in the air, the way he was doing, but she could feel herself starting to cry. They wouldn't stop.

"Tell me those are tears of joy," he said.

"These are *whatever* the marquesa wants them to be," said Ainsley.

Gabriel turned around. "Good, she is watching us. Juan Carlo has kept his promise."

"Can I look at her?"

"No, look forward."

Biting her lip, Ainsley forced herself to face the final act. The matador held the cape low, stood perpendicular to the bull, then drew his sword back in a wide arc and aimed it. He peered at the bull down the long blade, as if it were a telescope. Then he rustled the cape. The bull took a step forward, the matador made a flurry of small steps with his feet—

"The *volapié*," said Gabriel.

—and, leaping in the air, thrust the sword into the animal's upper back.

The bull halted. The matador released the weapon, took two steps to the side, and turned to the crowd, holding a regal hand out.

The crowd roared, Ainsley among them. She thrust her arms into the air, trying to feign joy.

Next to her, Gabriel applauded firmly. "That was authoritative," he said, "and clean."

Meanwhile, the animal's front legs had lowered. Its head and neck had angled upwards and stiffened. Ainsley could see its sides pressing in and out like a pair of bellows, its breath coming in stertorous grunts. She felt the tears coursing down her cheeks now but her hands kept applauding.

"This is a brave bull," said Gabriel. "He won't give up. Look, here comes the *descabello*."

A different matador had stepped to the twitching body of the bull. He poised what looked like a short dagger above the animal's neck, paused—

—and rammed it down into the animal's spinal column. The bull tipped over sideways onto the sand, its four legs sticking straight out.

It was dead.

The audience cheered. Not loudly—no bloodlust at all—but politely, as if for a job well done. A team of three horses was trotted out, all yoked together and dragging a long horizontal pole. Using ropes and chains, the assistants tied the bull's body to the pole, and a moment later, the dark corpse was being dragged across the sand like a plow, leaving a thick trail of wet blood, and then it disappeared out the gate.

The *corrida* was over.

Ainsley looked around. At first glance, all she saw were people slapping each other on the backs, leaving for the bathroom, checking their phones. As though a public execution hadn't just occurred.

And this was only the first bull. There were five more to go.

"I hope it wasn't too traumatic," said Gabriel.

Ainsley wiped her eyes with a tissue. "It was."

He nodded. "If it's your first, I can understand that. But when you are raised in the tradition, you don't have a problem with it. Truthfully, though, most Spaniards don't care for the *corrida*. Many of these people are visitors. Tourist money is what keeps the doors open on many bullrings."

Ainsley peered more closely at the people around her. This time, she noticed several shocked faces, some crying, a few slinging purses over their shoulders and running towards the exit. She wondered if it was fair to say that the most affected people seemed to be blonde women of Anglo descent. It would stand to reason that they would be drawn to the bullring for its sense of transgression, based on the standards of their own cultures.

Then she felt a pair of eyes on her. Ainsley looked up. Seven rows above, the old marquesa was watching her, a smile slowly curling at the corners of her mouth.

A bugle announced the second matador's entrance. Ainsley plopped down in her seat. "Do we really have to stay?"

"Do you want the marquesa to trust you?" said Gabriel.

"Yes."

Ainsley noticed a familiar figure at the end of their row. It was Juan Carlo, standing in the aisle, and he was explaining something to the people on the outside edge. He jotted something on a piece of paper, handed it to the people, and gestured to them to pass it down to Gabriel.

A moment later, the paper arrived. Gabriel opened it. Ainsley peered over his shoulder.

The marquesa will see you tomorrow at ten o'clock am.
Call me to confirm in the morning.
–Juan Carlo

"She trusts us now," said Ainsley.

Gabriel made a small two-finger salute to Juan Carlo. In the aisle, the *mayordomo* nodded back, then climbed the stairs and sat down next to the marquesa.

"Excellent," said Gabriel.

Ainsley smiled. "Now can we go?"

He shook his head. "No, it would look suspicious."

Ainsley slumped in her seat as the next matador enter the arena.

There were five more killings to go.

CHAPTER THIRTY-THREE

Though Ainsley had always been a light sleeper, she'd never woken up to the sound of a paper sliding across the floor.

It'd been a restless night. A nightmare that had stubbornly persisted—a dream that she was walking through a dark primeval forest populated by large animals. Mostly it'd been sounds, the whistling of claws as they rent flesh, the gnashing of teeth as the victors dined, and the long bellows of dying creatures.

That's why, at seven-thirty the next morning, the tiny sound of a note being shoved underneath Ainsley's door jerked her awake.

She stumbled out of bed and went over to the door and picked it up. It was from Gabriel.

Change in plans. Call me when you wake up. Room 204. —Gab.

Ainsley sighed. Nothing was going to go smoothly in Madrid. Sitting through the *corrida* the night before had been a wrenching experience, not too different from watching two hours of snuff films. The art was there, true, the *faena*, and even a touch of beauty too, but the four stiff legs that invariably pointed sideways at the end of each sequence blotted out everything else.

Ainsley thought about it. The civilized world had outlawed public executions of humans over a hundred years ago. Why, then, was this practice still conducted on animals, and celebrated in such a flamboyant way?

On the other hand, after a few hours in a front-row seat, she could finally understand why people gravitated to the *corrida*. It carried a special visceral power, one as old as humanity itself, and to deny that would be to deny our own heritage.

The *corrida* is a vestige of those old ways. It's our last remaining connection with our Paleolithic ancestors and their cave paintings of humans chasing bulls. This is notable by itself because, other than cooking our food over open flames, humans haven't preserved much else from this ancient past. Ainsley remembered reading once that one out of two people ever born died of infectious disease before reaching five years old.

And then there was the thorny question of whether bullfighting was *right*.

Was it *moral*?

Ainsley didn't have the answer to that question. All she knew was that it was an exceptionally difficult event for a newbie spectator to watch. In fact, it was like suffering through a too-vigorous massage—despite the pain, she knew that it hadn't been *all* bad, and she would probably find herself still thinking about the experience, days, weeks, months later.

She opened the curtain to let in the morning light. Then she picked up the hotel phone and dialed Gabriel's room.

He picked up quickly. "Ainsley?"

"Yes."

"I didn't think you were awake."

"You woke me up. What's happening?"

"The marquesa has decided to leave for her estate in the country. She was only in Madrid for the *corrida*."

"So is the meeting cancelled again?"

"No," said Gabriel. "Juan Carlo says that we are welcome to visit the marquesa's country estate instead."

Ainsley sat down on the bed, distraught. She was starting to feel like a greyhound on a track, chasing a rabbit that could never be caught.

"This woman is very difficult," she said.

"Absolutely."

"Is it worth it to drive out to the country?"

"Probably. It's not every day you get the chance to talk to someone like her. She has a lot of knowledge of swords and the *corrida*."

Ainsley thumped the mattress and stood up. "Then let's go."

"There is another problem."

She stopped. "What?"

"I cannot go with you. Pepito needs me."

Ainsley felt her stomach drop. Gabriel had been an invaluable guide—reliable, knowledgeable, a little mysterious. Plus, he was one of the few humans on earth who could match Ainsley's own high level of energy. Immense stamina was probably a job requirement for working for Pepito.

"So you have to leave right now?"

"Yes. Pepito called this morning and begged for me to return to him. There is a *corrida* tomorrow in Granada."

"And you answered his call?"

"Working with you has been my penance. I am ready to serve him again."

Ainsley sighed. "So what am I supposed to do? You won't be able to go for at least two days, and we don't know if the marquesa will meet me alone."

He thought about it. "I will call Juan Carlo and with God's blessing, she will meet you alone."

Then Ainsley remembered another obstacle. "One more thing, Gabriel."

"What?"

"I can't rent a car."

"Why?"

"Pepito took away my passport."

Silence on the other end. Then: "Shit." He sighed. "Then you will have to come with me to Granada."

"But I don't want to go to Granada, Gabriel."

He spoke urgently. "Pepito has your passport, Miss Walker, and you will have to beg him to get it back. There is really no other choice. Be downstairs in thirty minutes."

"I have to shower and pack—"

"Thirty minutes. He's expecting me."

He disconnected. Ainsley stared at the television console, running through all the options in her mind. Her wild pursuit of a tourmaline sword, convoluted as it already was, was about to suffer a detour.

Then her phone rang again. She looked at the caller ID.

It was Joaquim.

She hesitated, her thumb over the red button to answer. Then she changed her mind, dropped it into her purse, and went into the bathroom and closed the door and turned on the shower. She didn't want hear the ringing anymore.

It was time to see Pepito.

CHAPTER THIRTY-FOUR

Standing at the end of the bed, Ainsley watched Gabriel kneel on the mattress and quietly pull the half-full whiskey bottle out of Pepito's drunken fingers.

It was four o'clock p.m., and the matador was sprawled facefirst across his bed in a suite at the Hotel Isabella. They'd arrived at lunchtime, but Gabriel had warned Ainsley that he was unapproachable on the afternoon of a *corrida* until he'd liquored himself up.

Ainsley checked her watch. He'd been drinking for three hours. It was now or never.

She stood up straight and cleared her throat.

"Pepito," she said.

The matador didn't move. The t-shirt across his broad back rose and fell gently with his breathing. Beneath his undershorts his narrow man-buttocks were pushed together like two small heaps of veal carpaccio.

"Pepito," said Ainsley, "I need my passport back. I have to rent a car."

A small muffled sound came from his face. Ainsley realized that it was a snore.

"If you wait outside the room," said Gabriel, "I will wake him up. I know what to do with Pepito when he's like this."

Ainsley left the bedroom and went out into the living room. Unlike its drunken occupant, the hotel room was elegant and even sophisticated. She sat down on a chair and crossed her legs and bobbed one calf. She feigned fascination with a fingernail.

Then she noticed the balcony.

Ainsley stood up and pushed open the doors and stepped outside. It was a narrow balcony, but it didn't matter, not with the city of Granada spread out around her—sloping hillsides, ancient structures, the white-tipped mountains of the Sierra Nevadas high above. She felt her breath catch in her throat. It was a beautiful site, and she understood why the Moors had clung so fiercely to it.

Below the hotel, on the other side of the narrow road, stood what appeared to be an ancient Islamic compound. Even from here she could see the shimmering arabesques on the column arcades, hear the water trickling into green reflecting pools, smell the lemon-scented air from the citrus gardens. And beyond the sheer escarpments that sloped down the other side of the fort were the busy but distant sounds of the commercial streets of Granada.

In the hotel room behind her, Ainsley could hear the *mozo de espadas* unlocking a suitcase. "He's almost ready," he said.

"Gabriel," she asked, "what is that?"

"What?"

"That fort across the street."

Gabriel stepped out onto the balcony and followed her finger to the fortification. Then he looked at Ainsley as though she'd just escaped from a mental asylum.

"You don't know it?"

"No."

"That's the most popular tourist site in Spain."

Ainsley's eyes widened. "What's it called?"

"The Alhambra. Three million tourists a year."

"Oh."

Ainsley had heard the name, of course, but she hadn't realized that the fortification was so famous. Maybe she could visit after she found the tourmaline sword. Maybe Joaquim would even agree to be dragged away from his ugly beach.

The *mozo de espadas* seemed to read her thoughts. "Forget about it. You have to buy tickets three months in advance."

"Where is she?" roared a deep male voice.

Ainsley found herself rolling her eyeballs. "Coming, Pepito."

She followed Gabriel back inside the hotel room. The matador was standing in his underwear and t-shirt, leaning against the frame of the bedroom door. His eyes were bloodshot. A full bottle of whiskey was in his hand. She wondered how it got there.

"Where have you been for three days?" he said.

Ainsley felt herself grow defensive. "Working."

"For who?"

"For you, stupid."

Gabriel laid a steady hand upon her arm. "Take it easy. Pepito is very drunk and doesn't know what he's saying."

"Ainsley," said the matador, "we made an agreement. I paid you to find the sword of Pepe. Do you remember the sword? It has a tourmaline in it."

He made a circle with his thumb and forefinger to illustrate the size of the gemstone. Then he lifted it to his eye and looked at Ainsley through it.

"Of course I remember—"

He cut her off. "And you take my money and don't deliver what you promised."

"Gabriel and I have been working like crazy—"

The matador roared. "But there is *no time*."

"Then give me my passport," she said, "and let me do my job."

Suddenly Pepito charged Ainsley like an angry boar, stopping a few centimeters short. This close, she could feel the snorting of his nostrils, smell the liquor on his breath, sense his rude animal vigor.

"This Saturday," he said, "there will be fourteen thousand people expecting to see me use that sword."

"I know."

"That's three days away. Bring it to me."

"Then give me my passport."

They'd reached a logical impasse. Ainsley felt like she was arguing with a toddler. Still, she gritted her teeth and tipped her chin upwards, standing her ground.

The matador stared at her, nostrils snorting. Then, with a satisfied grunt, he turned away. He lifted the whiskey bottle and took a deep drag of the stuff, then swaggered into the bedroom.

She looked at Gabriel, who had begun unpacking a travel bag. "You gave him another bottle of whiskey?"

"No, I filled the half-empty one with water."

Ainsley smiled at the trickery. "He doesn't notice?"

Gabriel shook his head. "It keeps him hydrated. This way, he never gets through a full bottle."

Ainsley understood their relationship. Pepito was the id, and Gabriel was the superego. Each needed the other to survive.

"Why does he do this to himself?" she said.

"It's the stress," said Gabriel. "He's addicted to risk-taking, but it hurts him."

"You can't stop him?"

"No," said the *mozo de espadas*. "Nobody can tell him

anything. Not God, not humans, not even himself. He's at the mercy of his instincts."

"You're a saint for dealing with him," Ainsley said.

An embarrassed smile passed across his face. "Only the pope can bestow that honor."

The bedroom doors burst open again. Ainsley slowly turned. Pepito was standing there.

He was competely naked.

"I'm ready," he said.

"Oh Jesus," said Ainsley. She quickly averted her eyes, trying to forget what she'd just glimpsed. Pepito was the hairiest man she'd ever seen, his body almost fully covered in thick mat of springy black hair. She wondered how he handled shaving his face. Maybe he picked an arbitrary point on his neck at which the razor would stop.

"Pepito, there is a *lady* here," said Gabriel. "Please lay down on the bed and wait for me. I'll bring the suit in a minute."

"Okay."

The matador disappeared into the bedroom. Ainsley heard the soft thump of a body falling backwards onto a mattress.

"Do you dress him too?" she said.

Gabriel nodded.

"What does he wear under the suit?"

"You were just looking at it."

"Nothing?"

He nodded. "It's a tradition. Matadors wear only the suit."

Deep within, Ainsley felt the stirrings of something powerful. It was that elusive creature known as sexual interest. It was oddly natural. After all, matadors were socially dominant and admired by millions. They even dressed like female performers—glittery sequins, tights that accentuated their sexual organs, and no underwear.

Gabriel opened a suitcase on the dresser. Inside was a beautiful *traje de luces*, folded in perfect rectangles. He unfolded it gently. It was light blue with white trim and silver sequins; the hosiery was gray. He threw everything over his shoulder, picked up a bottle of body lotion, and went into the bedroom and shut the door.

If Ainsley hadn't known the two of them, she would say that there was a homosexual tryst occurring in the bedroom. She could hear commands, groaning, and even a triumphant shout.

At last the noises stopped. Ainsley pressed her ear to the door and listened. Silence within. She rapped on the door.

"What is it?" said the matador.

"I still need my passport."

A moment later, the door opened. Pepito appeared, this time wearing a pair of gray pantyhose. Ainsley tried not to glance at the small bulge in the crotch.

His eyes full of passion, he pointed a stubby finger at her. "You will get your passport after you come to my *corrida* tonight."

Her jaw dropped. "Why do I have to go to your *corrida*?"

"Because you need to see the killing. Up close."

"No, I don't."

"Yes, Anglo, you need to understand our culture."

Gabriel appeared next to him, looking aghast. "You want her in the *callejon*?"

He grew insistent. "Yes."

"But Pepito—"

"It's good. She should learn to love the bulls like we do."

That was the booze talking. Ainsley wasn't remotely prepared to watch Pepito murder an animal up close. And she still couldn't understand how a matador could love something that he had sworn to kill.

She looked to Gabriel, who returned a sympathetic glance. The message was simple: *He's the boss*.

There was no choice. "Pepito," she said, "for the last time, just give me my passport, and I could be *this close* to finding your sword." She held two fingers a centimeter apart.

"And we will celebrate your work after the *corrida*."

Ainsley pinched the bridge of her nose in frustration. "My work isn't done, Pepito."

"You still have time," he said, taking another slug of whiskey.

She slapped one palm onto the other. "But you just said there *wasn't* time."

A weird drunken fire had begun to blaze in the matador's eyes, and she realized that he wasn't even listening to her. Pepito turned and disappeared into the bedroom, then reappeared with something in his hand. Ainsley recognized it.

Her passport.

"This," he said, "will be yours after tonight."

Then he stuffed the booklet into the back of his tights. Ainsley dropped her head and buried her face in her hands.

Her employer had just stuffed her passport in between his sweaty ass cheeks.

Gabriel threw a gentle arm across his shoulders. "Come on, let's finish dressing."

The *mozo de espadas* pushed Pepito back into the bedroom just as Ainsley threw her bag at the door.

CHAPTER THIRTY-FIVE

As Ainsley entered the service corridor of the Plaza de los Toros, the hair on her neck stood up.

It may have been the scent of blood that was somehow already in the air. Or it may have been the anticipation that zipped like an electric shock through the audience.

Most likely, though, it was the elegant matadors who were lined up in the waiting area, practicing their swoops and elongated poses. Trailing Gabriel, one of his duffle bags slung over her shoulder, Ainsley glanced at the men. Despite the suits of lights, none of these five guys were particularly good-looking, not up close. She was surprised to find herself feeling a little disappointed.

Ahead of Gabriel, Pepito stumbled in his light blue suit of lights. She couldn't tell if he'd sobered up, but it didn't matter. From the way he dominated the corridor, the matador had performed this routine hundreds of times. Maybe the hooch helped him feel more connected with his job, or with the animal. It probably didn't help his reaction times.

She followed them through an open iron gate onto the edge of the arena. Blinking in the sun, Ainsley held her hand over her eyes and gazed around. This bullring was a perfect circle, ringed by three tiers of seats, the uppermost being a shaded balcony section beneath a set of arches. All the seats were filled, the arena overflowing with spectators, many of whom were enjoying picnic lunches out of wicker baskets. Men, women, and children were sipping wine, slicing chorizo, nibbling on cheese, tearing off hunks of bread with their teeth. They seemed comfortable with what was about to happen.

It reminded Ainsley of the stories of medieval nobles who used to picnic at the sides of a battlefield, watching the mercenary soldiers slaughter one another.

Then Gabriel tugged on her elbow and led her to the *callejon*, the narrow corridor that ringed the floor. She threaded her way through the people who were already in the trench. They looked to be mostly support staff—other *mozos de espadas*, picadors, medics, journalists, assistants of various stripes. To Ainsley, it felt like wandering backstage at a Broadway production.

Every few meters, the wall opened up into an aperture that was half the width of a set of shoulders. Ainsley guessed that this was to allow humans sideways access to the sandy ring, and to deny the bulls access to the humans. She noticed deep scars on the edges of the wood. She guessed those were from horns. Could bulls sometimes get into the *callejon*? A pang of fear shot through her.

Gabriel set down his items, and Ainsley followed. He unfolded a hanging organizer that he hooked onto the wall of the *callejon* and began to slide the various swords into the folds of its fabric. It looked like a shoe organizer that Ainsley used to drape across the back of her bedroom door.

"How many will Pepito use?" she said.

"Usually two," he said, "but I have to be ready with all of them."

Ainsley smiled. It was the same as a roadie preparing the guitars for a rock concert.

Then the opening parade entered the arena. The top of the *callejon* was just low enough for Ainsley's eyes to peek over. She heard the bugle melody, watched the the six matadors stroll onto the sand. At the center, Pepito, looking vaguely ridiculous in the flat ballet shoes, took a bow in each of the four directions. He was apparently the star of the show.

As he walked over to the mayor to accept the *toril*, Gabriel whispered, "He is the most senior matador tonight, so he will start."

"That's bad news," said Ainsley.

"Why?"

"Because he's still going to be drunk."

"Oh no," corrected Gabriel, "he needs at least some alcohol to fight well. The bad news would be if he went in completely sober."

The *corrida* began. Pepito crouched on one knee in the middle of the arena, his head down at his knee. The gate was lifted—and in a flash the bull was out, running furiously. The crowd roared.

It galloped in a circle around the ring, and as it passed less than a meter away from Ainsley, she was drowned in a wave of its musky animal scent—its primitiveness, its violence, its passion, its rude health. Nothing had felt so frighteningly *alive* before.

Meanwhile, Gabriel was standing next to her, his arms on the high wall, watching the animal very closely. She could tell that he had a practiced eye.

"What are you looking for?" she said.

"I'm trying to identify the characteristics of the bull," he replied, "so that I know what Pepito is going to need. This one is slow and stupid."

Ainsley disagreed. As the animal thundered past her again, shaking the earth, *slow* was the last word that she would use to describe it.

She looked on as the bull tried to charge one of the horses, but the rider easily avoided the horns. Pepito was pacing a slow circle around the animal, keeping his distance, but tightening the distance between them nonetheless.

"See," said Gabriel, "he knows how to handle this one."

"Indeed."

Soon the *banderillas* arrived in the ring, and they began stabbing the animal in the hump. Ainsley averted her gaze. The sand was soon sprinkled with drips of black blood.

Finally, the third of death began, and Pepito walked over to them. He was sweating like an athlete, and his eyes carried the ferocious spirit of someone who has just communed with an ancient power.

"Ainsley," he said.

She gulped. Fifteen thousand people were watching him speak to her right now. She felt her ears beginning to burn.

"Yes?"

"You must watch the killing."

The matador's eyes drilled into her own.

"I will," she said.

Then his eyes flicked over to Gabriel, as though ordering him to verify that she watched the killing. He nodded.

The *mozo de espadas* handed him the red *muleta*. Then they exchanged swords, the caping for the killing. Ainsley watched the matador stride back across the sand to the bull. He raised the cape to the arena. The people cheered lustily. They knew what was about to happen.

Pepito used his cape to draw the staggering animal, over and over, across the sand. The people cheered every move. Slowly, however, it dawned on Ainsley that he was bringing the wounded beast towards her side of the *callejon*.

Towards her.

So she could see. Up close.

The wounded animal was pushed closer and closer until, finally, it stood less than five meters away, snorting, breathing. Pepito stood in front of its face, his own face screwed up into a tight grimace. His eyes flicked up to Ainsley.

He nodded. She found herself nodding back.

"Are you watching?" said Gabriel.

"Unfortunately," she replied. "Can I leave?"

"No."

"But I'm going to be sick."

"They've locked us in here."

He nodded towards the iron gate that both arms of the *callejon* led to, the same one she'd passed through upon entering the arena. It had been closed. A stolid guard stood in front of the handle.

She was stuck. Ainsley's hand clutched her stomach while her face reluctantly swung back towards the imminent murder.

Then it happened. Pepito swept the cape, the bull lunged low, and he came in high and hard with the killing sword. He plunged it with great precision into the space between the ribs, the most vulnerable part of the animal.

The bull stopped, wheezed, and fell over onto the sand. Four more hooves pointed sideways into the seats.

The crowd leapt to its feet, applauding. Stiffening her lip, Ainsley tried not to look at the murdered beast whose life was spilling onto the sand right in front of her.

"The crowd is satisfied," said Gabriel. "Pepito will get an ear for sure."

"It's horrible," she said.

"I know. Another beautiful animal, gone. After a while, though, you get used to it." He paused. "Death comes to all of

God's creatures. Every one of us. That's why what we do on earth is so important."

He broke off the thought as Pepito rushed into the *callejon*, flush with victory. His light-blue suit of lights was spattered with blood. Gabriel gave him a towel, then took the killing sword and used another towel to clean the bull's blood off the blade. It looked sticky and viscous on the towel's black fibers.

Pepito wiped off his face. "It was a clean kill. It was pure. Now we can celebrate. The women are coming to the hotel?"

"Yes, Pepito," said Gabriel wearily.

Looking at Ainsley, the matador lifted his eyebrows conspiratorially, then reached into one of the bags, produced another bottle of whiskey, and took a huge swig.

"My passport," she said.

"Later," he replied. "We drink first."

Pepito handed the bottle to her. Sighing, Ainsley lifted it to her lips and began to swallow.

CHAPTER THIRTY-SIX

Twelve hours later, Ainsley barely managed to kick shut the bathroom stall before she vomited into the toilet.

Partying with Pepito was going to kill her.

It'd been useless to resist. She could've more easily stopped a tornado with an outstretched palm. The matador's appetites were enormous, unstoppable, and the last ten hours had been a blur of food, flesh, alcohol, drugs, screaming, singing, swearing, dancing, and destruction. Ainsley herself boasted a love of life, but the matador's *joie de vivre* outweighed even her own.

Her hand scrambled around the toilet, found the handle, and flushed it. Then she slowly hoisted herself up, sat down on the lid, and hung her head between her legs, elbows on knees. She mentally reviewed everything that had happened since the *corrida* had ended.

First there'd been a happy hour at the hotel bar, which had kicked into high gear when the Pepito had appeared, showered and changed. Among the fifteen people waiting for him was a pair of middle-aged heavyset women. Gabriel had explained that these were his Granada groupies, local women who'd once spent a decadent year in London and had picked up the type of open sexual appetite that Spanish women didn't often indulge in. Pepito had taken both upstairs, then returned sweaty and disheveled a half-hour later, the two women giggling like schoolgirls behind him, tugging their skirts down after them.

"He always gets lucky when he gets an ear," Gabriel had explained. "No ear, no sex."

Then, at nine o'clock, the group had begun to head out to the bars, one after another, two, three, four, a drink and a tapa at each. She'd noticed that the cost of the tapas decreased for the Spaniards and increased for the tourists around them. Gabriel had called this tiered pricing system *tapartheid*.

Meanwhile, Pepito had collected even more admirers along the way, all drawn to him like pale winter creatures crawling towards the dawn. Boasts and toasts from the host— and then, at two o'clock in the morning, he'd announced that he was heading up to the gypsy caves for flamenco, and that the entire congregation was following him, no exceptions. A jabbed forefinger into Ainsley's sternum had underscored his seriousness.

Which was how she'd found herself with a group of twenty strangers, hiking up the steep hill just outside of town. She'd been barefoot, both heels dangling from the fingers of her left hand, thirty minutes of sweaty exertion. On the opposite ridge, the orange Alhambra lit against the black night like the fires of an enemy encampment.

Pepito had led them into a gypsy *cueva*, an old mountain dwelling that had been used for hundreds of years. It'd been basically a large living room, two lines of twelve chairs running parallel to one another along opposite walls. On a stool in the center of the room, a wild-eyed man had been playing an impossibly fast lick on his nylon-string flamenco guitar, his foot tapping swiftly in time with an arpeggiated line of sixteenth notes. Before him, a beautiful dark-haired woman in a heavy red dress had been singing, the thick kohl creating the smokiest of smoky eyes.

Ainsley had leaned forward on the edge of her chair, listening. She was no vocal coach, but she always knew soulful music when she heard it—and this had most definitely been it. The woman's heart-wrenching voice rose and fell and dipped and quavered and strengthened. Ainsley had wondered why the best music came from the most marginalized groups in societies.

Then, after the performance had ended, there'd been more wine, and a drunken twenty-minute stumble back down the hill and into the Albayzín, the Moorish portion of the city. By four o'clock in the morning, they'd wound up in this bar, an Arab-themed depravity with copper pots hanging from the blue *azulejo* tiles. Without warning, Ainsley had found herself drinking another glass of sherry, and soon she'd known it was time to kiss the porcelain god.

Now she was feeling better. She staggered out of the stall, stood up, checked her hair and makeup, and returned to the bar.

In the center of the bar, Pepito was standing upon a chair, commanding attention. His shirt had somehow been slashed down the sides, from armpit nearly to the waist. A necktie was wrapped around his sweaty head and a madness burned in his eyes.

"Friends," he said, "it's getting cold. We need some *heat*."

Gabriel stepped forward. "No, Pepito, please don't—"

The matador threw a shot of heavy-duty rum into his mouth, flicked a lighter—

—and blew a meter-long tail of orange fire across the room.

The entire bar applauded vigorously. Pepito took a deep bow, then fell off the chair, facefirst onto the floor.

Ainsley watched five different people descend upon him. *Are you okay, Pepito, please, don't you might be hurt, Pepito, let me help you, Pepito.*

She backed away from the scrum, near the window, and that was when the snarling caught her ear. She looked outside.

In the alley was a tall dog with a short neck, black mask, and heavy bone structure. Its lips were back and it was exhibiting a fearsome snarl.

She squinted. That was Pepito's dog, the *alano español.* Cowering before the animal was what looked like a cocker spaniel.

Gabriel appeared at her side. "Oh no," he said.

"Did Pepito bring his dog here?"

"Yes," he said, "he travels everywhere with us. Pepito ordered me to bring him here an hour ago."

"I didn't see the dog in the hotel room."

The *mozo de espadas* nodded. "I keep him in the bathroom. Otherwise, he gets in the way."

Suddenly the animal leaped onto its opponent, and what followed wasn't a friendly tussle. The *alano español* was snarling, its teeth gnashing, its head buried in the other one's neck. Ainsley could practically smell the blood.

She couldn't watch another attack.

Snatching a copper pot off the wall, Ainsley ran out of the bar and into the narrow Arabic alley of the Albayzín. She approached the *alano español*, lifted the kitchenware, and struck the dog on the head with it. Not hard, but enough to cause it to yelp and release the other animal. It glared at her.

She crouched down to examine the cocker spaniel, but it snapped at her and limped away into the night, whimpering.

Pepito burst out of the bar, holding a towel to his face.

Ainsley could see the blood streaming down his chin from a split lip. Surrounding him were the rest of the merrymakers.

His eyes went to the *alano español*. Then they went to the copper pot in Ainsley's hand.

"You don't have to defend my dog," he said. "He can defend himself."

"I wasn't defending him," replied Ainsley. "I was attacking him."

"Why?"

"Because he was trying to kill another dog."

Pepito blew an exasperated breath from his mouth. "You want to be Mother Teresa and save all the animals from dying."

"Yes," she said, "I care about life."

"You think I don't?"

"Your job is to kill animals."

"But I love them too. I want them to live."

Ainsley shook her head. "It's not natural."

"That," said the matador, "is wrong. It's *very* natural. People like you can never understand this. Bulls, dogs, birds, fish, insects—they're not humans. They're lower than us."

"No, they're not," said Ainsley.

"Yes, they are. On the great chain of being, they are *below* us. That's why we don't give them names."

Suddenly he reached into his mouth and removed something small and white. It looked like a pebble. Then Ainsley realized that it was a tooth.

Ainsley stood her ground. "You're losing control of yourself."

"I never lose control."

"You fell off a chair facefirst."

"I never lose control *inside the arena*," he corrected.

This was a chance to get Pepito to address his own excesses, so Ainsley grew more insistent. "The bull you chose for this weekend's *corrida* is a Miura. It's fast and intelligent and highly dangerous. You said so yourself."

Pepito's face changed. Worry etched itself into the fleshy folds of his face.

"Yes," he said.

"You don't have to face this bull."

"I have to," he said. "It's an addiction."

"Just cancel the performance," she replied.

He shook his head. "The audience will be disappointed—"

"But you'll still be alive. That counts for something."

She held his eyes. To her surprise, Pepito broke the gaze first, dropping his head sadly. Behind him, the patrons shifted and murmured. Ainsley could tell that they wanted the life of the party to come back.

"Sometimes I want to become a farmer," he said in a quiet voice. "I want to grow almonds and watch the seasons pass in my field."

"You can do that."

"No," he replied, "my body won't let me. The *corrida* is more than what I do. It's who I *am*. I have no choice in the matter." The matador looked at her with firm respect. "The same way that *you* need to find gemstones."

That was a jab to her soul. Ainsley realized in a flash—she was guilty of the very same compulsions as Pepito was. She was powerless to resist, even leaving her boyfriend to pursue this tourmaline sword. She couldn't even call it selfish, since the matter was outside her control.

To judge Pepito would mean to judge herself.

Suddenly the matador whistled. His dog, which had been licking itself nearby, leaped to its feet and trotted over. He stroked it roughly across the back.

Then he approached her. "Here."

Ainsley looked down. In his hand was her passport.

"Is it clean?"

"It was in my pocket. I only shoved it in my ass for show."

"You're such a matador."

"And you are going to find out what happened to my sword. You have three days."

Pointing a thumb at Ainsley, he walked backwards, never breaking eye contact, until his group of admirers surrounded him, closed ranks, and pulled him back into the bar.

In the alley, Ainsley felt the copper pot slip from her fingers and clatter on the cobblestones. It was five o'clock in the morning, and she was coasting on fumes, but she was absolutely sure of two things.

One, she was going to get a cup of coffee.

Two, she was going to rent a car.

CHAPTER THIRTY-SEVEN

Two hours later, Ainsley popped the clutch of the rental sedan, slipped into first gear, and pulled into the maze of urban Granada.

The *mozo de espadas* was sitting beside her. "Turn left here," he said. "Now, look over there, that's the artery that leads out of town."

"But we have to go back to the hotel first."

"Yes."

Gabriel grew quiet. Ainsley was aware that he was watching her shift gears.

"What is it?" she said.

"You drive like a man."

"And you still talk like a woman."

He laughed. It was the first time she'd heard him lighten up. "Pepito's a terrible driver. He's always watching girls on the sidewalk. And he would run over an archbishop if it meant beating the car next to him. He has no respect for those who do God's work. Turn right here."

As Ainsley cranked the wheel and drove the car up the

one-way road that wound around the Alhambra, Gabriel began to relax a little.

"I called Juan Carlo yesterday," he said.

"Everything is good?"

"Yes. He is holding a room at the marquesa's country estate."

"I didn't know she runs a hotel."

"She doesn't. She accepts certain overnight visitors."

"I didn't know that wealthy people like her needed to do that."

"You would be surprised," said Gabriel. "Her husband has been gone for nearly twenty years. Somebody has to pay the bills."

In her exhausted state, it took Ainsley a minute to process what he'd just said. "Wait a minute. Did you say he is holding *one* room?"

"Yes."

"But we need *two*. One for me, one for—"

Gabriel shook his head. "I asked him but he said no. Pepito needs me more than ever right now. We have many preparations for the *corrida* on Saturday."

Ainsley's throat went dry. She felt the full weight of the deadline fall upon her shoulders alone.

The *mozo de espadas* seemed to understand her fear. "You'll do well by yourself. Here, look." Gabriel reached into his coat pocket and pulled out a map and unrolled it on the dashboard. "The marquesa's country estate is near a mountain village called Aguadever. It's located here." The tip of his pencil touched on the spot on the map, about a hundred kilometers southeast of Madrid. "Juan Carlo said that, from the plaza at Aguadever, her estate sits in the saddle between the head and the tail."

"What does that mean?"

"I don't know," he replied, "so you'll have to ask somebody when you get to the village."

Ainsley crinkled her brow. "Gabriel, what do you think I should ask her?"

His fingers massaged his forehead. "Oh, I don't know. Ask her about the *corrida*. Just start her talking. A person that age has lost all the filters on her mouth. Eventually she will reveal something about the sword of Pepe."

Ainsley understood that phenomenon all too well. Her own loose tongue had embarrassed herself on more than one occasion, and her friends loved this aspect of her personality. She was the funny one, ready to mouth off at anything. Privately, though, Ainsley regretted this characteristic, since strangers, especially uptight ones, sometimes found her off-putting.

Ainsley circled the rental car past the Alhambra until she saw the hotel looming on the right. She pulled into the drop-off lane, throwing the stick into neutral and pulling the parking brake.

The *mozo de espadas* folded the map and solemnly handed it to her. "Good luck," he said. "I will call if I have time, but Pepito is demanding right now."

"Okay," replied Ainsley. "I want to thank you again for not helping me *at all* the last three days."

Gabriel grinned at the sarcasm. "I was glad to be of no service."

It looked, for a moment, as if the *mozo de espadas* wanted to hug her. Ainsley respected his space, however, and didn't attempt to touch him. He looked at her with a vulnerable look in his eyes.

"What is it?" she said.

"Nothing."

Ainsley studied him. "Can I say something, Gabriel?"

"Of course."

"You're hiding something."

Gabriel froze. Then he suddenly left the seat. The door shut behind him, and then there was only silence in the vehicle.

As Ainsley watched him walk into the hotel, he didn't look back. She felt as though she'd just ended a promising but nonetheless disappointing date with a very puzzling man.

Then she took off the parking brake and began to drive out of Granada.

———

An hour later, she had escaped the medieval maze of urban roads, and found herself on a freeway headed north, away from Andalucía. On either side of the road sped thick oaks, green rolling hills, and blue snaking rivers.

Hands on the wheel, Ainsley thought about Pepito. Choosing a Miura was viewed, even among matadors, as a foolishly brave decision, made by someone with a death wish, but you couldn't stop a man from killing himself. There was no legislation, no intervention, no restriction that could prevent that, ever, as the families of countless drug addicts have experienced.

Ainsley could, however, refuse to *assist* in that process.

She forced herself to confront the facts. If she were *truly* concerned about Pepito, she would stop driving right now. She would turn around and point the car towards the Costa del Sol, towards Joaquim. By lunchtime, she would be on the beach, the pursuit of the tourmaline sword a fading memory.

But she wouldn't be happy. This adventure had given Ainsley a taste of real Spanish culture, and of real mystery, and those were the two most powerful drugs in the entire world. She couldn't turn her back on them. Besides, she wasn't going to contribute directly to Pepito's injury or death.

She was just bringing him the sword that would allow him to satisfy fourteen thousand *aficionados*, many of whom remembered his father well.

At stake was Pepito's livelihood and his self-esteem. That was the very heart of everything, and they justified her quest.

At least, that's what Ainsley told herself.

She glanced down at the clock. Another hour had rolled by, and off to the left a low mountain range had appeared. She consulted the map that Gabriel had left on the passenger seat. Her fingertip confirmed it: Up there, among those snow-capped peaks, was the village called Aguadever.

Ainsley turned off the freeway and followed a twisting side road as it wound its way up the flanks of the range. Below her lay a valley cut by a wriggly line of blue water. That was snowmelt, and even from here she could feel its iciness. A thick mat of green growth curled around the river. She guessed that was the spring clover.

Finally, after a half-hour ascent, her ears popping in her skull, Ainsley found the nose of her car gliding into a small village.

AGUADEVER

CHAPTER THIRTY-EIGHT

The road had narrowed to a one-way alley over uneven cobblestones, the aperture barely wide enough to accommodate her vehicle.

Her stomach tightening, Ainsley gently eased into the narrow space. The sound of her engine was magnified as it bounced off the walls. She steered carefully, there being no more than two handwidths between her rearview mirror and the ancient plaster.

Then she squeezed out of the alley into a central plaza, the one mentioned by Gabriel. A dry fountain stood in the middle of the stones, a stray dog nipping at its haunch next to it. Ringing the fountain was a classic Spanish design—an upper gallery resting on a lower arcade of highly-stepped arches. On one wall were torn, faded posters advertising decades-old bullfights.

Ainsley parked the car at one end of the plaza and stepped out. The air smelled cold and clean here, the sky was bluer than an ice crystal, and the sun bore upon her eyeballs with the glaring whiteness of high altitude.

Near the edge of the plaza, a group of four old men were

gathered around a chessboard at a small table. They wore black berets and were nursing small glasses of a pale yellow liquid. The label on an uncorked bottle on the table read *amontillado*. They were sitting in front of a humble flat-fronted structure with metal grates over the square casements.

It was the local bar.

Ainsley loudly cleared her throat.

The men glanced at her, then returned their attention to the game. It was silent except for the distant *caw-caw-caw* of a crow.

"Excuse me," she said, "do you know where the saddle is?"

"*Señorita*," said one, "if you don't know enough to stay silent while the men are playing chess, then there is no saving you."

Next to the fountain, the stray dog circled itself twice, flicked its tail, and fell over with a sigh.

"You're obviously busy," she said.

"No," said one, "and we are much too old to be helping you. The younger men come during the evening. You should talk to them."

Stymied, Ainsley knew that she had no choice. The only solution here would be to play up her foreignness, and the best way to do that was to simply be very direct, even insulting.

"If this is Aguadever," she said, "then what they told me is true."

"What did they tell you?" one said.

"That its men have no pride," she said. "That the mothers control their sons from birth to death."

All four men looked up at her.

"This one," said one of the man, "has impaled herself upon the horns of the devil."

"And from that one's mouth," replied Ainsley, pointing at

him, "flows a river of shit. Maybe one of your friends will swim through it and find me."

It was aggressive, and judging from the shocked expressions on their faces, Ainsley felt that they'd never heard a woman speak quite like that. After all, this wasn't Madrid, and these weren't sophisticated men.

Ainsley stalked past them into the bar.

She waited for her eyes to adjust, then studied the room. It looked like it hadn't changed since at least the nineteen fifties. Chunky wooden chairs and rough-hewn wooden tables stood in the room like a team of beaten-down mules. The bar itself was nothing more than a wooden plank set atop two stacks of crates, and on the plank were lined seven green bottles.

Standing behind the plank was a matronly woman dressed entirely in black, wrists to ankles. Her mouth was a grim little slit in her face and her hands were placed palms down on the plank. Her black hair had been pulled back tightly into a bun. Her lips were pursed tightly, evidence of some inner issues.

"Are you the owner?" said Ainsley.

"Yes."

"Those men won't help me."

"Of course they won't," she said. "You didn't ask them about church. It's the only thing they'll talk to outsiders about." She huffed. "*Que aburrimientos*. They don't even buy drinks from me."

"I'll buy a drink," said Ainsley, "and maybe you can help me."

"That is fair."

Ainsley pulled out a stool and sat herself on the edge of it. "What are you pouring?"

"Wine, sherry, and anis."

Ainsley cocked her head. "What is anis?"

The woman didn't ask permission. She uncorked a bottle,

pulled a small shot glass from under the table, and poured half a slug. Then she pulled a cold glass bottle from a small refrigerator and filled the rest of the small glass with icy water. She used her finger to mix it until the liquid turned milky white, then shoved it towards Ainsley.

"*Una palomita*," she said.

Ainsley lifted it to her lips. It was thick, sweet, and burned her throat like fiery licorice.

"I like it," she said, coughing.

The woman poured her another. "What is your question?"

"I'm looking for the saddle."

The widow set the bottle down and drew her head back, as though she were surprised that a foreign visitor would know of something that familiar. "It's up the road," she said.

"Where?"

She nodded with her head to the left. "There."

"Show me."

The woman circled the bar and walked to one of the casement windows. Ainsley followed behind her. Leaning over, the woman pointed at two low mountain peaks above the town, one of which was dusted with a long trail of white snow.

"That rock is the head of the horse," she said, "and that snow is the tail."

"And in between—"

"—is the saddle."

"Exactly."

Ainsley studied it. "How do I get there?"

"Just go out of the town and keep to the left."

"Thank you," she said.

The woman stepped away and began straightening the battered chairs, wiping down the tabletops with a wet rag.

"What is your business in the saddle?"

"I'm going to see the marquesa."

"Which one?"

"There is more than one?"

"We have three."

"I have an appointment with the Marquesa de Grantruca."

She nodded. "Of course."

"Should I know the other two?"

The woman shrugged. "No, they are dead."

Ainsley tried to process this. Why this widowed bar owner thought that Ainsley would be trying to find a dead person was a mystery, but mountain people were often eccentric, and experienced time in ways different from the way that flatlanders did.

"What should I look for?" she said.

"A stone arch. It marks the entrance to the property."

"Do you know the marquesa well?"

"No," said the bartender, "she keeps to herself. Nobody speaks to her except one of the nuns."

"There is a convent here?"

She nodded. "The Carmelites."

Ainsley pulled a ten euro note from her purse and laid it on the plank and put her shot glass on top of it. "What is your name?" she said.

"Maria."

That was easy to remember. Throw a rock in the air in Spanish-speaking countries, and nine times out of ten it's going hit a Maria. For a while it was even stylish for men to carry it as a middle name.

"Maria," said Ainsley, "you've been an immense help."

CHAPTER THIRTY-NINE

Twenty minutes later and five hundred meters higher, Ainsley's stomach floated as her car crested a blind rise in the dirt road—

—and when her tires touched down again, she stepped on the brakes, slowing the car to a crawl.

This was the saddle.

It was a meadow, dotted with green pine trees, studded with chunks of granite. Early springtime, and wet piles of white snow still pocked the brown earth, hiding in crevasses, huddling beneath boulders like traitors hiding themselves in hostile territory.

It was beautiful.

Straight ahead, the road ran beneath a stone arch, its twin pillars just wide enough to admit an automobile. Running to the left and right of the arch a low stone wall whose craggy surface would be called *rustic* in the Anglosphere. Here, that word didn't exist. It was just an old stone wall, it had always been there, and nobody gave it a second thought.

Ainsley passed beneath the arch and rolled into the marquesa's property. The road wound through a dark glade, and Ainsley's cheeks began to feel chilled. She rolled the window up.

Shortly the house came into view. It was a quiet structure, recessed slightly into the side of the mountain. A set of yellowed curtains hung inside a large window that peered upon a wide flagstone porch, which was empty of everything except three rusted iron chairs. It looked like the home of an elderly person; nothing had been changed in decades.

Another car, a red Mercedes, was parked in the driveway. Ainsley parked next to it and stepped out and slammed the door. The sound echoed across the grass. A moment later, a figure appeared on the patio, wearing a red sportcoat with a white scarf around his neck. He looked dashing and a little flamboyant.

It was Juan Carlo.

He stepped off the patio and quickly crossed the grass. "I didn't think you would make it," he said.

"Surprise," said Ainsley.

He clasped her hands and kissed her on each cheek. She appreciated his good manners. "I am sorry for all the confusion. The marquesa has a strong will."

"It's my pleasure," said Ainsley.

"You will experience an even greater pleasure," he said, "if you look behind you."

His hands gently turned her shoulder. Ainsley spun around in a circle—and felt her breath pulled out of her body.

Behind and below her was a magnificent view of the *meseta*, the Iberian peninsula's central highlands. Green plains, brown patches, blue squiggles. There was little detail at this distance, but that was the beauty of it.

"It's unbelievable," she said.

"Do you see that?" said Juan Carlo. He was pointing at a brown fog on the distant horizon.

"Yes."

"That is Madrid."

"Really."

"The marquesa likes to know that the city is far away—but close enough that she can keep an eye on it."

"She is from Madrid, correct?"

"Yes," he said, "but some people cannot reconcile themselves with the place where they are born. Please, come inside."

Ainsley found herself being through the front door and into the house. It felt like walking into a museum dedicated to royalist Spain. The decór was a riot of Córdoban leather, regal chairs, and clawed armrests. In one corner perched a stuffed hawk. In another stood a suit of armor that was barely half of Ainsley's height, its open left hand outstretched as though grasping for a long-gone weapon.

"Please wait here," he said, "while I go prepare the marquesa for your visit. Do you have a list of questions?"

Ainsley ran a nervus hand through her hair. "No, I don't."

"The marquesa needs to have a list."

"We can't just talk?"

The *mayordomo* shook his head. "She doesn't like surprises."

Ainsley grew frustrated. "Please let the marquesa know," she said, "that it's common decency to speak to her overnight guests."

"Excellent way to put it," he said. "One moment, please."

Juan Carlo disappeared, and Ainsley strolled through the rooms marveling at the the décor. White walls and black studded chairs. A red-and-gold embroidered candelabra. Iron chandeliers.

The *mayordomo* reappeared in the room. "The marquesa is ready. Would you like coffee or tea?"

"Tea," said Ainsley.

He nodded. "This way."

Ainsley followed him into a corridor and walked towards the rear of the house, the sound of her footsteps ricocheting off the walls. She noticed that the corridor was lined with three closed doors. The prospect of sneaking into them tantalized her. Even as a child, Ainsley had never been able to resist the urge to snoop.

A fourth door at the far end of the hallway, however, was their destination. His hand on the doorknob, Juan Carlo turned to her and lowered his voice. "The marquesa is very opinionated," he said, "so it is best to agree with her."

"That won't be necessary," replied Ainsley, "I have very thick skin."

"Like a crocodile?" he said.

"Absolutely."

"Suit yourself," he replied, turning the doorknob.

CHAPTER FORTY

Though the marquesa's room was closed to the outside air, Ainsley sensed that something was very different.

It was decorated in the same royalist manner as the rest of the house—white walls, blood-red carpet. A dark brown sofa with gold fringe sat in the middle of the room, a small circular glass coffee table before it. Diffused sunlight streamed through yellowed lace curtains.

Ainsley took a deep breath and paused. The air held an unfamiliar smell. It was rich and full, yet somehow foreign, bold, even defiant. She tried to identify the scents using familiar words, but she couldn't. The strongest notes were hidden below the scent, concealed almost beyond recognition.

"Ainsley Walker," said Juan Carlo, "this is the Marquesa de Grantruca."

Ainsley turned. In the corner, cloaked in darkness, was the old lady. She was quietly resting in a settee and her hands were crossed upon the blanket that had been tucked around her lap. She resembled a dusty museum exhibit.

Except for one thing.

Her eyes.

They were bright blue, clear, undimmed by age—and they were boring straight into Ainsley's skull.

"Marquesa," said Ainsley, crossing the carpet, "it's a pleasure. Thank you for speaking with me."

The elderly woman lifted a hand. Ainsley grasped it. Then the marquesa turned her cheek. Ainsley leaned over and kissed it quickly. She smelled like camphor.

"Please seat yourself," said the old woman.

Juan Carlo had brought over a chair, and Ainsley perched herself primly upon the edge of it. Beneath the chair, she crossed her feet, and on her lap she folded her hands, mirroring the marquesa's body language.

Ainsley leaned forward and spoke loudly. "I don't know how much Juan Carlo told you about me," she said, "but I am working for Pepito."

"I can hear you," replied the marquesa, "you don't need to scream."

Ainsley lowered her voice to normal. "Sorry."

"I know Pepito," said the marquesa, "but I knew his father much better."

Ainsley felt her heart leap. "That is why I am here. I was told that you know something about the sword of Pepe."

The woman's blue eyes grew very still. "Of course I do, but only because that sword meant everything to Pepe."

"I meant," replied Ainsley, "that you know that it was stolen from Pepito last week."

She grew defensive. "Who told you such gossip?"

"Samson."

"The crazy swordsmith in Toledo?"

"Yes. He said you were searching for the sword too."

The marquesa touched her fingers to her cheek. "That would take a miracle. At this age, I can hardly move from this room."

She was interpreting the statement too literally. "No," said Ainsley, "he said that you knew somebody who was looking for it."

The marquesa turned her head. "Juan Carlo, what do you think?"

The *mayordomo* had returned from the kitchen bearing a tray. On it was a fearsome iron teapot, two ceramic cups, and a plate of sugar cubes.

"About what?" he said.

"How did Samson learn that we were searching for the sword of Pepe?"

"I don't know," he replied. "People talk."

"It's supposed to be a secret."

"It is." He set down the tray between the two women and poured tea into a cup. He smiled at Ainsley. "Sugar?"

"Yes please."

He dropped a single cube into her cup, then handed it to Ainsley. She tried to stir it without clinking her spoon against the ceramic. It was that kind of room.

"What happened to the man we hired to search for it?" she asked.

"I don't know," said Juan Carlo.

"Did you call him?"

"He isn't returning my calls."

Ainsley interrupted. "Can I ask a question?"

"If you would like," said the old woman coolly.

"Why are you so concerned with the theft of the tourmaline sword? It doesn't belong to you."

The marquesa looked at Juan Carlo. "She doesn't know?"

The *mayordomo* turned to Ainsley. "Did Pepito tell you the story of the tourmaline, Miss Walker?"

"No," she answered.

"He said nothing at all?"

"No."

The *mayordomo* sighed. "Marquesa, would you like me to tell her?"

The old woman nodded and made a small wave with her fingers, then settled back in her chair.

Juan Carlo pulled up another nearby chair and seated himself lightly. "The tourmaline embedded in the sword of Pepe has a special history."

"Okay."

"It's not a history that the public is really aware of, so you must keep this confidential."

Ainsley sighed quietly. Pepito and Gabriel had made the same demand. She wondered how loose the tongues must be on the Iberian peninsula for so many people to insist upon so much secrecy.

"I will," she said.

The marquesa looked at Juan Carlo. "Can we trust her?"

He nodded. "*Va a misa.*"

Ainsley translated: *She goes to mass.*

"Pepe was given the tourmaline by a very famous person," he said. "One of his supporters."

Ainsley nonchalantly reached for a second sugar cube. "Really? Who is that?"

The marquesa caught her eyes. "Franco's wife."

Ainsley dropped a sugar cube into her tea, but missed the cup entirely. "You're joking."

"No."

Ainsley took a moment to digest this news. The wife of Francisco Franco, one of the twentieth century's most infamous dictators, had given Pepito's father the tourmaline. And then he'd set the gemstone into a sword.

And yet Pepito hadn't breathed a word about this. She wondered if he were ashamed.

"Why did she give it to him?" said Ainsley.

"Because Pepe had been loyal to the regime."

"And because he was an excellent matador," added Juan Carlo. "He collected seven hundred ears in his career. Many of them at Las Ventas."

Ainsley remembered what she meant by *ears*. At the *corrida*, she'd learned that if the matador had performed exceptionally well, he was presented with the ear of the bull as a prize. It wasn't easy to get an ear, especially not in Madrid, since the audiences were so jaded there.

"It was the year after Franco passed away," said Juan Carlo. "She was broke and very unpopular, so she began selling her jewelry to survive. But she didn't sell the tourmaline. She made it a gift to him. It was a reward for his loyalty."

"Bless their hearts," said the marquesa. "She and General Franco were good Christian people. The pride of Spain."

It took every ounce of Ainsley's energy to avoid blowing hot tea all over the table. Could she have heard that right? The *pride of Spain*? From what Ainsley understood, it was nearly impossible these days to find a supporter of Franco. They'd all passed away or ashamedly recanted their beliefs. There was no rug large enough to sweep the bones of thousands of victims beneath. They were proof enough.

The marquesa, it seemed, was one of the last remaining Francoists in modern Spain.

"Is it fair," Ainsley said, "to say that the sword of Pepe is a symbol of the Francoist regime?"

Juan Carlo affixed her with a long, knowing look. "Yes. But only to those who know its history."

"Do you think this is perhaps why it was stolen?"

He nodded.

Ainsley turned to the old lady. "And you, marquesa, want to help recover the sword because you still support the memory of Franco."

The marquesa's eyes were so alive that they seemed to be vibrating. "That is correct."

Ainsley set down her tea. "Then it's a good thing that you invited me here."

"No," said the marquesa, "it's a good thing that you accepted."

"What does that mean?"

Her small tongue snaked out and wetted her lips. "You've been investigating in the wrong way."

Ainsley had never been offered career advice from a Spanish noblewoman in her tenth decade of life. "Then please tell me."

"Who is this man that was with you at the *corrida*?"

"Gabriel."

"Gabriel should know better. We Spanish don't reveal sensitive information so easily." The old woman's jaw worked itself into a near smirk. "In our country, nobody trusts you until you prove yourself. Then, afterwards, you share some wine, and people begin to talk."

Ainsley smiled to herself. The second part was exactly what Gabriel had recommended that she do with the marquesa.

"Would you like to take some wine with me?" said Ainsley.

"I am not the one you need to speak to," said the marquesa, "and I don't drink until dinner anyways. There is, however, a person closer to the theft than I am."

"Who?"

The marquesa glanced at Juan Carlo, who cleared his throat. "A man named Don Vasquez," he said. "He is a retired landowner. A bull breeder."

"He enjoys working," said the marquesa. Her voice dripped with disdain.

Ainsley watched as the woman literally lifted her nose into the air. She was witnessing firsthand that famous Spanish aversion to manual labor—the same aversion that, centuries earlier, had driven them to import millions of slaves to the New World.

"And what did he tell you?"

"He isn't calling me back. I don't know."

Ainsley pulled out her notebook. "I'd like to compare notes with him. I have some very interesting leads."

"Such as?"

Ainsley described for them the hazy morning spent in the tearoom in Seville, the mysterious text message from Isaac luring Gabriel away from the hotel in Córdoba, the confrontation with Javier about the storage closet.

When she was finished, Juan Carlo and the marquesa traded quick glances. The old woman measured her words carefully. "You are a good investigator," she said, "especially in an unfamiliar country. I think you should definitely talk to Don Vasquez."

"Let's do it."

"I must warn you that breeders are difficult," said Juan Carlo. "They don't like telephones, and especially not the humans who hold telephones. They prefer animals."

Ainsley had a flash of insight. "What if I go to visit him?"

"You?" said Juan Carlo.

"Yes. I have a car."

"But he lives very far away."

"I have a map too," she said.

The *mayordomo* shrugged. On the settee, the marquesa seemed to be lost in thought. Ainsley sensed that her mind was running over all the possible ramifications of such a visit.

"Yes," she finally said, "we can arrange that. Let's call him right now. Juan Carlo will do it."

"Excellent," said Ainsley.

"And later," said the marquesa, "we can talk over dinner."

Energized, Ainsley leapt to her feet and grasped the old woman's hand. It felt oddly cold.

CHAPTER FORTY-ONE

As night fell, Ainsley stood before the full-length oval mirror in her second-floor room, preparing for dinner.

Juan Carlo had asked the estate's maid to clean her outfit, the one that she'd purchased in Córdoba. She applied lipstick and then spun in front of the mirror, looking at herself. It wasn't exactly flattering, but it was still eye-catching.

Her heels clicked on the wooden steps as she headed downstairs, imagining how she was going to begin picking the brain of the marquesa. Would it be during the first glass of wine? Or should she wait until the second? Would there even be a second glass of wine for someone so elderly and frail?

Ainsley entered the formal dining room. There was a long table with a row of candles lit. Around the table were arranged ten chairs.

At the head of the table was a single place setting.

"You are the only guest tonight," said a voice.

She turned. It was Juan Carlo, standing behind her in the doorway.

"Where is the marquesa sitting?"

"She isn't feeling well," he explained, "and she won't be dining tonight."

Ainsley felt crestfallen. "That's too bad."

The *mayordomo* nodded.

"There aren't any other guests?"

He shook his head. "No, it's the slow season. But next week a couple from Barcelona is visiting. Would you like a gin-and-tonic?"

"Sure."

He disappeared, and Ainsley walked around, inspecting the knick-knacks, the crucifixes, the photos of stiff matadors swiping their capes around blood-smeared bulls.

Juan Carlo returned with a pair of clear drinks in tall glasses. A wedge of green lime floated amongst the ice cubes. Ainsley took the glass and sipped the liquid. It was tart and citrusy, perfectly balanced.

"We love gin-and-tonics in Spain," the *mayordomo* said.

"So I understand."

"It's a gift from the Anglos. Now, a toast." Juan Carlo hoisted his glass. "To dinner tonight."

"Which is?"

"Paella."

Ainsley felt her stomach rumble to life. "Really?"

"Of course."

Her eyes lit up. "I am excited, Juan Carlo. This is my first paella in Spain."

The mayordomo nodded courteously. "You have come to the right place. Only here is it authentic."

"Nowhere else?" she said, smiling.

He shook his head. "I make it the correct way."

"Where is it cooking?"

He looked at her curiously. "Follow me, and I will show you."

She nodded. A moment later, she'd followed Juan Carlo

outside to the patio. The air had chilled noticeably; tonight's temperature would probably dip below freezing. In the far distance, as the orange sun plummeted down towards the purple horizon, the plains of the *meseta* were a painter's palette of a dozen different pastels.

Then her eyes found it.

On the edge of the stones, squatting on a low fire made of branches, sat an enormous dish of paella. Over a meter across, nearly the size of a gong, the copper dish was laden with the finest bounty of Spain—*calasparra* rice, rabbit legs, sausage, fava beans, saffron, and other ingredients.

Ainsley walked over to the dish and leaned over. Her nose took in the sweet scent of the burning branches, her ears absorbed the quiet crackling of the rice. It was cooking beautifully.

"Do you need me to stir?" she said.

The suggestion caused Juan Carlo's face to darken. "No, we don't stir it. We don't even *look* at it. We just let it cook. Your nose and your ears will tell you when it's ready."

Ainsley studied again at the enormous dish. "I can't believe this is all for one person."

"You Americans love large portions," he said.

Ainsley noticed that his mouth had taken on a slightly mocking smirk, so she decided to agree and amplify. "You're right. In fact, this won't be nearly enough for me. You'd better bring a loaf of bread and a few roasted chickens too."

He smiled, and as they waited for the food to finish cooking, Juan Carlo began to explain to Ainsley the history of this iconic dish. How the debates raged about where exactly the word *paella* came from. Some said it derived from *patella*, the Latin word for pan. Others said that it was a shortening of the phrase *para ella*, meaning *for her*, since it was traditionally cooked on Sundays by men who wanted to give their wives a day off from the kitchen. Either way, he said, one thing was absolutely sure: The dish had been invented in the rice fields just south of Valencia, part of Catalunya, by hungry laborers who were forced to trap, shoot, or pick whatever foods were available and cook them together in a big pan.

Ainsley thought about that. Most of the famous dishes around the world had been invented by poor people who had used whatever simple foods they could scrounge up. True, the cooking techniques had been tested and retested, each generation refining the dish, so that the world's most beloved recipes were, in fact, what would today be called *crowd-sourced* —but the process always started as simple peasant fare, born of necessity.

Then they fell silent. Ainsley felt the mountain night air beginning to chill the tip of her nose.

"Miss Walker," said Juan Carlo, "Don Vasquez has finally replied to my phone calls."

"It's a miracle," she replied.

"That is no exaggeration. I had to call his neighbor, who walked into the pasture and personally reminded him to reply to me."

"So what did he say?"

"He said that he has some information about the sword of Pepe."

Ainsley felt her palms start to sweat. "Is he willing to talk to me?"

"Maybe."

"Why maybe?"

Juan Carlo fed more branches to the fire beneath the paella. "He didn't sound very enthusiastic about hosting an American woman."

She grew frustrated. "Did you tell him that I went to the *corrida* at Las Ventas in Madrid? Did you tell him that I'm working for Pepito?"

"Yes," he said, "but he is still uneasy about the situation."

"How can I persuade him that I am trustworthy?"

He shrugged. "Somehow you will have to prove yourself."

Ainsley felt defeated. She wasn't going to be an insider in this peninsula, certainly not after four days, and maybe not ever. Spain felt like the type of country where, even after decades of full-time residency, a person would probably still be considered a newcomer.

"What can I do?" she said, growing agitated. "Put on the *traje de corto*? Eat raw steak?"

"Our people don't eat much steak."

"You know what I'm saying."

Suddenly Juan Carlo held up a finger. His nose twitched. "Do you smell that?"

"Smell what?"

His face grew serious. "The paella just told me that it is finished."

Ainsley inhaled. Wafting through the air was a delicious, earthy, redolent scent—but it was the same one that had enveloped her from the moment she stepped outside.

"If you say so," she said.

"Trust me," he replied. "The call of the paella cannot be mistaken for anything else. Now I ask that you help me carry the pan into the house."

"But it's huge."

"Of course. It's traditional."

Juan Carlo stood on one side of the dish, Ainsley on the other. Together they lifted the enormous dish and carried it into the dining room. It wasn't easy. Her lack of sleep, her wooziness from the cocktail, her wobbly heels—none of it was a recipe for strength.

They lowered the pan onto a pair of metal trivets on the long dining table. Juan Carlo pulled out her seat. "Please, sit."

Ainsley lowered herself into the chair. She watched the mayordomo use a large metal spoon to spoon a generous helping of the paella into a low cylinder, then deftly tip it onto a clean white plate. It left a perfect cylinder of paella.

Then he laid it before her.

"Enjoy," he said.

Then Juan Carlo left the dining room, his footsteps dying away in the hallway. Then Ainsley was alone with an enormous paella. As she picked up her fork, she realized something.

There *was* such a thing as paella for one.

CHAPTER FORTY-TWO

An hour later, after two plates of paella, three glasses of wine, and a slice of flan, Ainsley slowly rose from the table like a blimp cut loose from its rope moorings.

Juan Carlo had cleared her tableware and silverware. She clutched the edge of the table and used it to hoist herself to her feet. This was how a pregnant woman in her third trimester stood up. Ainsley had seen it in her girlfriends.

She looked down. From her belly hung a squishy little half-sphere of half-digested food.

That was the paella.

One hand on the back of her hip, Ainsley waddled out of the dining room and into the living room, among the Córdoban leather, the regal chairs, the clawed armrests. She drew a finger along the rusty suit of armor. It felt sticky. She wondered how you polished something like that.

She ambled past the black studded chairs, beneath the golden chandelier, near the tall candles on the red-and-gold embroidered stand. The air smelled thicker, mustier, heavier than it had in the daylight. Here, the only sound was the ticking of a grandfather clock in a corner.

Then, turning her head, she saw the hallway.

And the three doors.

Deep within her soul, that small insistent animal that went by the name of curiosity lifted its mischievous head. Ainsley had never been able to resist a closed door. The urge to snoop ran strong in her veins. It always had.

She slipped out of her heels, placed them tidily on the carpet next to a floor lamp, and then tiptoed quietly down the hallway.

At the first door, she gripped the knob and turned it. It didn't budge. Firmly locked.

She found the second door, gripped the knob, and turned it. It didn't budge either. Juan Carlo had dotted all his i's, crossed all his t's.

But there was still the third door.

Ainsley tiptoed lightly towards it. To avoid making any sounds, she placed her hand on the knob and pulled it as close as possible to her. Then she twisted to the right.

This time, the knob turned. There was an audible thunk, she felt something pop inside the mechanism, and the door sprang open.

Like a secret that couldn't be held back.

Though the hinges had been well-oiled, Ainsley's arm stayed tense on the door to insure its silence. At last, she slowly released the knob. She'd been gripping it so tightly that her palm had begun sweating.

She took a tentative step into the pitch-dark room and stood there, breathing. She felt beads of sweat popping onto her forehead and waited for her eyes to adjust.

Then: a dark black shape against grayness of the window. It looked like a lamp.

Ainsley felt her way across the room, reached out, and touched the object. That was a lamp; she was touching the shade, could feel its fabric. Her hands ran down to the base of the lamp and found an electrical cord. Her fingers found the switch embedded in the cord.

She pressed it, and a half-second later an explosion of white light erupted before her eyes. Ainsley staggered back, covering her face.

Slowly, she lowered her arm and took a better look around. She was standing in a mostly empty room. A pair of curtains covered the window. A large tarp, like a white painter's sheet, had been cast over what appeared to be a large chair.

Ainsley went over and lifted the tarp. Underneath was a chair, but this was no ordinary one. It was fascinating—fluid lines, irregular curves, and the organic shapes that reminded her of mushrooms, caves, and elfin villages. Bits of blue and purple stained glass were embedded throughout the item.

She stepped back and studied it. This chair was stunning. Ainsley wondered why the marquesa wasn't displaying it. It clashed with the rest of the house, true, but for something this gorgeous the old lady should've made some accommodations—maybe decorated around it—or else sold the piece to a museum.

Then something else caught Ainsley's eye.

A pair of sandals.

They were on the floor, beneath a side table, nearly cloaked in darkness. As a shoe lover, Ainsley and her roving eye never missed an interesting pair of boots, heels, wedges, or sandals.

She crouched down and pulled the sandals out from beneath the table. They were navy blue on the sides, but the toes were white. A pair of two long white fabric strips dangled off each heel, presumably to be tied around the ankle. Strangest of all was the fabric. It felt reedy, even grassy.

Ainsley stared at the items for a long while, feeling the

lightness in her hand. This was the most curious footwear she had ever discovered.

"Put that down," said a voice.

Startled, Ainsley fought to contain a yelp. She turned. Juan Carlo was standing in the corridor. She wondered how he'd managed to sneak up so quietly. She noticed that he had changed into slippers.

"We invite you into our residence," he said, stepping into the room, his fists clenching, "to enjoy our hospitality, and to hopefully help you on your quest. Not to help you snoop in our private rooms."

He seemed angry. Ainsley slid the sandals back under the table and stood up and faced him. The same height, they stood looking at one another over the bridges of their noses.

"It wasn't locked," she said.

"That was an oversight."

"You never said that I couldn't look around."

"Another oversight."

"And don't forget," she added, "that I'm an investigator."

He threw his left hand into the air in frustration. It was a very Spanish gesture. "It's my fault," he said. "I strapped a scorpion to my back. Now it has stung me, and I have no one to blame."

Ainsley crinkled her brow and stepped forward, bending a little to put her face in his line of vision. "I haven't stung you. I'm just looking at these items."

"*You should not be seeing anything in here*," he hissed.

Something in Juan Carlo's eyes made Ainsley back down a little. She folded her hands in front of her chest, as though in prayer. "I am sorry if I have offended you."

His eyes were two plugs of steel. She slowly circled around him, left the room, and headed down the corridor. She picked up her heels and walked towards the foot of the staircase. Then she paused and glanced back.

In the third doorway near the end of the corridor was the silhouette of Juan Carlo.

Watching her.

CHAPTER FORTY-THREE

The next morning, as Ainsley began to descend the stairs for breakfast, she heard a lively conversation coming from the living room.

As she reached the main floor, she was surprised to see a nun sitting on the sofa, Juan Carlo sitting opposite. The woman was dressed in the customary black ensemble, and on her head was the customary white wimple. Each of them held a small white ceramic cup. The brown rim on the rim told her that it was espresso.

"Miss Walker," said Juan Carlo, "this is Sister Dora."

He didn't seem to be upset with Ainsley any longer, so she slowly moved forward, unsure about how to approach a woman of the cloth. Did you shake her hand? Embrace her? Drop to your knees and make the sign of the cross?

The problem was solved when the woman stood up, took Ainsley's hand, and kissed her on the cheek.

"Join us," she said. "I insist."

"Sister Dora is a Carmelite and rarely gets to talk to strangers," said Juan Carlo.

"I'm better off than my sisters," the nun said. "They don't

leave the convent at all."

As Ainsley accepted a coffee from Juan Carlo, she remembered Maria, the bartender in Aguadever, mentioning the Carmelite convent.

The *mayordomo* seated himself again. "Sister Dora always visits the marquesa on Tuesday mornings."

The nun nodded. "I am the convent's ambassador to the outside world."

"An ambassador," said Juan Carlo, "who tries to steal money from the marquesa."

"Stop it," said the nun. "I'm just being nice."

"It's true," explained Juan Carlo. "The Carmelites can't sustain themselves only by raising fruit and gathering honey and baking sweets. So Sister Dora walks around Aguadever every morning, shaking pockets, seeing what kinds of coins fall out."

"He exaggerates," said the nun, sipping her coffee. "I'm not a total mercenary."

Ainsley was surprised by her comments. Beneath the habit, Sister Dora was a shrewd, sophisticated fundraiser.

"But it's true, sister," said Juan Carlo.

"No, it's not," the nun answered. "Look, I have nothing to gain by visiting with you this morning. The marquesa isn't even coming out of her room."

"She's not feeling well," he said, glancing at Ainsley.

"Yes, that is unfortunate," said the nun, "and so now I'm drinking coffee with you, trying to be nice, even if you don't deserve it."

Ainsley couldn't help but smile at the riposte. The elderly nun was full of piss and vinegar.

Then the woman set down her small ceramic cup. "That's enough flirting for one day. See me out?"

"Forgive me, Sister," said Juan Carlo, rolling his eyes.

She stood up. Ainsley followed suit, shook the nun's hand,

kissed her on the cheek. The nun pulled back and studied the American visitor.

"I can read people like books," said Sister Dora, "and you're one of the good ones."

Struck speechless, Ainsley rooted around for an appropriate response. "How can you see that?"

"It's in the eyes," she replied. Ainsley was reminded of how, the first time she'd met Pepito, he had judged her in the same way.

Then the nun swatted Juan Carlo on the head. "Next Tuesday. Maybe the marquesa will be feeling better by then."

"Maybe," he said.

Sister Dora moved out of the living room and left through the front door. When it had closed behind her, Ainsley ran to the window and peeked out. The black-clad nun was walking down the long road towards the stone arch.

Ainsley turned to Juan Carlo. "She really did walk up here, didn't she?"

"She walks everywhere," he replied. "She says it keeps her young. The Carmelites used to have a bicycle, but she doesn't use it."

She watched the nun for a moment longer. Women like Sister Dora made her smile—individuals who boldly forged their own path, no matter how many tongues clucked. Ainsley hoped to become one of those women.

Then she turned to Juan Carlo. "About last night—"

He held up a hand. "Please, it was nothing."

"It didn't seem like nothing. You were very upset. Why? It was just a room with a chair. And it's beautiful, by the way. Where did—"

Ainsley stopped midsentence. The *mayordomo* had suddenly shot to his feet and stormed out of the living room. She'd angered him again. Ainsley stood there, smelling the musty, heavy air, the curtains guarding against the morning light, wondering what sort of bug had crawled under Juan Carlo's skin.

Just as she began to go upstairs, he returned.

In his hand was a piece of paper.

"On this paper," he said, handing it to her, "are the directions to Don Vasquez's property. He will be able to tell you much more about what has happened to the sword of Pepe."

She looked at the handscrawled directions, making sure they were legible to follow. "And he's expecting me?"

"I've already let him know."

"Thank you," she said.

"You have persistence," he said, "and I think that it will pay off at Don Vasquez's *finca*."

"I hope so."

He offered a handshake. Ainsley shook it. The hand felt thin and cold but strong. The type of hand that shouldn't be underestimated.

"Let me know what you find," he said.

"I will."

"Our maid put out a light breakfast in the dining room."

Ainsley shook her head. "Thank you, but I'm still full from last night."

Ainsley smiled and walked upstairs to her room. There, she quickly packed the small bag that she'd brought. It took all of two minutes. There was something to this idea of travelling light. She would have to do it more often.

She walked downstairs. The *mayordomo* was nowhere to be found. The marquesa wasn't coming out of her room. Ainsley wondered if she should make a big deal of her departure. That would entail wandering through the house, and she'd gotten in a lot of trouble for that the previous night.

She slung her bag over her shoulder, went outside to her car, and slipped behind the wheel.

A moment later, Ainsley was driving down the road.

FINCA VASQUEZ

CHAPTER FORTY-FOUR

Two hours later, Ainsley was flying across the rural pastures of Andalucía, springtime brown on the ground, green buds on the branches.

Juan Carlo's directions lay on the seat beside her. She rolled the window down and felt the brisk breeze on her face.

At last the front end of the automobile rolled up to the gates of the *finca*. An arch over the entrance read *Vasquez*. A small iron bull had been stamped on either side of the name.

Ainsley sat there, the engine running, lost in thought. Don Vasquez. The bull breeder whose father didn't like Pepito's father.

And yet, according to Juan Carlo, this man had also seen the sword of Pepe.

Cautiously, she motored through onto the property. On either side of the road ran a pair of long white fences. Stretching away on either side of the fence were wide, rolling meadows dotted with patches of green spring clover.

And standing in the meadows were bulls.

Hundreds.

It was unnerving, so many ancient beasts watching her vehicle. Ainsley kept her eyes on the narrow road.

She curved around an oak tree, and a warren of rural buildings came into view—thick walls, ochre paint, blue trim. A welcoming patio featured bowls of ferns that hung from a pergola. Below it, a long rustic table with wooden benches awaited the next family meal.

Ainsley parked alongside a white truck. Giant scrapes ran along its side panels. One window had been smashed. The grill had been utterly crushed. She wondered what could've caused such damage.

She stepped out, stretched her legs, and inhaled deeply. The air smelled fertile and earthy. Somewhere a pair of birds chirped.

"Are you lost?" said a voice.

She turned. It was a young man, about her own age, with a length of rope around his right shoulder. He was approaching her cautiously, as you would an intruder.

"Is this the finca of Don Vasquez?" she answered.

"Yes."

"I'm Ainsley Walker. Don Vasquez is expecting me."

He looked confused. His eyes looked up and down her person for a clue. "You have some business with us?"

"Juan Carlo sent me. He works for the marquesa."

"Which marquesa?"

"The Marquesa de Grantruca."

The young man nodded. "One moment."

He turned and crossed the patio, then disappeared into the house. Ainsley clasped her hands behind her back and strolled around a nearby pair of olive trees, rolling the leaves between her fingers. She dug the toe of her boot into the earth and nudged up a clod of red dirt.

A few minutes later, the young man returned. "I am afraid that Don Vasquez is busy right now and cannot see you."

"I was told that he was expecting me."

"Yes, but he is out in the *campo*."

"I can wait."

"He will be busy all afternoon."

"Pepito needs to find his sword, so I will wait."

His eyes reappraised her. "You know Pepito? The matador?"

"I'm working for him."

"You poor girl."

She laughed. "Maybe I can join Don Vasquez in the field and talk to him there?"

The young man wagged a finger and assumed an arrogant manner. "It's not possible. These are *toros bravos* and they must be approached only on horseback."

"Maybe—"

"And furthermore, the *vaqueros* are conducting the *acoso y derribo* today."

She didn't recognize that term, but he looked at her as though this were a significant event.

"Oh," said Ainsley.

Then the young man softened. "But you can watch from the fence, if you would like."

"I would. What is your name?"

"Iker. Don Vasquez is my father. Come this way."

She followed him along the fence to a small gazebo that stood atop a platform. She hiked up the small staircase and leaned against the railing. Perched up here, two meters high, Ainsley could see more of the meadows, and it took her breath away. By her estimation, at least a thousand acres of uninterrupted nature stretched out beyond the house.

Iker stood on the staircase and gestured out to the fields.

"Fortunately for you, the *acoso y derribo* is happening right over there. Look."

He showed Ainsley where to look, off to the right.

"Do you see?"

Ainsley squinted. Then she saw it: In an open part of the field, two riders were positioned on each side of a small yearling bull. Each carried a four-meter-long wooden lance that Iker called a *garrocha*. They used the lances to steer the bull down a long straight line at a gallop. Then, at the right moment, one of the horsemen used the end of his *garrocha* to knock the animal off its feet. It crashed to the ground, struggled to stand, then shook off the interruption and kept running.

Suddenly Ainsley understood the term *acoso y derribo*. Literally translated, it meant *to harass and bring down*.

"Why are they doing that?" she said.

"To determine the character of the bull," he said. "They are testing its speed, its intelligence, its spirit, its tenacity. When it is ready for the *corrida* at age four, we can recommend to the matadors an animal with whatever personality is desired."

"How do you remember each one?" she said. "You must have hundreds."

"We brand a number into their flanks, and we keep a list." He lifted his phone. "I keep it updated on here."

Ainsley nodded. Before, Pepito's request for an intelligent, fast bull hadn't make any sense, but that was because she hadn't known that you could order a specific type of bull as easily as ordering a sandwich on wheat or rye. Now she realized that the bull breeding industry of Andalucía was probably more complex, and modern, than she'd imagined.

"I need to work now," he said, "but I will have some refreshments brought to you. Please make yourself comfortable."

He smiled at her, then descended the small staircase. Ainsley watched him walk towards the far side of the house.

CHAPTER FORTY-FIVE

An hour later, her mouth feeling drier than a stretch of sand, Ainsley was grateful to see the pair of figures on horseback galloping across the field towards her.

As the two *vaqueros* drew closer to the gazebo, she got a better look at their outfits. Each wore the traditional Andalucían costume of high-waisted gray trousers, low-heeled leather boots, a short jacket, and a flat-brimmed hat cocked to the right. Their triangular steel stirrups completely encased the front halves of their feet, which Ainsley presumed was for protection against charging horns. Thick sheepskin that covered their saddles.

A hundred meters behind them rode a strapping older man. His equestrian style was compelling to watch. His barrel chest rose and fell, and as one hand held the reins of the horse, the other elbow was held straight out to the side, bouncing up and down. Even from this distance, she could see his pebbly teeth gleaming in his mouth like a cave full of diamonds.

That was Don Vasquez.

Ainsley knew it without even being told. She watched him

gallop across the meadow, the greenery flattening itself before the hooves of his horse.

The two *vaqueros* approached a gate near the gazebo. One looked around nervously, dismounted, unlatched the gate, and led his horse through it. The other vaquero followed. A minute later, Don Vasquez rode through the gate and dismounted. They quickly closed it behind him.

Ainsley saw her chance.

She gulped the last of the water, stood up, descended the steps, and quietly crossed the dirt. She stopped a few meters away, close enough to be noticed, distant enough to not be intrusive.

She watched Don Vasquez hand the reins of his horse to a stable boy, then peel the short jacket off his enormous ribcage. His servant handed him a towel, and he wiped his face and hands with it. Then the servant said something.

Alarmed, Don Vasquez quickly looked over towards Ainsley. His moustache twitched as he studied her. Aware of the scrutiny, she leaned against the fence, pushed a hank of hair behind her ear, and tried to give him her winningest smile.

"Miss Walker," he said in a booming voice.

"You are Don Vasquez," she said.

"Yes," he replied, "and you believe that I have some information about the sword of Pepe."

"Do you?"

He glanced at her. "I don't usually talk to Anglos."

"I'm American."

"That's even worse."

She tried not to scowl. People around the globe had a love-hate affair with Americans, usually loving the culture but hating the government.

"I am going inside to eat lunch," he said, "and then I will sleep. Maybe we can talk a little after I awaken."

"Okay."

He turned away brusquely and headed for the house. Ainsley was left standing alone at the fence. He'd never shaken her hand, or even come close enough to do so.

This was going to be difficult.

CHAPTER FORTY-SIX

Two hours later, Ainsley had passed out in the chair on the gazebo when the sound of footsteps woke her up.

Groggy, she lifted her head. It was Don Vasquez, climbing the stairs. Behind him was a servant carrying a tray with a jug of orange juice, two glasses, and a small plate of *madalenas*.

Ainsley panicked. Her eyelids felt fuzzy, her skin felt oily, and her lips felt dry. She quickly cranked the back of the chair to an upright position and attempted to comb her hair.

"The siesta," he said, "is a civilized practice that the barbaric world has lost."

"I don't know what came over me," she said.

"It's easy to sleep in this gazebo," he replied.

Ainsley watched him lower his bulk into the other chair. He barely fit between the armrests. Meanwhile, the servant deposited the tray onto the small table between them, poured two glasses of juice, and left.

Then Ainsley noticed a small cloth that had been neatly folded on a plate. It looked damp and had been presented on the side nearest to her. Don Vasquez saw her noticing it. "It is for you," he said. "To clean yourself."

That was very considerate. They'd evidently noticed her sleeping outside. Ainsley quickly wiped her face and hands and arms and then refolded the wet rag. She was aware of Don Vasquez watching her every movement.

"Is this your first visit to Andalucía?" he said.

"Yes."

"Is it pleasing to you?"

"I'm happy wherever I go," she said.

He nodded. "You are a good diplomat. That's unusual for an American."

She ignored the gibe. "This is a very historic area."

Don Vasquez reached forward and lifted the glass of orange juice. His hands moved with surprising delicacy.

"This *ganadería* has been in my family for seven generations. We are the stewards of the land. It is our *dehesa*."

"How many bulls do you have?"

"Six hundred. The *toros de lidia*. They are historic too."

"How?"

"They contain ancient blood of aurochs."

"What's an auroch?"

"The same bull that the Romans used in the arenas."

That took Ainsley by surprise. She looked out at the fields, towards the herd that had ambled closer to the fence, grazing. She pictured the ancestors of these same animals grazing here two thousand years ago, being taunted and captured by soldiers who wore knee-high latticed sandals and spoke a new and unfamiliar language called Latin.

All of that happened on these very fields.

"Can I be direct?" she said.

He nodded. "If you wish."

"Juan Carlo said that you probably wouldn't want to talk to me about the sword of Pepe," he said.

The barest hint of a smile crinkled one side of his mouth. "Why?"

"He said that it was because I was an American. And that you don't trust American women."

"That's true."

"Why?"

"Because Anglo women judge this lifestyle, this tradition, without knowing about it."

"I'm not judging."

He shrugged. "What have you heard about the bulls?"

"They're killed at age four."

"True. But it's better than being killed at eighteen months for food." He looked at her significantly. "Should we talk about your American system of livestock production?"

Ainsley dropped her head. Her own country had much to apologize for. Keeping animals living nose-to-tail inside pens. Standing them in their own feces. Injecting them with antibiotics. Rendering them on assembly lines. The history of the American relationship with meat was scarred with disrespect.

"No," she said, "let's not."

"So what is better for the bull?" said Don Vasquez. "Our way? Four years in the field, living free, becoming powerful, and ending with fifteen brave minutes in the arena? Or your way—eighteen months in a filthy prison ended in a pathetic minute in the abattoir?"

"Your way," Ainsley admitted.

He leaned forward and emphasized the next sentence with a finger on the table. "*This is the best existence these bulls can have.*"

Ainsley cleared her throat. "Some people say—not me, Don—but some people say that the bulls shouldn't be killed at all."

Frustrated, he waved away the comment. "Then this life wouldn't be possible. Look around." He swept a hand towards the rolling fields. "Last year, I invited a naturalist to come to this *ganadería* to study the wildlife. He told me that there are one hundred and fifty species of animals living on this land, and probably more that he couldn't count."

"But—"

He overrode Ainsley. "This type of wildlife conservation only exists because of the *corrida*. I could not continue my stewardship without it. The bulls are unsuitable for meat. They're unsuitable for milk. They are strong, aggressive creatures that are fit only for fighting."

"But the way they are killed in public—"

He took a sip of his orange juice and stared at her. "These bulls also kill each other, Miss Walker. Did you know that?"

"No," she said.

"They fight each other constantly, often in the late afternoon. Once you hear a fight, you will never forget it. Personally, I hate it."

"Why?"

"Because it's senseless, and because I lose a lot of money every time one dies."

"What do you think about the ban?"

"The killing of bulls will never go away. As long as there are bulls, humans will fight them, because they represent the powerful other. My God, one of the popes tried to ban the bullfight five hundred years ago, and not even he could make it stick."

She thought back to what Gabriel had taught her earlier. "But Catalunya banned it."

"What the Catalans do doesn't matter," he spat. "This is Andalucía, and we will *never* ban the bull."

"I've heard stories about—"

"About mistreatment of the bulls?"

"Yes."

"That's propaganda. It rarely happens."

"I've heard—"

Don Vasquez politely interrupted her. "Believe me, I

know the stories better than you, Miss Walker. I've heard that we shave the horns to destroy the bull's balance. That we overfeed bulls to make them fat and slow. That we beat them with bags of sand." He waved it away. "It's all lies, and the biggest reason is that *aficionados* don't tolerate those things. They can spot shaved horns from the stands, and when they do, they cry out for a new animal. They want to see the bull die honorably and bravely."

Ainsley stared at the animals, thinking hard. Then she stood up and leaned against the railing of the gazebo. "What can I do to prove to you that I'm not going to judge you?"

He shrugged. "I don't know."

"I would like to remind you that Pepito hired me."

"Nobody trusts Pepito. He's an egotist."

Ainsley had to admit that she didn't trust the matador's judgment either, so she tried a different tack. "Can I remind you that Juan Carlo recommended me?"

The breeder smiled. "Okay."

"That doesn't seem to matter to you."

"Not really."

"But he works for the marquesa. She is respected."

"By some."

The breeder was acting very weirdly. Confused, Ainsley decided to use the nuclear option. She would leave.

She picked up her bag. "All right then. If you won't talk, there's no point to my staying here. I should go."

"If you desire it, you may leave."

He looked unruffled by her departure. He wasn't telling her to go, but he wasn't telling her to stay. He seemed truly unconcerned. Ainsley paused, trying to figure out his angle. Don Vasquez was clearly a decent man, someone who loved nature, who treated people with respect. He was hiding something behind his faultless manners.

"Well then," she said, "there is nothing to say but good—"

The sound of an unearthly bellowing suddenly cut off her sentence. It was coming from the fields.

Don Vasquez turned his head quickly, his mouth open. He listened very closely.

Then he said, "Oh no."

"What is it?"

He stood up, alarmed. "The bulls are fighting."

CHAPTER FORTY-SEVEN

As the bellowing echoed across the field once more, Ainsley listened closely. It sounded like nothing she'd ever heard before—guttural, uncivilized, the primitive howl of an ancient and wild force blowing across the centuries.

Don Vasquez immediately shot to his feet, a worried look seeping onto his face like a pool of blood creeping across a floor. His fingers massaged his forehead. "*Maldito sea*."

Then the bellowing stopped abruptly.

"It's over," she said. "That was short."

"When it ends so quickly," he replied, "it means a fast victory. I have to go."

Don Vasquez turned and moved down the stairs, his rushed gait indicating the severity of the situation. He placed his fingers into his mouth and executed a short whistle. The two *vaqueros* materialized from somewhere behind the house, already holding the reins to their horses.

"Don Vasquez—" said Ainsley.

"Once again, you can stay here," he said, "or you can leave. It doesn't matter to me."

"I'm staying here."

"Fine, but don't come inside the fence. It's not safe."

That was like reminding Ainsley to keep her feet out of a lava flow. There was absolutely no way she was going to enter a meadow filled with hundreds of brawling bulls.

She watched the three men saddle up. One unlatched the gate, let the others through, then closed it behind him. All three cantered off down the fence to the right.

Curious about the royal battle that had just occurred, Ainsley began to run along the fence, following the riders. Her legs stretched out in long strides, her arms pulled at the invisible handrails before her, her cheeks puffed out. Ainsley was familiar with running, especially after four years of being an all-state competitor in high school track-and-field.

She ducked her head beneath low-hanging branches, leaped over mounds of red earth, and sidestepped a couple of ditches. Then, during a clear straightaway, she hazarded a sideways glance at the field.

She saw the *vaqueros*. They were surrounded by a group of seven bulls.

Ainsley stopped running. Approaching the fence, she placed her arms on the upper slat and watched the performance. The Spanish cowboys were wheeling and circling on the grass, using their long sticks to poke the bulls that dared approach them. It was an elaborate, dangerous, improvised ballet performance.

Soon she noticed the subtle rhythms to their work. With each prod, the bulls were being driven farther away from a small copse of woods. Inside that copse, nearly hidden in the shade, was Don Vasquez on his horse.

And on the grass below him was a bull. The animal was on its side in the grass, its legs kicking weakly.

From this distance, Don Vasquez was unreadable. His body language betrayed nothing. He wasn't a demonstrative man. Ainsley guessed that there was little reason to express emotion to livestock. In fact, the wordless expression of pride and courage had probably saved his life more than once.

Then she understood the wheeling and prodding of the *vaqueros*. Much like police officers who set up flares around a traffic accident, they were steering the other bulls away from the scene.

Then Don Vasquez turned towards her. She saw him tilt his head, as if in curious recognition. He appeared to be staring straight at her.

Then he turned his horse and began to ride across the grass, his bay mare's head bobbing up and down. Ainsley realized that he was heading towards her. That was very weird. She straightened herself and smoothed her hair.

The breeder pulled up alongside her on the other side of the fence.

"You decided to stay," he said.

"It's not every day I get to see something like this," she replied. "Is the bull going to be okay?"

"No, it's not. But I know which one did it." He gestured into the distance. "Number four-eighty-seven. He is too solitary. He gets aggressive when other bulls draw near, and this one probably got too curious."

"I'm sorry," she said, then noticed that he was watching her oddly. "What is it, Don?"

"I would like to make a request of you."

"Okay."

"I want you to get on this horse with me."

Ainsley took a step back and lifted her palms. "No no no, wait a minute. I've been told to stay out of the field—"

"There is something that needs to be done," he said, "and if you help me, I will tell you everything I know about the sword of Pepe."

"But I have to get on your horse."

"Yes," he said, "climb this fence and get onto this horse

with me." He smacked its rump to show where Ainsley should sit.

Ainsley tried to contain her fear. She'd never liked horses, not since she'd been bucked in middle school and shattered a forearm. To her, no good thing ever occurred on horseback.

"But the bulls—"

"Don't worry, the *vaqueros* will keep them far away. It's their job." Don Vasquez grew very serious. "This is your chance to win my trust, Ainsley."

Horses and bulls: strikes one and two. But she couldn't honestly back out now, not without losing her dignity. Furthermore, if she did, Don Vasquez's opinion of Western women would remain just as low as it always had been, which bothered her. Something drove her to prove herself to this man.

Ainsley felt as though she'd been shoved into a long hallway, and every escape route had been blocked, and the only way out was to go forward.

So she would go forward.

Taking a deep breath, Ainsley placed a foot on the lowest slat in the fence. Don Vasquez maneuvered his horse so it was parallel with the fence, then held out his arm. Ainsley reached the top slat on her knees and grabbed his arm to steady herself. The rump of the horse was right there, a meter away.

"Can you bring it closer?"

"Not without injuring my leg," he replied. "You have to jump."

Tensing her abdominal muscles, she placed her other hand on his shoulder and threw herself through the air, swinging her left leg in a large arc.

To her surprise, the seat of her pants came down perfectly on the horse's rear. The bay mare staggered a little under the new weight but regained its footing.

"She's not used to carrying double," said Don Vasquez.

"I can get off."

He ignored the comment. "Now, put your arms around me and don't let go. If you fall off, I can't save you."

At that warning, Ainsley felt panic rip through her body. Nonetheless, she wrapped her arms around the breeder's midsection and locked her hands together. His torso felt hard and sculpted, which was surprising for an older man. That was the pleasant result of decades of working outdoors with enormous livestock.

"Hold on," he said.

The breeder spurred the horse with his boot, and the animal took off like a shot.

Into the field of wild bulls.

CHAPTER FORTY-EIGHT

As they galloped across the green field, Ainsley felt a wild thrill race through her body.

The sight and scent of fresh green clover was sprouting from the loamy earth, and the chill spring breeze whipped her cheeks red. To her left, the *vaqueros* were on their steeds, wheeling and leaping and swinging their long *garrochas* in wide arcs, jabbing the bulls when they got too close.

She tried not to notice that, on the other side of the *vaqueros*, milled no less than thirty large bulls.

And the animals' eyes were following her.

Ainsley buried her face into the back of Don Vasquez's coat and squeezed her own eyes shut. She never should've agreed to this. It was an excellent way to end up dead meat. And she didn't even know what type of task the breeder had in mind.

With little notice, Don Vasquez halted the horse. He reached into his pocket, produced a small radio, and spoke into it quickly. A voice radioed back. Ainsley recognized it as Iker.

"*Bueno*," he said, then put the radio away.

"What's happening?"

"My son is bringing us some equipment."

"For what?"

"You will see."

He spurred the animal forward again, and a minute later Ainsley found herself in the small copse of trees.

Below her, snorting on the ground, lay the injured bull.

It had been gored in the flank, in the chest, and in the right eye. Circular gashes of shredded red flesh flapped from its body. Its chest was still rising and falling, but even an outsider like herself could see that the bull was dying.

"See, this is what they do to each other," said Don Vasquez. "Humans are no better, no worse."

Unsettled by the gore, Ainsley turned her head away and stared up into the blue sky. "Why did you bring me here, Don?"

"You will see shortly," he said, then fell quiet. Ainsley noticed his body stiffen. "There he is."

"Who?"

He pointed. "Four eighty-seven."

Ainsley followed his finger. A solitary bull was prowling the grass less than fifty meters away, unconnected to any other part of the herd. It was large, its short trunk thickly muscled, its hooves stepping with authority.

And it was watching them.

"That's the one," said the breeder, "too solitary."

"Why don't you sell it for the *corrida*?" offered Ainsley.

"There is no chance," he said. "Not even a lunatic would fight that bull. It's too dangerous to the matador. I cannot deceive the buyer either. When they found out the truth of the bull, I would lose my reputation." The breeder spat on the ground. "Either way, I cannot win. All he does is cost me money."

Ainsley thought for a moment. These animals weighed at

least half a ton, and half of that was pure muscle. They were the type of animal that Pepito was going to voluntarily face this Saturday. For the first time, Ainsley felt a shiver of fear.

"He doesn't look afraid," she said.

"Exactly. He's the type of bull who would ignore everything in the ring except the matador, and charge him, again and again, until the human is ground to a piece of meat under his feet."

Beneath them, the horse shifted uneasily, as though something had made it uneasy.

"There there," said Don Vasquez, petting its head. Then there was the sound of galloping hooves, and he turned his head. "Ah, here comes my son."

Ainsley twisted around. Iker was cantering across the field towards them, holding a long *garrocha* tucked beneath his left arm like a joust. He slowed down as he approached, then stopped.

"That," said the breeder, "is what we were waiting for."

"Why?"

"It's a special one. Look."

Iker lifted the *garrocha*. On the end was a sharp blade, at least half a meter long, that had been cemented into the wood.

"Is that a *sword?*" she said.

"Essentially."

It didn't take long for Ainsley to put two and two together. "You're going to use it to kill the wounded bull, aren't you?"

"No," said Don Vasquez, turning his head to look her in the eye, "*you* are."

CHAPTER FORTY-NINE

Ainsley froze. With her legs splayed wide across the powerful rear haunches of Don Vasquez's horse, she wanted to slide backwards off the animal, drop to the grass, and run like hell.

But she was in a field of wild bulls. In the best case-scenario, she somehow safely made it back to the gate, unscathed. But even then, since the animals had seen a woman standing on her two feet, according to Spanish law, the bulls would be rendered useless, unable to be sold to the *corrida*. That would cost the breeder hundreds of thousands of dollars, and she would be flayed alive by Don Vasquez and his *finca*.

The worst-case scenario was something she preferred not to think about.

Iker was eyeing her carefully. "Can you do it?"

Ainsley crossed her arms and tightened her lips and shook her head. "No."

"You can do it," urged Don Vasquez softly, "if you remember that you are helping to relieve the bull of its pain."

"You are giving it an honorable death," added Iker.

"I can't kill anything," she said. "It's inhumane."

"But this bull isn't human."

"It has a soul," she said.

"No, it doesn't," he replied.

"Yes, it does."

"No soul," he insisted, with a curt wave of his hand. "Nobody has ever been haunted by the spirit of a bull."

This was really the crux of the issue. Ainsley remembered having the same argument with Pepito. She was starting to glimpse the Spanish hierarchical view of life—the great chain of being. Humans dwelled at the middle of the chain. Below us lived animals, plants, and minerals; above, various levels of angels and other higher powers. This was the long history of Catholicism: a vertical classification. And the Spanish had an equally long history of imposing a vertical class system upon their overseas colonies as well.

All of this stood against Ainsley's own American psyche, which wouldn't admit to a hierarchy even if it toppled over and buried her in its rubble. Her upbringing had taught her that not only were all humans created with equal and inalienable rights—but, lately, so too were animals. She thought about the millions of dogs, cats, birds, rabbits, and turtles back home who'd been named, dressed up, photographed, cooked for, fussed over, anthropomorphized, and treated as actual children.

The Spanish didn't really think like that.

Iker was holding the *garrocha* out to her. She glanced at the stick, then looked at his face. It was impassive.

Don Vasquez clapped a meaty hand on her leg. "You can do it," he said, "if you have pride."

"I have pride," she said, "and I don't have to kill this animal to prove it to you."

"But if you do," said Iker, "he will tell you where you can find the sword of Pepe."

Ainsley stared at him.

"You're joking," she said.

"No joke," said the breeder's son.

She tapped Don Vasquez on the shoulder. "You know where the tourmaline sword is?"

"I do," he said. "And killing this animal will show me that I can trust you. It will show me that you understand the truth of life."

"Which is?"

"That with life comes death."

Ainsley felt herself being drawn closer to the center of a dark vortex, and she didn't know what she was going to feel like after she passed through it. She chewed on the heel of her palm, thinking about Juan Carlo's statement about the breeder. *Somehow you will have to prove yourself*, he'd said.

This was her opportunity.

Evidently Iker had guessed her decision, because he tossed the *garrocha* through the air towards her. She caught it in her right hand and held tight. It was heavier than it seemed.

She expected Don Vasquez to smile at her decision, but he didn't. Killing was a serious business, she imagined, and shouldn't be taken lightly.

"Show me," she said.

"You have to plunge it into a very specific spot," he explained. He tugged on the reins and maneuvered the horse around the bull's twitching, dying body. Ainsley gazed down. Its nostrils were opening and closing, its thick hide seeming less glossy already. Its head was lolled backwards, exposing the soft hide of the throat.

"Right there," said Ainsley, "on the neck."

"Never," said Don Vasquez. "That is assassination. The only place to kill a bull is in the same place that the matadors do."

"Which is?"

"In its aorta."

"How do you reach that?"

He took the *garrocha* from her. He ran the tip of the lance alongside the upper part of the bull's back, just above the shoulder. "It's there, between the third and fourth rib," he said. "But not centered—it has to be a little to the left. You plunge the blade here, as deeply as it can go, with force, and the deed will be done."

He handed the lance back to Ainsley.

"Do it," he said.

"Right now?"

"Yes," he replied, "and hurry, because four-eighty-seven looks interested."

Fifty meters away, the solitary aggressive bull was pawing the ground, snorting, watching the humans claiming his vanquished enemy.

Ainsley took a deep breath and began counting ribs. *One ... two ... three*. Below her, the wounded bull was holding itself stock still. Its single visible eye had rolled backwards in its skull and was looking upwards at her. She positioned the tip of the lance in the spot that Don Vasquez had shown her.

"Here?" she said.

"Yes," he answered. "Grip with both hands."

She twisted her torso to the right and interlaced the fingers of both hands around the lance.

This was the moment. Ainsley paused, unable to breathe.

"Don't hesitate," said Don Vasquez.

But all she could see was the bull's eyeball looking at her, and Ainsley noticed an odd light staring back at her from the inky depths of its alien cornea. It showed something like awareness, certainly, but deep within herself, Ainsley felt a stab of revelation.

The bull *was* alive, but it wasn't human.

"I'm sorry," she whispered.

Then Ainsley lifted the *garrocha*—

—and, with all her might, plunged it into the animal.

CHAPTER FIFTY

The blade entered the bull's body like a knife into a tub of butter.

Ainsley didn't know why that should surprise her. After all, she'd prepared meat for much of her life, cutting chicken breast, slicing bacon, chopping cubes of beef. She was familiar with the sensation. It was always soft.

"Good," said Don Vasquez, "now pull it out."

Ainsley leaned over, tensed her abdominal muscles, and prepared to lift—

—when a thudding sound made the hair on her neck stand up.

Bull four-eighty-seven was charging across the grass.

Straight towards them.

Shit.

Their horse, neighing, immediately bolted. Caught off-balance, Ainsley felt the seat of her pants sliding backwards with the sudden velocity—

—she tried to lock her legs around the horse's torso, but the hide was too slick with sweat—

—and, in the blink of an eye, she felt her body hit the

ground. The fresh brown scent of rich earth in her nose, the blades of grass tickling her cheek. And next to her, pointing at her face like accusing fingers, the four hooves of the dying bull.

It took a moment to realize that she'd fallen off the horse.

The thudding grew louder. She looked up. Four-eighty-seven was closing in fast. Its head was down and its white horns glinted in the sun. Ainsley's forebrain instantly shut off, and her reptilian hindbrain took over. Without hesitation, she tucked her arms around her head and rolled herself into the belly of the dying animal, like a child into its mother's arms.

Her nostrils were immediately assaulted by an overwhelming stink. It was an ancient smell, a primitive blend of blood, animal, wildness, violence, and death. Ainsley felt it trigger a wild sense of exhilaration in her own body.

Then she looked into the face of the animal for the last time. In the inky depths of its alien cornea, she saw that undefinable light flicker ... and then extinguish. A short breath expelled itself from the animal's mouth.

It was dead.

And she felt an enormous jolt shake the bull's carcass. It was lifted up, high enough to slide an arm underneath, then dropped again with a thud.

Beneath the four stubby legs, Ainsley quavered in fear, burrowing her face into the grass. She knew what was on the other side of the carcass. She knew that it was bull four-eighty-seven, toying with its dead rival. She heard the beast grunt and wallop the corpse again. Ainsley squinched her eyes shut. She hadn't been planning to die like this.

Then she heard the light pounding of hooves on grass, and a man's guttural shout. The carcass of the dead bull suddenly lay still. Ainsley lifted her head and peered over the carcass. Bull four eighty-seven was right there, a couple of meters away—and the *garrocha* had been sunk into its back.

It let loose a horrendous cry, so loud that Ainsley buried her face and covered her ears. Then the sound of tortured breathing reached her ears.

Ainsley lifted her head again. Bull four-eighty-seven had fallen to its knees. This time, she saw Don Vasquez on his horse, circling the animal. He leaned over and yanked the *garrocha* out of its back. It was the same spear that she'd used. He must've grabbed it as Ainsley fell off the horse.

Only a few seconds later, bull four-eighty-seven fell over onto the grass. Dark red blood was pumping out of a gaping hole between the third and fourth ribs on its back, staining the green grass. Its eyes stared out into infinity.

Don Vasquez circled over to Ainsley, leaned way down from his saddle, and extended a strong hand. "Take my hand," he said, "but don't stand up."

She grabbed the breeder's hand and felt herself hoisted into the air. A moment later she was laid out on her belly across the back of his horse.

She hoisted herself up to a sitting position, turned around, and grabbed Don Vasquez's shoulders. Then she thunked her forehead against his back and shut her eyes.

"I don't know what just happened," she said.

"You were almost killed," he replied, "but your bravery allowed you to live."

"I wasn't brave," she said.

"Playing dead is brave. It was the best option you had."

Ainsley stared at the two carcasses. "You killed four-eighty-seven."

"And you showed mercy to the other bull."

She thought for a moment. "Do you trust me now, Don Vasquez? That I'm not an activist?"

"I do."

The breeder turned in his saddle and cupped Ainsley's face in his hand. It wasn't a sexist or creepy gesture. It was the movement of a powerful older person showing approval to a younger one.

Then he released her face and looked down at her shirt. "Your clothing is dirty," he said.

Ainsley looked down. Her shirt had been totally splattered in bull's blood and stained with grass.

"Your face too," he said.

Ainsley touched two fingers to the side of her face. They came away sticky and red. She was too shocked to complain.

"We'll go back to the house and find some clothing for you. Tonight, Ainsley, you are my welcome guest. Hold on."

Ainsley wrapped her arms around his midsection again. He spurred the horse forward, and they rode across the grass, past the *vaqueros* still wheeling around and fencing with the bulls and rode through the gate.

Back to safety.

CHAPTER FIFTY-ONE

With the claw-footed bathtub nearly filled, Ainsley dropped the towel from her torso and stepped into the hot water.

A sigh escaped her lips as she lowered herself into the hot water and laid her head backwards upon the porcelain. A single thought was pinging back and forth across her mind.

I am a murderer.

Twenty-nine years of life, and until this afternoon, Ainsley Walker hadn't so much as squashed a spider. Now, by driving a sword into the heart of a mammal that was ten times her own weight, she'd betrayed everything that she'd supposedly believed in. She'd heard Don Vasquez's reassuring rationalizations, but they hadn't registered. Ainsley was too preoccupied with her own treason.

I am a murderer.

Using the pitcher, Ainsley poured water onto her head, massaged shampoo into her scalp, scrubbed the dirt off her hands and arms with a sponge, and rinsed everything off.

There was a knock at the door. "*Señora*," said the servant's voice, muffled through the wood, "we are almost ready for dinner."

"Thank you," said Ainsley.

"Does the dress fit?"

"I don't know yet."

Ainsley unplugged the tub and stood up. There wasn't any time for a leisurely hourlong soak, or for a true accounting of the ledger of the soul. She had to make her way into some clothing and get to dinner.

There, the breeder had promised to tell her the location of the sword of Pepe.

She toweled off, quickly blow-dried her hair, and applied a little bit of makeup. Then she picked up the dress that had been folded on the chair in the corner of the bathroom. She unfolded it.

It was a *traje de gitana*, the traditional sevillana dress, white with large blue polka dots and white ruffles around the neck and hips. She laughed. This was going to look ridiculous, but it was her only choice. She slipped into the garment, adjusted the tight bodice, and looked into the mirror.

She was taken aback. The Andalucían dress was flattering to her own modest figure. The woman who stared back at her was a much more attractive human being than the one who had been rolling around in the grass with dying bulls earlier in the afternoon.

Ainsley left the bathroom, went down the hallway, and entered the *finca*'s great room. It was solidly masculine, filled with oversized Córdoban furniture, a massive fire roaring in the hearth. A bull's head was mounted above the flames, its hollow, glassy eyes staring quietly at the opposite wall. The room smelled of mesquite and leather.

A small group of four men were conferring at the far end. One of them was Don Vasquez. He was wielding a glass of red wine in one hand and a black iron poker in the other.

He saw Ainsley enter. "There she is," he said, "the *matador*, Miss Walker. Ainsley, these are my neighbors." To the others: "This woman killed a wounded bull from horse-back. Her first time on the *finca*."

The other men nodded in appreciation. Don Vasquez continued: "But there is more. She fell off the horse and had to hide beneath its corpse while a *negro bragao* attacked from the opposite side. She was almost meat for the bulls." He sipped his wine. "In other words, an ordinary day."

The other men laughed at the understatement. From their eyes, Ainsley could see the fact that they seemed to know full well, despite his attitude, the danger they'd both faced.

"Thank you, Don," said Ainsley.

"You deserve a glass of my best wine," he said.

Don Vasquez produced a wine glass from the cabinet, cleaned it carefully using a fresh cloth, and filled it with vino tinto from an unmarked bottle. "It's a garnacha from a friend's vineyard. Not available in any store."

Garnacha. The word took Ainsley back to the liquor store on the Costa del Sol, with Joaquim, just a few days earlier. It felt like a lifetime ago.

Thinking about Joaquim caused Ainsley to bite her lip. She fought back a tear. She hadn't talked to him in days. It would be a miracle if he didn't dump her after this was all through.

She threw the wine into her mouth and swallowed half the glass in one gulp. The men looked at her with amused expressions on their faces, then resumed their conversation.

Ainsley went over to the bottle and filled it up again. Then she eavesdropped on the men as they discussed the details of rural life on the *huerta*, and Ainsley noticed that there were mild negotiations burbling beneath the conviviality. Which man would change the water sluice on Tuesdays. How many hours of water each landowner would be allotted per week. Whether to build a new *alcantarilla* if the *chirrascal* flooded this spring.

A few minutes later, they'd decamped for dinner at the long farmhouse table beneath the pergola on the patio. The danger of the day and the heat had conspired to restrict Ainsley's hunger, but now it came roaring back with a vengeance, and Don Vasquez served a rough but hearty Andalucían feast —jamón, bread, olives to start. Then the servant brought out the *cazuelas*, adorably small pieces of glazed crockery. Each was filled with a stew of chickpeas, tomatoes, and tripe.

Iker had joined the dinner too, sitting directly opposite Ainsley. She'd given up trying to follow the rural terms such as *trapío* and *cornadura* that were being bandied about. She noticed that Iker's eyes kept landing upon her.

Then something broke inside the breeder's son. With his eyes upon Ainsley, he suddenly leaned forward and said, "It's time that we discuss something that the *señorita* can understand, gentlemen."

"Lipstick," said a neighbor.

"No," said Iker, "and show some respect. She proved herself the equal of a man today."

"Miss Walker, what is the purpose of your visit?" said one man.

Ainsley was instantly at attention. This was her opportunity to direct the conversation towards something useful. "Don Vasquez promised a friend to help me find something."

"What?"

Don Vasquez cut in. "The sword of Pepe. Pepito needs it for his *corrida* tomorrow."

"How do you know where the sword of Pepe is?" said a neighbor. "You own a *finca*."

Ainsley had been thinking the same thing, but hadn't dared to ask it so bluntly. She'd never quite understood how a rural breeder would have any knowledge of a tourmaline sword stolen from a hotel in Córdoba. She'd trusted Juan Carlo.

All attention swung towards Don Vasquez. He swallowed the last of his stew, set down his spoon, and wiped his mouth. Then he laid two meaty hands upon the wooden tabletop.

"The truth," he said, "is that I don't know where the sword of Pepe is."

His eyes met Ainsley's own. There was sadness in them. She felt her stomach perform a double backflip off a ten-meter board.

"Are you joking?" she said.

He shook his head no. The table had fallen silent.

Ainsley looked at her food and wine. She'd just lost her appetite, for two reasons. One, Don Vasquez had just purposefully wasted her entire day. That was sobering. Equally sobering was number two—the knowledge that she'd murdered an animal for no good reason.

Ainsley felt the anger rising inside her like mercury to the top of a heated thermometer.

"But before my guest becomes upset," the breeder continued, "I would like to propose a toast."

He hoisted his glass. The other men did likewise. Her face a tight mask of politeness, Ainsley nonetheless lifted her own glass and waited for the next traitorous words to come out of Don Vasquez's mouth.

"To our friends and enemies," he said, "and the perpetual confusion between them."

He looked at Ainsley and lifted an eyebrow. She cocked her head slightly. What the hell was that supposed to mean? Don Vasquez *wasn't* a friend? Or was he? Could he be an *enemy*? Or was he *both*? Her suspicions began spinning in her head like a hamster upon a wheel. Had Don Vasquez *himself* stolen the tourmaline sword?

The men sipped wine from their glasses, unaware of the massive frustration building up inside of their guest. One of them ventured a new topic, and soon the conversation veered back towards agricultural matters.

The dessert was served, a dish of chocolate custard, but Ainsley barely tasted it. She pushed back her portion of the bench, stood up, and excused herself. Iker saw her leave and stood up too.

He caught up with Ainsley just as she was passing the fireplace in the great room.

"Miss Walker, please wait," he said.

Ainsley whirled. Her face was the picture of rage. She wasn't going to be finding out anything here at Finca Vasquez.

"Your father wasted my time," she said, "and I don't have much left. I have to find this sword by tomorrow."

"Excuse my father," said Iker. "He doesn't like to speak openly about such matters."

"Clearly."

"He prefers that you read between the lines."

"Okay."

"So can you do it?"

Ainsley shrugged. "What do you mean?"

Iker's eyes narrowed but stayed friendly. "Ask yourself something—who recommended you to come here? Who told you that my father was involved in the theft of the sword?"

"Juan Carlo."

"And who does he work for?"

"He works for the Marquesa de Grantruca."

Iker looked at her. "Think about that."

Ainsley stared back at him, the gears whirring inside her skull. "So Juan Carlo—"

"—was lying to you. I'm positive."

Ainsley scrunched up her face. "Why did your father agree to play along?"

Iker regarded her with a cunning expression on her face.

"I know that he and the marquesa have had a very long relationship. She introduced him to many important people in Madrid during the dictatorship."

Ainsley thought about that. She, in fact, could read between the lines very well. Maybe Don Vasquez had owed the marquesa a debt of gratitude for long-ago favors, and he'd agreed to play along with the deception.

The question now was simple: *Why*? Why had Juan Carlo and the marquesa tried to deceive Ainsley in the first place? Why had they asked Don Vasquez to pretend that he'd been investigating the theft? Why had they warned her that the breeder didn't like to pick up the phone? Why had Juan Carlo said that she was going to have to prove herself? And why had Juan Carlo grown so upset when he'd caught her snooping around that room?

The answer struck her like a bolt of lightning.

They had been trying to distract her.

"Your face tells me that you understand the situation better now," said Iker.

"Yes," Ainsley replied, "your father did help me. Just not in the way that I'd expected."

"He's very indirect," said Iker. "But I have no allegiance to that old woman, so I can speak directly."

"Hm."

"Now, will you be staying the night—or leaving immediately?"

"Leaving immediately," said Ainsley. Then a huge yawn escaped from her face, and she leaned against the fireplace mantel. The wave of exhaustion that swept over her body surprised even herself.

The breeder's son smiled. "No, you will stay. I'll have the servant wake you at six."

As Iker guided Ainsley back towards her room, Ainsley

couldn't summon the energy to resist. And as her head hit the pillow, there was only one thing running through it, the place that held the key to the mystery, the place that she would be headed towards first thing in the morning.

Aguadever.

AGUADEVER

CHAPTER FIFTY-TWO

The next morning, Ainsley drove her rental car through the narrow alleyway, over the rough cobbled street, and entered the plaza of Aguadever.

She parked her car and stepped out, admiring the ancient design of the plaza. She didn't know why she'd expected it to have changed in two days. It had probably been there for five hundred years, ever since the Christians came crawling up this road, swords in their hands, looking for Moorish blood.

The same four old men were circled around the chess board, wearing the same black berets. They were still drinking the pale yellow *amontillado* from small glasses. It was nine o'clock in the morning. The same dog slumbered next to them.

Ainsley cocked a hand on her hip and said, "Would any of you drunks like to make twenty euros?"

The men ignored her.

"How about forty?" she said.

Still nothing. She looked at the bar, which was closed. Good for Maria. The widowed bartender saw no point in opening at nine in the morning for a group of old men who brought their own liquor.

Then Ainsley remembered Maria revealing that the men would, as far as she knew, respond to only one thing.

"Well," said Ainsley, "if nobody will tell me where the nearest church is at, I guess I won't take communion this morning."

That got a response. The men rose up, and a chorus of creaky voices and pointed knobby arms began directing her to leave the plaza, turn left, go down by the cistern, look for the chapel beneath the bridge.

She held up a hand. "No," she said, "you don't understand. I need to know that other people are praying for me. I need a *community* of holy people."

"The Carmelites," said one.

The others nodded, humming agreement.

Ainsley smiled. That was exactly who she was hoping to find. "Where are the Carmelites?"

The chorus of creaky voices sounded again, this time giving her directions to head up to the fork in the road, bear left, follow it for two kilometers until she saw the chips of black stone in the road, and the convent will be built into the embankment above.

"And when you go," said one, "you must say *sin pecado conceibida* to enter."

The others nodded agreement. Ainsley translated: *Conceived without sin.*

"Why?" she asked.

"It's their rule," one said. "They won't let you in unless you tell them that."

"Thank you," said Ainsley.

As she slipped into her rental car, she looked back at the men. They'd returned to the game of chess, as if she'd never been there.

———

Ten minutes later, she was outside the town, wheeling around a doubletrack dirt road along the side the mountain range. Below her was a field of yellow sunflowers that had just begun to reveal themselves to the world. In the road lay thousands of tiny chips of black stone.

The Carmelites. She looked up at the embankment. A row of seven arches marked the front porch of the convent. It was a surprisingly small structure. She'd seen mansions in the United States that were bigger than this.

Ainsley slowed down, looking for the driveway up the slope. Then she realized that there was no entry driveway because the nuns didn't own any vehicles.

She parked the car in a small turnoff, then stepped out and peered around for the easiest access. She spotted a walking path that led up the slope, plainly visible amidst the brush.

Ainsley took a deep breath and started up the steep slope, through the scrub. Running through her mind was a single name.

Sister Dora.

If anybody knew anything in this town, it would be Sister Dora. Ainsley thought back to her brief encounter with that lady of the cloth a few days earlier. The nun had been quite discreet, apparently trustworthy, very sophisticated, and an admitted social butterfly. Women like that usually became a repository of people's secrets. Ainsley glanced up at the remote, forbidding convent. Secrets had a way of crawling into silent, rocky places like this anyways, where they curled up in dark corners and waited to be discovered.

By the time she reached the top of the embankment, perspiration had beaded on her upper lip. She wiped it off on her sleeve and stood there, breathing.

Under the row of arches was a long, empty porch. Just a flat tiled floor, nothing else, not even so much as a single chair. Given the view over the valley below, Ainsley would've suspected at least a wet bar for a glass of communion wine at happy hour. Apparently the nuns took the meaning of *cloistered* very literally.

At the far end stood a thick wooden door, a heavy knocker hanging from the middle.

Ainsley approached the long tile entryway and began walking down it. Her feet made heavy thuds that fouled the pure spiritual air.

At the door, she lifted the knocker and rapped three times. The sound echoed and died.

Then a small slat in the door flipped open. A wrinkled hag's face appeared in the rectangle. Ainsley didn't recognize it.

"*Va con dio usted?*"

Ainsley remembered the response. "*Sin pecado conceibida.*"

"Do you want to buy some desserts?" said the nun.

"I want to discuss the marquesa."

The rectangle slid shut, and silence returned to the porch. Ainsley felt worried that she might have been too forward. It was her Achilles' heel.

Then the heavy door moved slightly. Then it moved again. Someone on the other side was trying to open it. Deciding to help, Ainsley grabbed the handle, planted her feet, and yanked.

The door swung open, sending Ainsley tumbling backwards onto the floor. Stunned, she felt a shadow fall across her. Standing over her was a black-robed nun wearing a white wimple—and framed inside the wimple was the intelligent face of Sister Dora.

"Miss Walker," she said, "I was wondering when you would find me."

CHAPTER FIFTY-THREE

Sprawled on the floor, Ainsley groped around for a reply. "Why were you expecting me?"

The nun smiled. "Because Juan Carlo told me that you were investigating the sword of Pepe. I thought that if you were halfway decent at your job, you would eventually find your way here. And now you have."

Sister Dora offered a hand, and Ainsley grasped it. The woman's grip was remarkably strong. In one swift move, she pulled Ainsley to her feet.

"Thank you," said Ainsley.

"I was just about to finish my morning prayer. Do you want to buy some desserts after?"

Ainsley brushed off the seat of her pants. "Yes."

"Then come this way."

She followed the nun through the doorway into the convent. It'd been designed in the classic Spanish manner, with a square courtyard bounded on four sides by covered passageways. In the center of the courtyard was a stone grotto featuring a statue of the Virgin Mary, next to which was a low bench.

The nun gestured for Ainsley to sit down on the bench. She obeyed. Then Sister Dora dropped to her knees before the grotto, clutched her rosary, and dropped her head. Her lips began moving silently.

Ainsley waited, crossing her legs. Somewhere overhead a bird chirped. Behind her, a trickle of water burbled from a small fountain. Ainsley felt a strong sense of peace here, a respite from the aggression of daily life.

At last Sister Dora made sign of the cross, kissed her rosary, and stood up. "Now that that's finished," she said, "let's have breakfast in the refectory."

Ainsley followed the nun out of the courtyard, down the covered passage, and into a bare stone room. It had an ancient wooden table that was long enough to seat thirty people, but there were only four place settings laid out. She guessed that the number of sisters in the convent had been dropping for decades.

She pulled out the long bench and sat down. Before her were a chipped ceramic plate, a single fork and knife crossed over it.

Sister Dora went into a small side kitchen, rummaged around, and emerged with a plate. On it were eight crackers and two globs of honey.

The nun sat down across from Ainsley and poured each of them a half-glass of water from a pitcher. Then she scooped a spoon of honey onto a cracker and handed it to Ainsley. "Please," she said, "I want you to enjoy it."

Ainsley accepted the delicacy. She noticed that it wasn't the type of honey that drizzled or stretched. It glopped, which meant it was fresh, straight from the honeycomb. To be given this might be an honor.

Sister Dora's eyes watched her chew. When Ainsley had finished, the nun said, "Talk to me."

"I think the marquesa lied to me," said Ainsley.

"She lies to many people," replied the nun, fixing herself a cracker, "including herself."

"She and Juan Carlo said that Don Vasquez had been investigating the theft of the sword of Pepe. I went to his finca and killed a bull because he asked me to prove myself. Then he told me that he didn't know anything. It was a setup."

Sister Dora looked at her cunningly. "All for the sword of Pepe."

"Yes."

"Pepe was Franco's favorite matador."

"So I hear."

"The tourmaline had—"

"—belonged to his wife," finished Ainsley. "I already know all this. My question is simple: Why did the marquesa lie to me?"

Sister Dora was about to put the cracker in her mouth. Then she stopped, seeming to regard Ainsley from a great distance. Then she returned the cracker back down onto the plate. "Miss Walker, I can show you something that might answer the mystery."

Ainsley felt the thrill shoot all the way down to her feet. "Show me what?"

"A picture. Do you want to see it?"

She looked at the nun curiously. "Of course."

Sister Dora stood up, left the refectory, and disappeared. Ainsley listened to her feet softly padding away. She sat alone in the room, listening to the rock walls moisten.

A minute later, the padding sound returned, and the nun reappeared. In her hands was a black-and-white photo.

"Here," said Sister Dora, "look closely."

She slid the photograph across the table. Ainsley peered down. It was a photo of a group of people standing on barricades that had been erected in the middle of a street. The young people were holding handkerchiefs over their noses. Some were holding what appeared to be homemade bombs. Others were waving knives and guns.

This wasn't make-believe. This was a real photo, from a real war.

"I don't understand," she said.

"Turn it over," replied Sister Dora.

Ainsley flipped over the photo. On the back, in small handwriting, was scrawled the name *Beatriu Fons, Juliol 1936*.

"*Beatriu Fons?*" said Ainsley. "*Juliol?* What language is this?"

Sister Dora reached out and flipped the photo over again. Her finger landed on a figure on the barricades, close to the left margin of the photo. It was a very young woman, no more than fifteen years old, her mouth open in an angry shout, her thin arm thrust to the sky. A striped flag was wrapped around her shoulders.

"That," said Sister Dora, "is the marquesa."

"She was a *protester?*" said Ainsley.

"It was July of 1936."

"So?"

The nun remained patient. "You don't know what happened in 1936?"

Ainsley racked her brain. She enjoyed history, loved to learn about it, had even majored in it for a short while in college—but some events just fell through the cracks.

Suddenly she remembered. "It was the Spanish Civil War."

Too late she realized that calling it the *Spanish* Civil War was pointless, since she was in Spain.

"Yes," said the nun, "and this picture was taken in Barcelona. The Nationalist forces, who would eventually rule the country through Franco, defeated the Republicans."

Ainsley nodded. She remembered learning about that, once upon a time.

"Do you understand yet?" said the nun.

"No."

The nun reached across the table and clasped both of Ainsley's hands. Their eyes met.

"The marquesa is Catalan," she said.

CHAPTER FIFTY-FOUR

Ainsley's mouth worked itself in circles. Her tongue played along the edges of her teeth. Her eyes roamed across the nun's face looking for answers.

Then she pulled her hands away. "But that doesn't make sense. She loves Madrid. And she loves the *corrida*. Those things are Castellaño."

"No," said the nun, "not in her true heart." She sighed and checked the clock on the wall. "I have to make the *suspiros de monja*. Follow me to the kitchen and I will tell you more."

A moment later, Ainsley stood in the doorway of the tiny kitchen and watched the nun use a match to light the burner of an ancient, tiny stove. Then she opened the door of a three-quarter-sized refrigerator. It looked nearly a century old. She removed a bowl and peeled open the lid. Inside was raw batter.

"You make the desserts," said Ainsley.

"Every week," she said. "I made the batter this earlier this morning but didn't have time to fry them. Come, help."

Ainsley tentatively stepped into the kitchen and washed her hands at the ancient marble sink.

"What can I do?"

"You can shape the batter into balls," replied the nun, "but no larger than a man's testicle."

The surpise must've registered on Ainsley's face, because the holy woman gave a sly grin. "I took a vow of chastity, but that doesn't mean I can't talk about them."

Ainsley smiled as she plunged her hands into the cool batter and began to form small lumps. She handed them, one by one, to Sister Dora, who dropped them into the hot pan of oil. The browning and sizzling started immediately.

"The marquesa," said the nun, "wasn't born a marquesa. She was born Beatriu Fons in 1921. She was from a poor family in Barcelona."

"What happened?"

"The war happened. She was a passionate advocate of the Catalan cause. But when the Nationalists triumphed, she fled the city, hiding out in mountains with other rebels. When she realized that life wasn't going to change, that the Nationalists had won, she decided to change herself instead."

"She became Castellano," said Ainsley.

"Yes. She came down from the mountains, moved to Madrid, cleaned herself up, changed her accent—she's very good at accents, you should've heard her when she was younger, she would've been a good actress. And, honestly, she was an attractive woman, the perfect age for marrying."

"The people bought it."

"Apparently. Young women like her can get away with a lot."

The nun was right. At age twenty-nine, Ainsley was getting old enough to remember when she too could get away with nearly anything. Then the skin on her face had begun to grow a little more wrinkled, her movements a little less sprightly, the propositions from random men fewer and far between.

"So how did she become a marquesa?" she said.

"She married a man in Madrid," said the nun, "I can't remember his real name. He was almost forty and owned the Grantruca textile company. The regime favored the company, and so Franco gave him an honorary title: the Marquess de Grantuca."

Ainsley stopped forming the balls and stared at Sister Dora. "You're joking."

"No."

"So Grantruca is the name of a textile company?"

"Yes."

"You're telling me Franco just made up the title."

The nun seemed nonplussed. "Yes, he did that for many loyalists. What else did you think?"

Ainsley didn't want to admit the truth. She'd assumed that Grantruca had been a family of famous sixteenth-century Spanish nobles. Or maybe the descendants of a long-lost branch of the Habsburg or Bourbon dynasties. After all, the marquesa had filled her home in Aguadever with a hundred different props suggesting such a backstory.

"So how long were they married?"

"Fifteen years. Her husband died of a heart attack. With his mistress."

"Oh."

"But that was over fifty years ago. After his death, to maintain her position, the marquesa remained a Francoist, and even today she continues to hold the illusion. I've tried telling her that there is no point to the deception, that she could live openly as a Catalan now. But she's too used to the double life."

Using a pair of metal tongs, Sister Dora expertly turned each *suspiro* until it was a deep brown. Then she lifted each one onto a plate lined with paper towels. The oil formed wet rings around each dessert.

Ainsley studied at the nun. "Why are you telling me all this?"

"Because the marquesa has decided to cut this convent out of her will," said Sister Dora. The intensity on her face reflected the fierceness of this betrayal. "When you came downstairs the other day, that's what I had come over to discuss."

"Oh," said Ainsley.

She threw another *suspiro* into the pan, spattering hot oil on the walls. "That old bitch led me on for twenty years."

"I'm sorry," said Ainsley.

"I wish that she were. This convent is barely standing. And we had an agreement."

"Oral or written?"

"Oral."

"That's not worth anything, especially not with bad people."

"True. But you're one of the good ones."

Ainsley smiled. She remembered Sister Dora using those same words a few days earlier.

"Yes," Ainsley replied, "I try to be. But I have a question."

The nun began turning over the second batch of *suspiros de monja*. "You want to know what any of this has to do with the sword of Pepe."

"Yes."

Using the tongs, the nun pulled the remaining desserts out of the pan. "You can figure it out."

"I can?"

She nodded. "The sword of Pepe, a Francoist treasure, is stolen. An old Francoist woman sends you to a *finca*, lying to you, saying that you can find a clue there. Now you find out that the lying old woman is actually a Catalan—the autonomous region that was oppressed by Franco."

Ainsley felt as though she were in a helicopter that had

just pulled her out of a deep chasm, and now she was peering down onto the landscape that had defied understanding for so long.

"The marquesa stole the sword," she said.

The nun fixed her with a warning stare, as though Ainsley were crossing into dangerous territory by stating it so directly. "I didn't say that," she said.

"But it makes sense," said Ainsley. "The sword of Pepe is a symbol of the Francoist regime because of the tourmaline. Since the marquesa is a Catalan at heart, she doesn't want to see the tourmaline sword be used as public entertainment. So she orchestrates its theft."

"I didn't say any of that," repeated the nun, reaching for a sifter of powdered sugar, "but I'm not disagreeing with you either."

"But how did she arrange it?"

The nun shrugged. "It's a mystery. Only God knows." She used the tongs to drop five *suspiros* into a paper bag. "Now, the suspiros cost five for three euros. I can offer you ten for five, if you'd like."

There was no response except for a door slamming shut. Sister Dora turned around. A twenty-euro note was on the table, but Ainsley was already gone.

CHAPTER FIFTY-FIVE

A plume of dust billowed up behind the rental car as she tore away from Aguadever and up the road towards the saddle. Ainsley's mind was racing nearly as quickly as the vehicle.

The marquesa.

Catalan.

Franco's sword.

The scenario was certainly plausible, but she didn't have any proof, she didn't know how the marquesa had achieved the theft, and—most importantly—she still didn't know where the sword was.

But today was Pepito's *corrida*. There was no time to waste.

She arrived in the saddle, passed through the meadow dotted with green pine trees and studded with gray chunks of granite. The wet pockets of snow had melted, revealing the dark, hidden crevasses of the terrain to the bright daylight.

Ainsley passed beneath a stone arch, reaching out and dragging her fingertips along the pillar on the left. Winding her way through the dark glade, she felt her cheeks become chilled once again, but this time she kept the window down, forcing herself to feel the cold.

Then the quiet house came into view.

She pulled off the road well before reaching the house, hoping that nobody had heard the engine. She parked deep in a copse of trees, hidden in the shadows, and made sure not to slam her car door after she exited.

Then she began to creep towards the house.

Tiptoeing through the forest, Ainsley took care to avoid fallen branches, treading softly instead upon the brown pine needles that muffled her footsteps. She took in the scent of mushrooms and pine resin and granite.

Coming alongside the house, she crouched down behind a boulder and peered over the rock at the marquesa's house. Two yellowed curtains stared out of the front window like the unblinking eyes of a watchful cat. The residence was utterly still. Even the flagstone porch itself was empty—the three rusted iron chairs and paella grill had been pulled inside, covered, hidden.

Ainsley clenched her fist. She was here to uncover things.

Secrets.

Then she noticed that two cars were parked in the driveway. One was the red Mercedes, which belonged to Juan Carlo and the marquesa. The other was a battered Toyota. She didn't recognize it.

Ainsley leaned against the boulder, chewing the inside of her cheek, and reviewed her options. She could continue squatting out here in the woods, peeping on the house like a pervert, until both cars disappeared. Then she could sneak inside and ransack the house. That, however, might not happen for several days.

The other option was to ring the front doorbell and be very forthright. That, however, could end spectacularly badly. After all, Juan Carlo hadn't invited her to return, certainly not after he discovered her snooping in that weird room. She thought about that room again.

As she vacillated between the two choices, she heard a sound of a door open. Staying low, Ainsley turned around and peered over the rock.

Two men had strolled out onto the patio. One was Juan Carlo, dressed in a stylish yellow scarf and burgundy suede smoking jacket. Ainsley thought he looked nearly unrecognizable without his grey suit. His face was down, and he walked with a bizarrely informal shuffle.

Behind him was a man with hunched shoulders, salt-and-pepper hair, and a lavender scarf. Unlike Juan Carlo, he kept his head up and moved with some confidence. He looked comfortable with his own body. She noticed his hand resting on Juan Carlo's shoulder. Whether it was for reassurance or friendship or something else wasn't entirely clear.

When Ainsley looked at his face, she sucked in her breath.

The man had a lantern jaw. A massive chin.

She thought back to the patio of Renopedes in Córdoba, back to something Dolores, the wizened woman with the gnarled hands, had mentioned. The man who had visited her son Javier. How had she described him?

The tall Catalan with the big chin.

And her son Javier had been the bellhop at the Hotel Maghrebi.

All this was circumstantial evidence, of course, but coupled with the recent revelation about the marquesa's Catalan roots ... Ainsley couldn't see any other solution to the mystery.

She looked back to the patio. Juan Carlo and the man with the lantern jaw stood with their backs to her, arms across each other's backs, gazing out across the plains towards the brown haze that signified Madrid. Ainsley ruefully noticed that they stood in the exact spot that Juan Carlo had educated her about paella earlier. He was a decent man.

But she needed to know the real story.

Then they stepped off the patio, slipped into the red Mercedes, started up the engine, pulled backwards, and drove away down the road.

Ainsley watched them go, praying that she'd hidden her rental car well enough. If she hadn't, they'd be tearing back this way in less than a minute, and the hunt would be on.

She waited behind the rock, listening for the Mercedes' engine, for the slammed door, for the hunt to begin.

But there was only silence.

They were gone.

Still, Ainsley waited nearly ten more minutes, until she was positive that they'd driven off the mountain. She was alone.

Except for the marquesa.

Maybe.

This was her opportunity.

Ainsley monkey-walked across the yard, crept onto the patio, and slunk up to the side door. She tried the handle, and it opened easily. Juan Carlo probably never bothered to lock it. There was no need, up here in the mountains.

She slipped off her shoes and went inside. She found herself in the servants' passage and walked lightly along the passage, her fingertips touching the walls for balance, until the corridor emptied out into the foyer. Then she was in the living room, amidst the burgundy leather and the silver antiques, trying not to breathe too heavily.

She glanced down the long hallway towards the marquesa's room. The fourth door down. She could hear the distant, tinny sound of a musical recording. Ainsley paused and listened to it for a moment. It was the small, weird sound of a penny whistle singing over a woodwind orchestra playing in 6/8 time.

Ainsley cocked her head. She'd heard that music somewhere.

Next to the marquesa's room, the third door was slightly open, a sliver of horizontal light cracking out beneath the door. It was the room with the strange furniture. And the odd shoes.

Ainsley quickly padded down the hallway. Keeping an eye on the marquesa's door, she gently turned the knob. It popped open with a loud *thunk* that echoed up and down the hallway.

Then she pushed into the room for the second time and stood there, surveying. Nothing had changed except for the daylight that now filtered through the curtains.

Straight ahead was the tarp. She lifted the fabric and looked beneath it. There it was—the gorgeous chair with the fluid lines, irregular curves, bits of blue and purple stained glass. The mushroom motif. Something was tickling the back of Ainsley's head, a vague recollection of this style. It might've been featured in some of the art history books that she'd read in college.

Still, there was no sword.

She lowered the tarp and looked over to the side table. The odd navy-blue-and-white sandals lay beneath it, the pair of white fabric strips dangling off the heel, waiting to be tied around a pair of ankles.

No sword there either.

Ainsley glanced around at the few other items in the room. Her shoulders slumped. She'd been so certain, more certain than she'd ever felt about anything.

Then a voice croaked, "It's not in there."

Ainsley turned and saw the marquesa.

CHAPTER FIFTY-SIX

The elderly woman was standing in the doorway to her private room, barely upright, her frail body tensed, one hand on the doorway lintel. Still, something in her eyes radiated pride. The tinny music somehow played more loudly now.

"How do you know what—"

The woman waved a bony hand. "I'm not an idiot," she said. "You went to Don Vasquez's finca, like I told you."

"And I proved myself to him," said Ainsley.

"And he told you that he knew nothing of the theft."

"Indeed."

"And that made you question my motive in sending you there."

"Yes."

The old woman sighed. "You played every move right, from the moment Juan Carlo pointed you out in the *barreras* at Las Lentas. Any mistake was due to poor planning on my part."

Ainsley touched a wall for support. Sister Dora had offered the possibility of this very solution to the mystery, then backpedaled. Now the theory was being proven to be real. Ainsley felt the ground beginning to shift beneath her feet, tearing apart, reforming into new and terrible shapes...

"So you're the one."

The old lady looked at her. "What do you mean?"

"You stole the tourmaline sword."

"I certainly did not," said the marquesa. "Look at my condition. All I do now is *buscar rincones*."

That meant *look for quiet corners*, but that was a cop-out. Ainsley wasn't going to be shaken off.

"I mean that you paid someone to do it," said Ainsley.

The old woman waved her off, then began to close the door. Ainsley shot her hand out and caught the door just before it clicked shut. With little effort, she pushed her way into the room.

The frail marquesa stared at her in shock while Ainsley looked around. The tinny yet familiar music was coming from a television in the corner. On its screen played very old black-and-white footage of a group of people dancing in a public square, in front the steps of a cathedral. They were circled together, holding hands in alternating sexes, and performing a slow but intricate series of steps with their feet. In the middle of the circle was a stack of bags.

And on their feet were those odd sandals.

It was the *sardana*.

The realization swung into Ainsley's midsection with the force of a sandbag. That was the same dance that the liquor store owner had been watching on his tablet, back at the Costa de Sol, the man who'd made it abundantly clear that he was not Spanish.

He'd been a Catalan.

This was another pebble added to the pile of evidence. What Francoist would spend her retirement sitting at home, alone, watching old footage of forbidden Catalan dances?

None. The marquesa was indulging in private nostalgia of a childhood in Barcelona.

"You're Catalan," said Ainsley. "You were born Beatriu Fons in Barcelona, 1921. You fought the Nationalists during the civil war and then you hid in the mountains. After that, you moved to Madrid and pretended to be somebody you weren't."

The marquesa grew very still. Her eyes searched Ainsley's eyes for weakness. Then, she slowly moved over to her chair and lowered herself into it. She seemed to have aged yet another decade. Her thumbs stroked her cane.

"The sandals were so pretty," she said. "I used to love to wear them."

"They are unusual," said Ainsley.

"The *sardana* used to be my favorite dance." She pointed at the television screen. "In fact, I used to be one of those girls, when I was very young. Our culture was so wonderful."

She seemed to be transported into the distant past. Then the woman's thumbs stopped moving, and her eyes found Ainsley. "I know how you found out."

"How?"

"You spoke with Sister Dora."

Ainsley said nothing.

The old woman nodded. "She's getting a piece of my estate. I don't know why she wants to shout my secrets to the world."

Ainsley didn't know what to say. According to the nun, her convent had been squeezed out of any inheritance, but the marquesa was singing a different tune. It seems that there had been a miscommunication between the two women—and Ainsley had accidentally exploited it.

"She told me that you'd reneged on your promise," Ainsley said.

"There was no promise," said the marquesa. "She's been

guarding my secret for decades and she thinks that she is entitled to some of my money."

"You aren't giving her anything?"

"Of course I am. But she needs to be patient." The marquesa shook her head. "I don't know why she entered the sisterhood. She should be running an international business."

Then Ainsley remembered something else. "Marquesa, tell me about that chair in the other room."

"It's a Gaudí."

Ainsley felt something heavy drop into the pit of her stomach. She cupped a hand to her ear. "Did you say—"

"Yes, Antoni Gaudí. He was an architect in Barcelona in the early twentieth century who—"

Ainsley interrupted her. "The whole world knows Gaudí, marquesa. But you *own* one of his chairs?"

"Of course," she replied, as though it were nothing to be surprised about.

"Why is it *here*?"

"My husband took it from Barcelona after the war."

"Why?"

"Because I wanted it."

Ainsley was taken aback. A greedy gleam had erupted in the marquesa's eye.

"So you have a stolen Gaudí?" she said.

"It's not stolen. It's mine. My husband told everybody that it had been destroyed during the war. The world thinks it's gone."

That sealed it. It seemed that, for the marquesa, theft had been a lifetime habit. If she'd asked her husband to steal a priceless Gaudí from her own homeland, then stealing the sword of Pepe would be a no-brainer. Ainsley wondered how many other *objets d'art* in this house had arrived here in the same questionable way.

"I need that sword, marquesa."

"I'm not giving it to you."

Ainsley read between the lines. If she had the sword to give, that meant that it was somewhere on the premises.

"Is it in this room?"

"No."

"Tell me where it is."

She crossed her arms. "You can search for it yourself. I can't stop you anyways. But you'd better find it before Juan Carlo comes back. He's my hands and feet."

An evil light glowed darkly in the old woman's eye. Taking the hint, Ainsley left the room and sped down the hall into the living room, the museum dedicated to royalist Spain. Ainsley turned in circles, her eyes roving the tall candles, the red-and-gold embroidery, the Córdoban leather, the clawed armrests. The air was stuffy here. She felt as though someone had thrown a bag over her head.

Then she saw it.

In the corner stood the pint-sized knight, the suit of armor that barely reached to Ainsley's chest. His arm was still outstretched, as though grasping—

—but the hand was no longer empty.

It was holding a sword.

Ainsley peered more closely. It was a long, thin weapon, and in the handle was set a deep red gemstone. As a ray of the midday sun struck the stone, bits of red light spattered across the wall like blood.

That was a tourmaline.

It was the sword of Pepe.

CHAPTER FIFTY-SEVEN

Ainsley ran across the floor and began to pry the sword out of the knight's cold grip. It took some effort. Maybe it was her imagination, but the long-dead warrior seemed to resist giving up the prize.

At last she yanked it free. Her heart racing, her breathing rapid, Ainsley stepped back and held the sword of Pepe across her palms.

She studied the weapon. It was heavier and colder than she'd expected. She ran her finger lightly along the blade and stopped when she felt her skin begin to split open.

Then she admired the tourmaline. It was an unusual cut, probably forty facets, almost like a geodesic dome. She imagined Franco's wife wearing it on a necklace alongside her husband as he stood before a microphone in the nineteen-thirties, declaring Spain united under his stern hand. She knew that there was even a controversial monument known as the Valley of the Fallen, near El Escorial north of Madrid, that he'd constructed to the memory of his regime.

This sword wasn't too different.

Holding the weapon, Ainsley suddenly felt the urge to use

it. She shifted the sword's handle into her right hand, pulled it back, and thrust forward towards an invisible enemy.

"Don't give it to him," said the marquesa's voice.

The marquesa had shuffled quietly into the room and was leaning against the doorframe.

Ainsley lowered the sword. "That's not my business. My job is to recover it only."

"He could die."

"All matadors face death. It's their job."

"This is a Miura. It's much more dangerous than an ordinary bull."

Ainsley gently pointed the tip of the sword into the carpet, held the handle with a single finger, and balanced it. She truly couldn't stop Pepito, even if she wanted to.

"Tell me how you did it, marquesa."

"I had some help."

"From Juan Carlo?"

The elderly woman nodded. "He knew the Catalan. The Catalan knew the Moroccan."

The Moroccan. Ainsley thought back to the man in the teahouse, the swarthy man who's brought out that *majoun*, the baked druggie hash, the man with the scar in the cleft in his chin.

"Hamza?"

"Maybe. I never knew his name."

"But he was just here. I saw him leave with Juan Carlo."

"They don't tell me much. Only what they think I should know."

The marquesa seemed to be filled with sadness. Ainsley sensed in her that feeling of profound uselessness that affects people as they reach the ends of their lives.

Then another question occurred to her. "How did Samson know that you were involved in the theft?"

"Samson? The crazy swordmaker in Toledo?"

"Yes, that one."

"I don't know," the old lady said. "Somebody must've been talking. Gossip moves fast. I only wanted to keep the sword away from Pepito until after the *corrida*. Tomorrow, I don't care."

"Sorry," said Ainsley, "but you failed."

"What do you want?" said the marquesa.

Something about the way that she said it caught Ainsley's ear. She cocked her head. "For what?"

"To keep it here." The elderly woman swept her arm around the house. "I have much to offer."

Ainsley blanched. This was a bribe.

"Nothing," she said.

"Do you want money? How much do you want? I can give you anything. A thousand euros."

"I don't want anything," said Ainsley.

"Two thousand."

"No."

"Three."

Ainsley crossed her arms. Accepting it would mean screwing over both Pepito and the fourteen thousand people who paid money to see him use the sword. And a week ago, she would certainly have sold out the matador in a heartbeat, just for being a matador. Ainsley was surprised to discover that her own loyalties had changed.

"The *corrida* is tonight," said Ainsley, "and Pepito is going to use this sword."

"You won't make it," replied the old lady. "It's already one-thirty."

"Watch me."

Ainsley turned, slipped on her shoes, aware of the marquesa's eyes upon her back. "All these years you hated Franco," she said, "while you had to fake admiration. What's it like to live like that?"

The marquesa didn't answer. Ainsley felt her suddenly grow hollow, her eyes glassy and unfocused. Maybe the woman had been living a double personality for so long that she'd forgotten her true feelings, that her soul had cleaved in two.

Sensing her precarious state, Ainsley quietly picked up the sword and went to the front door. She paused in the doorway and looked back at the marquesa.

The old woman was holding the wall, still as a waxwork, staring at nothing with empty eyes.

CHAPTER FIFTY-EIGHT

A few minutes later, Ainsley was behind the wheel of her car, tearing down the one-lane road and descending the mountain dangerously fast. Her eyes flicked to the clock on the dashboard. It read one forty-seven.

The corrida would begin in Seville in less than five hours. It was nearly a three-hour train ride on the AVE.

She would be cutting it close. Ainsley gritted her teeth and pushed down on the accelerator.

A moment later, she came tearing across the cobblestones into the central plaza of Aguadever. The same four old men in black berets were hunched around the chessboard, all nursing the same glasses of pale yellow *amontillado*. The fountain in the middle of the stones was still dry.

But there was a red Mercedes parked at the edge of the plaza. She saw Juan Carlo and the Catalan with the lantern jaw sitting on the edge of the fountain, their legs jutting out, lazily smoking, their phones beside them. A third man sat with them. He wore a casual beige linen suit. From this angle, his swarthy features looked almost Arabic. Then Ainsley caught a better glimpse of his face, the scar drawn into the small cleft between his lower lip and his chin.

It was Hamza.

The man from the tearoom in Seville. The man who'd poured her mint tea. The man who'd brought the *majoun* that had sent her head spinning and her body passing out.

The man who'd known Isaac.

All three of the perpetrators were perched here, in the plaza of this remote mountain town.

Ainsley rolled her car up alongside them, stopped, and rolled down her window. Juan Carlo looked up and recognized her.

"Ainsley?" he said. "What are you—"

She cut him off. "I have only one question. Why did you play both sides of the game?"

Confusion contorted his face. "I don't understand."

"I know that you work for the marquesa," she said, "but I also know that you were the one who told Samson that the marquesa was involved in the theft."

"No—"

Ainsley held her frame. "Don't bullshit me." She looked at the Moroccan. "Hamza, you remember me from your tearoom in Seville."

He smirked. "You couldn't handle the *majoun*."

"And you let Isaac try to steal my money."

He shrugged.

"And you texted Gabriel on his brother's phone to come to Seville so that the sword would be left alone in the Hotel Maghrebi for long enough for that asshole bellhop Javier to steal it."

"That asshole owed me a favor," he said.

Ainsley looked at the Catalan with the lantern jaw. "And you were the man in Córdoba. You knew Javier."

The man thrust his jaw out even further. "And you're the girl they've been talking about."

"I'm a woman—and I wouldn't trust any of you with a matchstick."

Juan Carlo wagged a finger. "Those two, no. Me, yes." He touched his chest. "I'm a Madrileño, born and raised, upstanding. I have to work for the marquesa."

"Who is herself Catalan."

He paused, regarding her with new eyes. "How did you find that out?"

"It doesn't matter how."

Juan Carlo shrugged. "Sometimes the marquesa asks me to do things that go against my tradition. I wanted that sword to be found."

"Cabron," said Hamza, "I stole that sword fair and square."

"So you called Samson," said Ainsley.

Juan Carlo nodded. "In the world of swords, all roads lead to Samson. So I visited him in Toledo and planted a clue for anybody who was brave enough to ask him about the theft. A person like you."

Ainsley didn't doubt this statement. She'd guessed that it had been a phone call, but Samson didn't seem like the type to reliably answer a telephone.

"Why don't you quit working for the marquesa?" she said.

The *mayordomo* shook his head sadly. "I need this job. It helps me support my mother and sister."

Ainsley understood that feeling all too well. Then she nodded towards her backseat. "By the way, look what I found."

Juan Carlo glanced into the window to where the sword of Pepe lay on the cushion. He smiled ruefully.

"It doesn't surprise me."

"And," said Ainsley, "and it's going to be delivered to Pepito in time for the corrida."

He ran a frustrated hand through his hair. "I'm afraid that we underestimated you, Ainsley."

"Don't worry," said Ainsley, "if the marquesa fires you, you can find a job cooking paella. And one more thing."

"What?"

"You never saw me."

"Of course not," he replied. "You didn't see me either."

"*Cuidate.*"

"*Vaya con Dios.*"

Ainsley popped the brake, slipped into first gear, and tore out of the plaza.

CHAPTER FIFTY-NINE

On the train to Seville, Ainsley watched the Andalucían landscape flash past her window, a blur of green grass, brown earth, blue sky, white towns, and black roads. It was like a film reel that had reached the end of the reel and had unspooled, the loose end flapping against the projector.

On the seat next to her was the sword. It'd been wrapped in white cloth and bubble wrap by an official at the train station. At first, he'd been unwilling to allow her to board the train with such a weapon, and she'd begun to argue, but when another official had recognized the item, she'd been escorted into an office while it was wrapped. They'd even persuaded the conductor to hold the train for two minutes so that Ainsley could board.

Now Ainsley had nothing to do but bite her fingernails, thinking about what she was going to do after she returned the sword. While she'd been searching, her boyfriend Joaquim had stayed on the Costa del Sol. She owed him a lot.

She heard her phone ring. It was Joaquim.

"I was *just* thinking about you," she said.

"Chalk it up to my incredible male intuition," he replied.

"Guess what? I found the sword."

"Let me guess—it was Colonel Mustard. In the billiards room. With the wrench."

"Don't be an ass. I'm coming back tonight."

"I'll believe it when I see it."

"I'm not kidding. The sword is right next to me on this seat." She paused, searching for the right words. "Do you still want to see me?"

"I do, but this Russian hooker sleeping next to me probably doesn't."

"You would never pay money for sex."

He paused. "Of course not. She wants to be paid in vodka."

Ainsley smiled, but deep inside, she wondered if Joaquim really had found another woman. She wouldn't have blamed him. After all, she'd promised to cook him a meal, then abandoned him before she could do that. A bitter pang of regret shot through her body.

"Baby," she said, "it's killing me that I haven't made you any—"

She cut herself off. A weird buzzing sound came from her phone. Ainsley looked down. Gabriel was on the other line.

She took a deep breath. "Look, I've got someone important on the other line. Can I call you back?"

There was silence. Joaquim's disappointment was palpable. She closed her eyes and dropped her head.

"Okay," he said.

"I'll call you right back."

"I'll be here."

Ainsley switched over to the other line. "Gabriel, my friend."

"We're giving up on you, Ainsley."

"Don't. I found it."

He paused. "Say it to me again, and swear it to the Lord our God."

"It's true," she replied. "I have the sword of Pepe. And I'm on the train back to Seville."

An odd sound escaped from the *mozo de espadas*. It sounded like he was choking on something. Finally he said, "How did you do it?"

Ainsley related everything that had happened since they'd separated in Granada—the arrival in Aguadever, the meeting with the marquesa, the snooping in the backroom, the trip to Don Vasquez's *finca*, the murder of the bulls, discovering the dupe, returning to Aguadever, learning the truth from Sister Dora, and the final unraveling of the mystery with the marquesa.

Gabriel listened to the story. When she was done, he said, "It is the will of Jesus Christ that this sword was found. Our good works derive from him above."

"Actually, it was *our* will," she said. "Yours and mine."

"No, the Lord worked through us."

Ainsley figured it wasn't worth the argument. "If you say so. What time is the *corrida*?"

"Six thirty. Pepito will go first because he is the most senior. When can you be here?"

"The train arrives at five forty-five."

Gabriel deliberated. "It will be close. If you take a cab, you can make it. I'll be waiting at the back entrance. Be sure you go there, not to the front, or else you will have to walk through the crowds at the *feria*."

"How is Pepito?"

"He's been a disaster. Yesterday he was trying to get me to ask Samson to build a replica sword."

Ainsley laughed. "That madman wants to kill you."

"And he doesn't set gemstones either. Pepito is talking out of his throat." Gabriel paused. "He's been drinking too."

"Even today?"

"Yes."

After the night in Granada, Ainsley knew all too well that Pepito wasn't capable of having a social cocktail. His appetites were going to be his undoing.

"That's suicidal," she said.

"He does it often. But never with a Miura." Gabriel sighed. "Whatever will be, will be. We cannot stop it."

"Maybe it's God's will that Pepito be killed."

She meant it as a joke, but the *mozo de espadas* took it seriously. "You could be right. I have to go, Ainsley. I will prepare the second half of your payment. Please hurry. Fourteen thousand people are waiting on that sword."

He ended the call. Ainsley looked at the bubble-wrapped package next to her. The entire *corrida* depended upon it.

Then she remembered Joaquim. She'd promised to call him back.

A red light beeped in the upper left corner of her phone. The screen read *low battery*. She watched it shut down.

Ainsley looked around. There were no electrical outlets on this train. If there was any way to disappoint her boyfriend even further, this would be it.

SEVILLE

CHAPTER SIXTY

As the crowds of people flowed around her stopped taxi, Ainsley could tell that she was drawing close to it.

The spring *feria*.

A famous event in Seville, the most popular event in Andalusia, the *Feria de Abril* grew out of a simple livestock fair in the eighteen-forties. Today it occupies an entire bank of the Guadalquivir River and lasts a week.

While the river of pedestrians continued flowing over the cobblestones, Ainsley checked her watch. It was ten after six. She had twenty minutes to get to the Plaza de Toros de la Real Maestranza, but she suspected that if she stayed in this taxi, she would be sitting here for the rest of the night.

"Señor," she said, rapping on the dividing window of the taxi, "how much longer?"

"To La Real Maestranza?" He shrugged. "Maybe an hour."

"I have the sword of Pepe," she said, "and Pepito is supposed to start the *corrida* in twenty minutes."

The driver's eyes grew wide, and he whipped around in his seat. She lifted the bubble-wrapped weapon.

"You have to run," he said. "It's the only way you will make it."

"I need to get to the service entrance."

"Follow the crowds and go through the fair. From here it's the only way."

"What do I owe you?"

He waved it off. "Nothing. Just go. Hurry."

Ainsley popped out of the taxicab, the sword under one arm, her bag over her other shoulder, and shut the door.

Drawing a deep breath, she began to run.

Her shoes beating on the cobblestones, Ainsley darted through the crowd, dodging pedestrians, weaving and bobbing, until she saw the two-story illuminated castlefront entrance to the fair.

She ran up to one of the entrance gates. The ticket taker looked at her and said one word.

"*Billete?*"

Gasping for breath, hands on knees, she said, "I don't ... have one ... how much ... does it cost?"

"One hundred fifty euros."

Ainsley blanched. Then she decided to appeal to his better nature. "I have ... the sword ... of Pepe."

The ticket taker cast a skeptical look at her. Ainsley ripped open the bottom of the package and slid the sword out. In the last rays of the setting sun, the red tourmaline shone like the eye of a wounded beast.

The ticket taker immediately opened the gate. "Go, quickly. People paid good money to see Pepito use this. We can't afford a riot."

Ainsley moved past him and into the *feria* proper. The concourse was a dizzying mix of lanterns, carnival rides, elaborately dressed horses and equally elaborate carriages. Women in their *trajes de flamenca*, men in their *traje corto* with the black *cordobés* upon their heads. The sight of glasses of *rebujitos*, sherry mixed with lemon soda.

Then she was running again, this time down two winding rows of *casetas*, large but temporary tents that were erected each year to host parties. Inside the tents, she glimpsed people dancing *sevillanas*, eating tapas, laughing. The women were adjusting their *mantillas*, tossing their *mantónes*, and waving their *ventiladores*. Overhead were long strands of brightly colored lights known as the *ferrocarrilos*.

She regretted passing up such fantastic parties, but she was in no condition to hope to be asked into a *caseta* right now. Her face was covered in a slick layer of sweat and dirt and she was, after all, holding a sword. Her lungs bursting, Ainsley forced her legs to power on through the fairgrounds.

At last she saw La Real Maestranza. The arena lay dead ahead, at the end of the long concourse. She checked her watch. It read six twenty. With a final burst of energy, Ainsley began to sprint at full speed, her arms pumping through the air. Her glutes and hamstrings strained with the effort. Passersby turned their heads to watch the girl on the run.

She slowed down and stumbled to a halt at the front gate. An attendant stood there, the ticket barcode reader in his hand, his mouth slightly open.

"I ... have it," she said, gasping.

"*Señorita*," he said, "who are you?"

She lifted the package. "I work for Pepito ... and ... I have his sword."

"Ah," he said, "you're the one."

The attendant hoisted his radio to his mouth, spoke something quickly, then helped Ainsley to her feet. He led her through the turnstile and into a small security cart. He slid behind the wheel, and soon she found herself gliding silently around the outside of the arena. She noticed that his foot had floored the accelerator.

"They're delaying the start of the *corrida* until you arrive," he said.

Ainsley tried to process this. An entire massive event, fourteen thousand spectators, was waiting on her.

As they arrived at the back entrance, she saw Gabriel waiting in front of the large aperture. His hands were clenching and unclenching. She saw rosary beads hanging from his fingers.

"Praise be to God," he said, rushing towards her. She stepped off the cart and hugged him. Then she handed the *mozo de espadas* the packaged sword. He slid it out of the bubble-wrap and inspected it.

"What do you think?" she said. "Any damage?"

"This isn't it," he said.

He fixed Ainsley with a serious glare. She felt her stomach pucker up into a tiny ball of fear. Then he burst out laughing. "I am joking. This is the sword of Pepe. Come in, quickly. Pepito wants to see you before he begins."

"I need my money first."

"Of course."

He handed her an envelope. She opened it. Inside was a stack of euros. She thumbed through them. Another thousand euros, as promised.

Ainsley shut the envelope, stowed it in her backpack, then followed him into the bowels of the arena. The walls were lined with the flyers advertising tonight's event. She stopped to read the words in dramatic font: *El regreso de la espada de Pepe.*

The return of the sword of Pepe.

"And you have returned it," said a booming voice.

Ainsley looked up. It was Pepito.

CHAPTER SIXTY-ONE

The matador was attired in the most stunning *traje de luces* that Ainsley had ever seen—blood red satin, heavy with gold trim. Even his slippers were gold. It looked ridiculous up close, overly foppish, but she knew now that these suits had been designed to project glamour all the way to the rear of the arena.

"With respect," she said, "you have no idea what it took to find this."

He slid the sword of Pepe out of the wrapping and hoisted it into the air. It caught the eye of the other matadors nearby. "Gabriel told me that you killed a bull."

"I did."

He glanced at her briefly. "And how did you feel?"

"It was awful."

"But it helped you understand the *corrida*."

Ainsley nodded. He slapped her shoulder with a meaty palm. It was a sign of affection. "You should come to the party tonight. We have a room at—"

Ainsley held up her palms. "Thank you, but it's not possible."

"No?"

"I have to go back to my boyfriend. I can't stay here with you anymore."

Pepito stood there, blinking, unaware that he led a special existence. "Stay where?"

She made a circle in the air with her finger. "Here, in all of this. The *corrida*. The slaughter. The machismo. The ego."

"It's just life," said Pepito.

Gabriel arrived with a full-length mirror and plunked it down in the dirt. He held it dutifully while Pepito twirled in front of the mirror, inspecting his own outfit, making minute adjustments.

"Come here," said the matador, "and stand next to me."

Lifting an eyebrow, Ainsley stood next to him, his shoulder butting into the middle of her arm. Gabriel angled the mirror so they could see themselves.

"Look at yourself, Ainsley," he said.

"I am."

"You're part of this culture now. You can't escape it."

"I can leave," she replied.

"Yes, but you will always carry the *corrida* inside you. No matter where you go."

In the mirror, he held her eyes. Then she noticed that the horses, the picadors, and the five other matadors had begun to assemble in the corridor. The *paseíllo* was set to begin.

"This is the greatest moment in my career," said Pepito. "I will avenge the death of my father. And you've made it possible."

From the arena, the loud, brassy entrance music began to sound. It gave Ainsley the goosebumps.

"This my job," she said.

The matador approached her, wrapped his strong arms around her ribcage, and hugged tightly. Ainsley felt the breath squeezed out of her lungs. Then he kissed both of cheeks, grinned, and turned away.

The moment was ended. She watched Pepito stroll to the end of the *paseíllo*. She flattened herself against the wall of the corridor.

Gabriel appeared at her side. "Ainsley, come this way." He nodded towards the outside of the arena. "If you want to leave, you have to do it now, before they close the outside gate."

"Thank you," said Ainsley.

"Zamorano will help get you to the train station."

"He's here?"

Gabriel pointed down the corridor. The small mysterious man stood near the outside gate, the white furze of hair curling up beneath his black beret. She wondered how she'd missed him.

"Go," said the *mozo de espadas*, "and may God light your way for all your future good works."

He shook her hand. Ainsley felt a catch in her throat. She clapped her other hand over her mouth to stop the cry from escaping. It surprised her that she should be feeling so emotional.

"But—"

"You will watch the news for the result?"

"Of course."

"Goodbye, Ainsley," he replied.

The *mozo de espadas* stopped walking, and Ainsley felt herself being pulled back out of the tunnel by something strong, an unseen force. Tears streaking her cheeks, she suddenly turned around—

—and flung herself upon Gabriel in an enormous embrace.

"I don't want to leave," she said.

He staggered backwards, apparently in pain. Ainsley

herself had felt something odd underneath his shirt. It felt like a row of studs.

She released him and backed away, her eyes glancing down at his chest. "What is that?"

The *mozo de espadas* had closed his eyes and was biting his lip in obvious pain. "That ... is my secret."

On his shirt, a horizontal row of tiny dots of blood had appeared. Ainsley's eyes widened. "What is that?"

He sighed and looked around to make sure nobody was listening. Then he lowered his voice and drew close to her. "Something between myself and the Lord."

"What is it?"

"It's a sign of my dedication."

"Show me."

Fumbling, his fingers unbuttoned the top two buttons of his shirt. He pulled the fabric aside.

Wrapped around his thin, pale torso was a leather strap studded with spikes.

And the spikes were pointing inwards. Lines of blood were starting to trickle down the skin of his chest from where she'd pressed down.

Ainsley clapped her hand over her mouth. "Oh my God."

"My secret," he said again.

"Why on earth do you wear that?"

"It's my vocation. It's a reminder of my purpose on this earth."

Then Ainsley remembered what Joaquim had mentioned offhandedly a week earlier. "Gabriel, do you belong to ... Opus Dei?"

The *mozo de espadas* was already buttoning his shirt. "I dedicate myself to the purpose of serving Pepito. By my works I will show my worth in the eyes of God."

That was no answer at all. It was the equivalent of a bureaucrat saying, *I shall neither confirm nor deny these charges.*

Ainsley stood there, panting heavily, speechless. What do you say to someone who reveals that he voluntarily chooses self-mortification as a manner of proving himself to the divine? She thought about all of the unusual behaviors that Gabriel had shown over the last week—the constant pious worship in the cathedral, the abhorrence of physical contact, the regular mentioning of God, the mysterious personal life that not even Pepito was privy to.

All the clues had been there. She should've put everything together.

"Gabriel," she said, "*quiere usted mantenerte en contacto?*"

He lifted a gentle hand. "*Usted no mas. Ahora estas conmigo.*" He smiled, then nodded to the tunnel. "Hurry, before the gate closes."

At the end of the corridor, the men were beginning to unlatch the giant gates. Zamorano was motioning to her. Ainsley felt the force dragging her away again, and this time she didn't resist, floating down the dark tunnel, towards the small rabbit, towards the white light, the real world outside...

Ainsley shot out of the arena and stood in the cool night air, gasping for breath. Behind her, the men swung the gate shut with a heavy thunk. She went back and hung her fingers into its square metal apertures and looked down the tunnel.

At the far end, she glimpsed the silhouette of the matador as he strode into the arena. She heard a deafening cry arise from the fourteen thousand spectators.

It was Pepito's moment.

COSTA DEL SOL

EPILOGUE

In the kitchen of the beachfront condo, Ainsley stood at the cutting board once again, carefully chopping a head of lettuce for a salad. In the oven was a roasting chicken. For their first homecooked meal together, she'd decided that simpler would be better.

Joaquim watched her from the doorway.

"Really," he said, "I had a good time without you."

"How so."

"I met some guys and we went out drinking."

"That's usually how your stories start."

"It was really fun."

"Good," said Ainsley.

He dropped his head. "I lied. It wasn't that fun." He sighed. "Okay, so are you ready for the good news."

"You have good news?"

He nodded. "You remember my collaboration with the New Jersey company? The one that was supposed to start Monday?"

"Of course."

"They postponed it another week."

Ainsley dumped the lettuce into the spinner and began pumping the handle. "So what does that mean?"

"It means we can stay longer."

She looked up at him. "For real? We're supposed to fly home tomorrow."

He pulled a sheaf of papers out of his pocket. "You were bored with the Costa del Sol, so I changed the location."

"To where?"

"We're booked for a week at a hotel outside of San Sebastián. In the north of Spain."

Ainsley stopped pumping the spinner. "You're kidding."

"Nope," he said, "and it's on the Atlantic, the Bay of Biscay."

"So more beaches."

"Yes. But colder, cleaner ones. And we get to learn the Basque language."

"I don't know Basque."

"Nobody does. And the Camino de Santiago is up there too."

"What's that?"

He casually poured himself a glass of whiskey. "A medieval pilgrimage route. It stretches hundreds of miles across northern Spain, and last I heard, thirty thousand people try to walk it every year. When's dinner going to be ready?"

Stunned, Ainsley couldn't answer. She had been getting ready, mentally, to face life back home again. Now her Spanish stay was going to be extended.

Joaquim walked to the living room, sank into the sofa, picked up the remote control, and turned on the television. A local broadcast reporter was speaking about the deteriorating health of the leader of a radical Catalan separatist group. Then the continuing legal aftermath of a massive train disaster in the northwest.

Ainsley shook up the bottle of Caesar dressing. She heard

the broadcaster say, "*Proximó, una tragedia a la Real Maestranza*."

Ainsley was using tongs to put the salad in a pair of bowls when she heard those words. Her hand paused.

Una tragedia a La Real Maestranza.

Joaquim grew silent. "Little spoon," he said slowly, "do you think it was—"

"I don't know," she replied.

"I mean, there are six matadors. It could've been any of them—"

She stood up. "Joaquim, could you hand me the remote control?"

"Using the remote control is a man's job," he said.

"I'm not joking. Give it to me."

He threw her the remote control. Ainsley hit the power button and the television snapped off. Then she threw it back at him.

Joaquim stared at her. "You don't want to know what happened?"

"No."

"Why not?"

"I can't change him. I can't change any of it." She finished the salads and threw them onto the placemats. "It's just ..."

"It's just what?" he said.

She collapsed in a chair and buried her face in her hands. "It's just a part of life."

"What is?"

"The *corrida*. The killing. Everything has to die."

Her boyfriend put his hand on her shoulder. "I'm happy that you can see it that way now."

"I still don't like it," she said, "but it's not my place to judge."

"I feel the same way."

She looked up at him. "But you love to watch the *corrida*. You said you go to them all the time."

"Nah," he said, "it was a lie. The one in Malagá last weekend was my first."

"Why did you lie?"

"I wanted to look manly to you."

She stared at him, confused. He grinned boyishly.

"Did you," she said slowly, "mean what you said before?"

"What?"

"Those three words you said."

"When?"

"A few days ago on the phone."

He struggled to remember. She knew that he was feigning forgetfulness. Then his face lit up.

"Now I remember," he said. "Do you want me to say them again?"

Ainsley felt her breathing quicken. "Yes."

Joaquim took her hand, leaned forward in his chair, and opened his mouth to speak.

"I ..."

Ainsley felt her heartbeat quicken.

"... am hungry."

She lowered her head and thunked her forehead on the table. Inside, though, she was amused. Joaquim knew exactly how to defuse important conversations with humor.

When she looked up, he was opening the oven. She watched him pull out the chicken and carried the steaming bird to the table.

"Are you ready to eat, Miss Walker?"

Ainsley held up a finger. "I have one request."

"What is it?"

"I want you to tell me more about the Camino de Santiago."

PLOTWORKS PUBLISHING

THE

CAMINO CRYSTAL

AN AINSLEY WALKER
GEMSTONE TRAVEL MYSTERY

J.A. JERNAY

THE CAMINO CRYSTAL

Midday heat.

As Ainsley lifted the water bottle to her lips, she felt the last drops of water trickle onto her tongue. She saw yellow waves vibrate across her field of vision.

Nobody had warned her that this part of the walk would be so hot, so flat, and so devoid of water. Maybe that's what the albergue owner had been trying to say. Maybe she should've listened to him. But that had been three hours and at least ten kilometers ago.

She turned around. She was in a plain covered with a low brown scrub. There had been sunflowers earlier, their yellow-and-brown faces following the orb overhead, but they were gone. The trail had trudged to a higher elevation, the vegetation had withered, and now Ainsley felt as though she had been transported into a two-dimensional landscape dreamed up by a team of science fiction landscape designers. Ainsley remembered a peregrino in the dormitory saying that the eerie landscapes of Spain had been the setting for many of the famous Sergio Leone spaghetti western movies.

She peered hard through her sunglasses. Straight ahead, the trail was a thin line drawn by a mysterious deity in the dirt. In the distance, a band of mountains hovered on the horizon in the heat and the haze.

That was it. Her fingers formed themselves into a fist. The pink cliff had to be there. It had to be.

But those mountains were at least a day away.

Upset, gritting her teeth, she wheeled her bag around through the air and smashed it onto the ground. Then she kicked it.

The kick went too far, and she felt her foot slide on a loose pebble, her hamstring hyperextend. Then it stopped, and Ainsley found herself caught in a leg-split. This was ludicrous. Arms stretched out, she strained with the effort of trying to scissor her legs back together, but they'd gone too far. She'd have to pitch over sideways on the trail to get out of this.

Then she felt hands under her elbows.

"My child," said a voice, "lift yourself."

"I can't. My legs are too weak."

"You can do it."

Drawing a deep breath, Ainsley managed to tense her abdomen, her glutes, her thighs. Her hyperextended front leg pulled back just enough to give her an extra centimeter of leverage. She was able to heel-toe her feet back together again.

Upright once more, she turned around to look at her mysterious helper. She sucked in her breath. It was a mendicant in a brown robe with a rope belt cinched around his waist, his hands folded around a Bible. She hadn't even heard him approach.

"Who are you?" she said.

"Nobody."

"Where did you come from?"

"Nowhere. I represent nothing."

"But you helped me."

He nodded. "That's what we do on the Camino. We help each other."

The mendicant reached into his sack and pulled out a bottle of water. He held it out to Ainsley. "I saw you drink the last of your own."

Ainsley hesitated. What was the purpose of this man's generosity? What was he seeking for himself? Did he roam the wild highlands of northern Spain, posing as a holy man, only to bind, gag, rape, and torture unsuspecting peregrinos?

As soon as these thoughts crossed her mind, Ainsley felt ashamed of herself. How poisoned had her soul become? How suspicious had modern culture made her? Out here, on the meseta, far removed from the anonymity of a large city, people actually helped one another, with no expectation of anything in return. She'd occasionally experienced this same generosity back home, in rural areas where passing strangers smiled at each other and neighbors asked about each other's grown children and people lost track of their own front door keys because why even bother.

"Thank you," she said.

He closed his own bag, then turned and began walking again. Ainsley felt a sudden irrational fear that this religious man was abandoning her to grapple with the harsh world.

"Wait," she said.

The mendicant stopped and turned back. His eyes were inscrutable. "You can't follow me."

"I just need help finding the pink cliff. Maybe you've seen it."

He paused. "You will find it."

"How?"

"When you're ready, it will present itself."

The man in the brown robe smiled, then turned and

walked away. Ainsley began to say something else, but the words caught in her throat. She watched the man disappear into the shimmering heat waves.

Then she began to walk too.

Towards the peaks.

PLOTWORKS PUBLISHING

Visit Plotworks Publishing to follow Ainsley Walker on her next exciting gemstone travel mystery!

Then explore a new series by J.A. Jernay—the Cosmo Bennett Mapping Thrillers!

Turn the page for another sneak peek—

J.A. JERNAY
BOUNDARY

A
COSMO
BENNETT
MAPPING
THRILLER

FROM THE AUTHOR OF THE AINSLEY WALKER
GEMSTONE TRAVEL MYSTERY SERIES

BOUNDARY

Cosmo and his assistant Noah shuffled down the dirt shoulder of the boulevard in the midday heat, sweating and miserable.

Each was lost in his own thoughts. Cosmo dreamed of hitting a heavy punching bag at his gymnasium. Noah dreamed of passing level nineteen of Operation Earlobe, an obscure RPG he'd abandoned last semester.

The morning's meeting had been a complete bust.

"I don't think we should continue," said Cosmo finally.

Noah didn't respond, but Cosmo took no notice. He continued: "I don't think anybody here takes our task seriously. I don't think this propaganda map was as influential as they say. I don't think this map has driven the civil unrest. I think social media and centuries of tribal warfare are more to blame for the unrest than anything else."

He looked over at Noah, waiting for a response. "What about you?"

The graduate assistant came back from his reverie. "Huh?"

"Did you hear anything I said?"

"No."

"I was just saying this is pointless and we should go home."

"I don't have a problem with that."

They arrived at Vida e Caffe. It was a chain café, with hundreds of similar franchises scattered across the southern part of the African continent. The branding was modern and inviting. A hundred people sat beneath umbrellas at small tables on the large outdoor patio.

An arm was waving at them. It was Christopher, their fixer, a cup of tea on a ceramic saucer in front of him. Two other cups awaited them.

"Hello sirs," he said. "I ordered us all a rooibos. It's a vanilla tea that is extraordinary."

Cosmo and Noah pulled out the chairs and sat down. The driver quickly sussed out that something was wrong.

"It was a bad meeting?" he said quietly.

"Yes," said Cosmo, "there was no progress made."

"I'm very sorry."

Cosmo sighed. "I think we have to leave."

The fixer looked confused. "But you just sat down—"

"The country," he clarified. "We have to leave Fabajouti. We can't seem to do any good here."

Christopher looked crestfallen. "I do understand your frustration."

Noah said, "If it's okay with you, we'd probably like to just get in the car and go back to the hotel."

The fixer rediscovered his manners. "Of course, as you wish—"

"But we'd love to try the tea first—" added Cosmo.

"You two enjoy the rooibos," said Christopher, "while I fetch the car. The parking lot is very jammed and it will take quite a while to remove. I've already paid the bill."

Before they could object, the driver had shot to his feet.

He clapped Cosmo on the shoulder and left the patio. They watched him cross the boulevard to an off-street parking area that was crammed tightly with vehicles. On his approach, the attendant began shifting other vehicles.

Noah sipped the tea. "This does taste really good. I don't drink enough tea."

"I like tea," said Cosmo. He sipped from the cup. "This one is good."

"What's your favorite?" asked Noah.

"Maybe pu'er."

"That one's bitter, right?"

"Yeah. It's fermented."

"What about Earl Grey?"

"A cliché."

"I think I'm more of a fruity tea guy," said Noah.

Cosmo nodded. "Yeah, they have their charms."

"You ever try chamomile?"

"It's good for sleeping," said Cosmo, "but otherwise it's—"

His comment was cut short by a massive fireball that erupted from the parking lot across the street.

———

In a split second, Cosmo and Noah instinctively rolled off their chairs and onto the ground beneath their table. Their eyes met. Each was filled with terror.

Then the shock of the overpressure hit. Cosmo felt the force of the blast wave hit the left side of his body. The highly compressed air rattled the left side of his skull. It even sent his lips and cheeks flapping to the right.

The initial sound of the explosion was deafening, but that was soon replaced by a symphony of falling destruction. A thousand pieces of metal, plastic, glass, and upholstery rained down upon the boulevard, the grass, the other cars.

A shower of tiny shrapnel hit on the patio of the cafe. One hit Noah in the hand and sizzled his flesh. He shook it off.

They waited another few seconds for the shrapnel rain to end. Then Cosmo and Noah lifted their heads.

The patio of the café was transformed into pandemonium. The patrons started to pull themselves up from the ground and flee out to the street and in the opposite direction. The street itself was coming alive with panicked people running in every direction.

"What the actual—" said Noah.

"Christopher!" interrupted Cosmo. "What about Christopher?"

He scrambled up to his feet. Without waiting for Noah, he sprinted out of the café and across the boulevard, weaving through the stopped cars. The air was acrid with chemicals and the heat had somehow intensified even further.

The parking lot was a field of wreckage. The bomb had exploded in the middle of the space, shredding every vehicle and person within twenty meters. Pieces of concrete and metal and glass had been blown across the scene.

"Christopher!" he shouted again. "Christopher! Don't do this!"

He saw a shoe with a foot still in it. He saw a red string of guts entangled in a hubcap. A wave of nausea gripped his stomach. He covered his nose with his t-shirt and backed away.

He tripped backwards over a piece of metal, stumbled, and fell to the ground.

That's when he saw it.

A long strip of shredded fabric. A yellow-and-green printed tropical shirt.

It was bloody and torn.

Cosmo turned his head and retched onto the asphalt. All the tea he'd just drank came out.

He somehow pulled himself to his feet and staggered back to the café. Noah was waiting at the far corner, on the sidewalk, pacing frantically.

"So?"

"I found him," said Cosmo. He forced the next words out. "A little bit."

Noah's face went white. "Oh my God."

Cosmo didn't say anything. He just gripped Noah by the upper arm. "Walk with me. And don't look back."

———

The pair moved briskly down the boulevard, away from the scene. People were running past them, mouths open, eyes full of fear, but Cosmo maintained a steady pace. His face betrayed an intense desire to appear as normal as possible.

"So we're just going to leave the scene?" said Noah.

"Yep."

"Why?"

"Don't make me answer that, Noah."

"I think we should talk to the police, cooperate, tell them everything—"

"In a different country," Cosmo replied, "in a different scenario, you'd be right. But not here, not now."

Noah looked back over his shoulder at the scene.

"Look straight ahead," Cosmo said through his teeth, "and listen to me. Our Mercedes is gone. Christopher is ... gone."

"Shit—"

"And I'm going to suggest something else that could blow your mind."

"What?"

"It's possible that we were the intended target."

"That's insane."

"Is it?"

"How do you know?"

"I don't. But it's a possibility. Here's another one. It's possible that we are going to be used as scapegoats. We were the last people seen eating with Christopher. Do you want to be put in a Fabajouti jail on suspicion of a crime?"

They walked for another half minute in silence. Behind them, the chaos grew distant.

"Where are we going?" Noah said finally.

"Back to the hotel."

"And then?"

"We're leaving, like we planned."

"We're not going home, are we?" said Noah.

Cosmo's mouth grew hard and his jaw jutted out. He stared straight forward at an invisible point on the horizon. "No, we're not."

PLOTWORKS PUBLISHING

Visit Plotworks Publishing today for all these titles—and more!